White Roses
Tabor Heights Year 1, Book 4

Michelle L. Levigne

www.MtZionRidgePress.com

Mt Zion Ridge Press
295 Gum Springs Rd, NW
Georgetown, TN 37366

https://www.mtzionridgepress.com

Published in the United States of America
Publication Date: February 15, 2024

Editor-In-Chief: Michelle Levigne
Executive Editor: Tamera Lynn Kraft

Welcome to Tabor Heights:
A friendly little town on Ohio's North Coast, where sweet romance is always in the air.

Here you'll be able to explore the lives of the members of the congregation of Tabor Christian Church in the space of two years. The stories overlap, and there's no one right place to start.

Just like any small town, you come in, you meet someone, you hear their story and get to know them, and they introduce you to their friends, tell you something about them, and you learn those stories. As you get to know these new friends, they introduce you to other people, and tell you about other interesting stories in town.

It's the same way with Tabor Heights. Start with the story that interests you the most, and then branch out.

Settle back and enjoy your visit.
Welcome!

<u>Year One</u>

THE SECOND TIME AROUND
DETOURS
COMMON GROUNDS
WHITE ROSES
THE FAMILY WAY
FORGIVEN
FIRESONG
BEHIND THE SCENES
THE MISSION
ACCIDENTAL HEARTS
A QUIET PLACE

<u>Year Two</u>

COOKING UP TROUBLE
THE WRATH OF BUBBLES
INVITATION TO A WEDDING
TRUCK STOP ANGEL
A BOX OF PROMISES
WHEELS
THE TEDDY BEAR DANCER

Chapter One

Wednesday, November 6

Toni Napolitano checked her rearview mirror as she pulled up in front of the little cottage tucked among the trees between Main and the curve of road down into the Metroparks. A single notch of tension eased away at the sight of the Tabor Heights Police Department sign and all those black-and-whites parked behind it, almost directly across the street from her new home. It wouldn't ease her parents' anguish and disappointment over all the lies she had told lately, especially over her returning to Tabor Heights, but she felt a little better. This had to be done. She owed it to Angel, more than anyone else.

Taking a deep breath, she unlocked her door and stepped out of her fourth-hand brown SUV. She chose to take the glorious sunshine on the sugar dusting of snow as a good sign. A promise for success.

"Okay, God, I know we haven't talked in a long time, but please... help me catch him? For Angel? For my folks?"

She reached back into the front seat and pulled out the canvas bag with all her paperwork for the cottage and the thick folder of printouts of newspaper stories taken off the Internet. She walked around the trailer hitched to the back of her SUV and up onto the curb, and grinned at the thought of the whirlwind she had made of her life since reading that first newspaper article just three weeks ago. Pride mixed with panic surged through her, and she kicked aside some fallen twigs on the slate sidewalk as she approached the cottage door. She had quit her job at the *Calumet Cyclone*, gave up her apartment, sold most of her belongings, and drove all the way from Iowa to Ohio without a job to cushion her landing.

Toni had told no one she was positive the White Rose Killer was the same boy who had killed her sister, Angel, twenty years ago. What use was all her education and being an investigative reporter if she spent her life reporting on small-town events, and didn't use the gifts God gave her to track down that boy, now grown into a sick, cruel man?

She pulled out the key her new landlord, Mandy Gordon, had given her and unlocked the front door. The scents of lemon, ammonia and honeysuckle greeted her as her boots made echoes on the bare, hardwood floor. The cottage was partially furnished: kitchen table and chairs, appliances, sofa, bedroom furniture in one room. That suited her perfectly, and she had chosen to take that as a sign of promised success and maybe God smiling on her plan. Toni had kept her pots and pans, her desk, TV, DVD player, stereo, books, and office equipment. Everything she now owned in the world was inside that trailer she had hauled for two days of silent driving. She was rather proud of herself for being able to get rid of so much, pull up stakes and go where her heart led her.

If she had to, she would do it again. If she could find Angel's murderer and bring him to justice after all these years, she could do anything.

It took her less than half an hour to walk through her cottage and go through the checklist Mandy had given her. Living room, kitchen, bathroom, two bedrooms. The empty one would be her office. There was a cellar with a deep freeze and the detritus of belongings previous tenants had left behind, which Mandy had said she was free to use. Toni laughed at the snowshoes, three bikes with flat tires, or no tires at all, gardening tools, and a big, old-fashioned picnic basket with the wooden flap top that could be used for a table. She thought of picnics and bike hikes she, her parents and Angel had gone on in the Metroparks, when they lived in Tabor Heights twenty years ago. Would she still be here in the spring, to use that basket and enjoy the park?

If she found the White Rose Killer and she was still in this cottage in the spring, she promised herself she would go on a picnic. She would visit all of Angel's favorite places. But she wouldn't go to that dead end road in the Metroparks where Angel had died. She could never go there, no matter how her hunt turned out.

Her first trip out to the SUV was to bring in her two suitcases and five grocery bags of clothes and shoes from the back seat. With the chill in the air, Toni chose to unpack all her clothes and put them away in the tall dresser and bedroom closet, soaking up the warmth of the cottage before heading out again into the breeze.

"Afternoon," a man called, as she stepped around the back of the trailer and reached for the padlock to unlock it. "Sorry," he added, when she jumped and stumbled. "Guess you didn't see me."

"No. I didn't." Toni pressed her hand over her heart. Her gaze fastened on the gold shield on the man's navy jacket before she took in his square-cut, cold-reddened face and dark gray eyes.

"Iowa, huh?" He gestured at the back of her SUV, where the license plate was barely visible behind the hitch. "What brings you to Tabor?"

"I lived here when I was a kid, and I decided it was time to come back." That was the truth, anyway. "I'm going to work at the *Picayune*." Actually, she hadn't applied at the newspaper yet, but she had met so much success so far, Toni dared to believe that part of her plan would work out as well. If it didn't, her next option was getting a job at the police department. She had worked as a dispatcher in college. Either job would put her in the center of the action, looking for the White Rose Killer, who had made Tabor Heights his hunting ground.

"Sounds like a plan. Well, welcome back to town." He held out a gloved hand. "I'm Duane Evans."

"Thanks, Officer Evans."

"Please, call me Duane." His grin had something almost shy, boyish about it. "Nice to see someone in the old Baker place."

"I remember walking past here when we'd go to the park." She cocked her head to the left and studied him. "How long have you lived here?"

"Feels like forever. My folks died when I was little and I came here to live with my dad's family." He frowned a little. "Why do you ask?"

"I was just trying to figure out if I knew you back then."

"Could be. What's your name?"

Toni laughed. "Sorry. I'm used to asking questions all the time-- hazard of the profession. I don't usually talk about myself. Antoinette Napolitano."

Duane's eyes narrowed and he looked her up and down, then shook his head. "Sorry. Must be getting old. Name doesn't ring a bell."

"Well, we only lived here two years, and there are how many elementary schools in Tabor?"

"When I was a kid, five." He glanced around when a car drove past. "Uh... sorry. I'm supposed to be out on patrol. Just thought I'd check out the new neighbor. If you need anything..." He gestured at the police station across the street.

"Why do you think I chose this house in particular?" Toni laughed with him and they made their farewells.

He strode back across the street and she got to work. She had to unload the trailer and get it to the rental store before they closed at five. More important, she wanted to find a florist and visit Angel's grave before it got dark.

~~~~~

He had to follow her. His Angel would have wanted it.

He knew her face, the moment he saw the stranger get out of the truck pulled up in front of the old Baker house.

His Angel's little sister.

It gave him chills and tied his guts into knots, to stand there in the shadows of the trees and watch her go from the trailer to the house, back and forth, carrying boxes. Now he knew what his Angel would have looked like if she grew up.

It was a gift. It was a sign.

His angel was the right one this time. He didn't regret killing the first one. She had appeared in his life to distract him, to trick him and make
~~~~~

him think Angel had kept her promise to return to him, no matter what. When they were children, they had promised to love each other forever, and not even death would keep them apart.

The first one had been false, a lying whore. She hadn't been worthy of his love, of his patience, waiting all these years for her to return to him. He had to kill her, to punish her. This new one, Katrina, was his Angel, returned from the dead just like she promised.

The return of Angel's sister had to be a sign.

He followed when Toni went to the rental station and had the trailer unhitched. He followed her when she went to Blooming Miracles and bought a bouquet of carnations and daisies. He followed her to the cemetery in Hyburg. He stayed by the gate, pulled out binoculars, and watched her put the flowers on a grave.

Angel's grave.

He was glad her sister didn't put roses on Angel's grave. Only he was allowed to put roses there.

~~~~

Snow frosted the stiff grass over Angel's grave. Toni shivered, seeing in her imagination the white roses that had been there every time she came to the cemetery, until her parents couldn't take the pain, the cruel, silent taunting from the unidentified killer, and moved them to Indiana. Shaking, she crouched and leaned against the simple cross that held Angel's name, and her dates of birth and death. She had a hole in the index finger of her driving glove, but she ignored the wet and cold to clear out the engraved letters in the gray and pink granite.

There were no roses on Angel's grave. She supposed she should be grateful. How long had the roses continued? Until he found a new true love to haunt with notes and roses and demands for eternal loyalty?

"He's doing it again," she whispered, and her throat tried to close up.

Toni blinked away tears that felt as if they had been building up for years, just waiting to burst out. Her head ached from the pressure. She rubbed the tears away with the back of her fist. Now wasn't the time for crying. Not yet. When the White Rose was caught, exposed, and punished, then she could cry. Then she could finally ask her parents to forgive her for keeping Angel's secrets from them. Why hadn't she tattled on her sister? Their parents wouldn't have approved if they found out Angel had a boyfriend. They would have made her break up with him. She wouldn't have gone to the park to meet her boyfriend. She wouldn't have died, strangled by fencing wire and left lying in the dirt.

Tabor Heights still felt small, quiet, and safe. Just like it had when Toni, Angel and their parents had moved here. She had liked her small classes in school and the quiet, tree-shaded streets. She had felt safe going anywhere she wanted.
~~~~

Toni hadn't felt safe since Curt Mehdlang went to the park to look for Angel and came back with the police, pale-faced and red-eyed from crying.

She had to get that job at the *Picayune*. She needed a job, and working for the local newspaper would give her all the information she needed, immediately. People expected reporters to ask questions.

"Please, God, if You're listening to me anymore, I have to have that job. I have to do it for Angel."

Standing, feeling a little wobbly in her knees, Toni stepped backward from the grave. She wondered where the other murdered girl was buried. She wondered what the current target of the White Rose Killer was doing right that moment. Did she feel curious about the man who wrote her those demanding, frightening love notes? Did she feel angry?

Toni thought about contacting the police, to ask to talk to the girl. Would they believe her, if she told them about Angel and her theories about the White Rose? Would they think she was a crackpot, capitalizing on someone's terror? Would it do any good to tell anyone?

Bottom line: she had to do something. Even if she had to do it alone.

Thursday, November 7

"Who's that?" Curt Mehdlang moved back from the table in the lunchroom at the *Tabor Picayune,* until his shoulders touched the top of the hatch window looking out over the river behind the building. It gave him the perfect angle to see through the gap in the curtain over the porthole window into Angela Coffelt's office.

A dark-haired young woman sat opposite Angela's desk while the editor looked through a sheaf of papers. As assistant editor for the twice-weekly newspaper, Curt would have known about any interviews. So what was she doing there?

"Hmm?" Max Randolph, one of the copyeditors, pulled her mug of hot water out of the microwave and stepped over next to Curt. "Oh. She's here for a job interview. I heard her tell Myrna she was a reporter at a newspaper out in Iowa somewhere."

"Job interview?" Curt shook his head. "When did we advertise?"

"We didn't." Max raked her fingers through her mop of dark hair and twisted her combs back into place to hold it out of her eyes. "I heard her say she just moved back to town. Takes a lot of guts, moving without a job to go to, in this economy."

"A lot of confidence," he muttered, still watching the composed, familiar-looking woman. "Not much going on to warrant new staff."

Something about her oval face, those big, dark eyes and the way she tipped her head to one side. He knew he should recognize her.

"Hmm?" He jerked, startled when Max touched his arm. "Sorry. A lot on my mind."

"I said, how can you say there's nothing going on, when the White Rose is still on the loose? That's kind of exciting. Sick, but exciting."

"You and Tony aren't going to use it for your next book, are you?"

"Spare me." Max rolled her eyes and ripped open two packets of raspberry hot chocolate mix for punctuation. "We write romances. Sickos preying on innocent girls, demanding love, sight unseen—that's not romantic."

"Maybe we should check the personal ads at the PD and any other papers, to find someone who's been advertising for months and can't find his true love." Curt's stomach twisted and his mouth tasted like he had bitten into moldy bread. How could he make a joke about the White Rose Killer? Gretchen McKenzie was dead, and now Katrina Harper alternated between terror and frustration.

"I don't think someone like the White Rose would waste time and money on advertising. He's the kind of guy who sees what he wants and punishes anyone who won't give it to him."

"The White Rose?" Ted Gruber, the senior advertising rep, sauntered into the room. "Bet you anything he got rejected by e-Harmony. Maybe we should get the cops to subpoena them to open up their records."

Curt and Max exchanged glances. She muttered about a queue full of stories that needed to be edited and hurried out of the lunchroom. Ted sidled up next to Curt and went up on his toes to see through the gap into Angela's office. He whistled.

"Who's the cutie? Looks kind of familiar... Hey, is she victim two? What's her name, Karen? Kate?"

"Katrina," Curt muttered. "That's not her."

His stomach twisted and he stared at the young woman, standing now and shaking hands with Angela. Make her hair longer, exchange that brown blazer for a fuzzy pink sweater, and make her twelve years old... she could be Angelique Napolitano.

But Angelique was dead. Nearly twenty years now.

Curt shook his head. He was seeing Angelique everywhere, lately. He had nearly knocked himself out on the basketball court two weeks ago, when he looked up in the stands and thought he saw her sitting there, cheering for Tabor Christian's team in the inter-church basketball tournament. The look-alike was Sheila McGuire, Officer Frank McGuire's niece. Her parents were Army doctors, both on duty overseas.

Ted stomped over to the coffeemaker and tossed a quarter into the donation jar. Everyone was supposed to put in fifty cents for the coffee. "Some loony thinks he's in love and plays Cyrano DeBergerac, spouting love poetry from the bushes. When the girls get scared, he gets nasty." He spilled coffee on the counter, then scattered as much sugar as he put in his coffee. He picked up the sponge from the tiny sink, made a half-hearted swipe at the mess, left it sitting there, and headed out of the lunchroom. "What happened to the good old days when a guy saw a girl he wanted, clobbered her over the head and dragged her back to his cave?" He disappeared down the hall to the front of the long, narrow office space.

"I bet you got rejected by e-Harmony, too," Curt muttered.

He heard the doorknob click and pretended to read the six-month-old copy of *Writer's Digest*. He sauntered to the doorway of the lunchroom, watching from the corner of his eye as Angela walked the stranger to the front of the office. The long hallway down the far side of the office unit went from front to back, giving Curt a clear view of the traffic at the front door. He watched Angela and the Angelique look-alike shake hands. Several knots of tension in his gut and shoulders loosened when the young woman walked out the door.

"Likely prospect?" he greeted Angela, as she came back down the hall. They paused in front of the large room where the reporters worked.

"Maybe. But we really don't have any openings. Something about her caught my attention. I'm not sure what." She rubbed her temples and attempted a smile. "Please tell me Dad isn't trying to install another arcade game on the file server?" She gestured at the cluster of workers gathered around the stacked unit of CPUs and printers, with a jungle's worth of cables leading out to the other computers in the office.

Andrew Coffelt had inherited the *Tabor Picayune* from his father and had gladly embraced every advance in technology. Curt sympathized with Angela, because her father was a little too eager to rest on his credits as publisher, semi-retired yet still in the office every day. His delight in trying out new software on the office system was a constant source of frustration for Angela. The only thing that kept her from banning her father from the office was the fact that his experiments hadn't interfered with the publication of the paper. Not yet, anyway.

Curt suspected that even if Andrew caused a power blackout of downtown Tabor Heights for a week, Angela still couldn't ban her father from the paper. They both loved it too much. He just wished she wasn't stuck with being the adult while her father enjoyed his second childhood.

"I think he's just checking out the FBI site that Loni decided to access. Tracking the White Rose and identifying him has become the favorite hobby here," Curt offered.

"Unfortunately." Angela's brown eyes lost focus. Then she shuddered, wrapped her arms around herself, and continued down the hall to the lunchroom, her shoulder-length black hair streaming out behind her with the impetus of her exit.

"Something wrong?" He followed her.

"Everything lately reminds me of the White Rose. That woman who was just in here —"

"Looks like both his targets?" He nodded when she stared at him. "I noticed. She reminded me of someone I knew when I was a kid."

"You might have known her. Toni said she lived here for a few years. Toni Napolitano. Sound familiar?"

Curt started to say no, then choked. "Short for Antoinette?"

He remembered Angelique's little sister, trying to tag along with them when their gang from school went to play kickball. A scrawny kid, she pouted a lot when Angelique told her to stay home. Curt thought she was four years younger than him, putting her in third grade while the rest of them were in seventh.

"Yes, Antoinette. Her credits are impressive. She brought a folder full of clippings." Angela sighed and put down the coffee carafe without filling her mug. "We can't really afford another reporter on staff right now. But it wouldn't be fair to just tell her no without at least examining her work."

"Look at it this way." Curt's smile felt stiff. "She looks so much like the White Rose's targets, would you feel right giving her a job that would have her all over town, letting him get a good look at her?"

"That's not funny." She dumped cream and sugar into her cup before reaching for the carafe again.

"I wasn't trying to be funny." He glanced toward the open door of her office. "So, those clippings she brought. What did she write?"

"Everything. Her specialty seems to be investigative reporting. If you ever feel like you need a partner, I'd seriously consider her."

"Nah, not yet." Curt stayed in the kitchen when Angela went back to her office.

Investigative reporter, huh? He felt sick with the certainty of what brought Toni Napolitano back to Tabor Heights. Somehow, she had heard about the White Rose, the two women he had terrorized, the one he had killed. She heard about the notes, demanding undying love and purity; the white roses left on doorsteps and even inside the victims' houses. The threats against any men who trespassed on his territory.

Just like he had done, had Toni made the connection between the White Rose and her sister's murder? Did she feel duty-bound to hunt him? Just like Curt felt duty-bound? After all, he found Angelique's body, left lying like so much discarded forest trash in the park.

Chapter Two

"This is Angela Coffelt at the *Tabor Picayune*, calling for Toni Napolitano."

Curt stopped outside Angela's office, his hands full of the layout sheets for the next day's paper. He stayed still, hoping Angela wouldn't see him.

"I'm just calling to say I'm sorry—"

Curt backed away, heading across the editorial room to his desk. He felt sorry for Angela, having to be the bearer of bad news. He had read Toni's clippings and she was quite good. The paper she worked for in Iowa was a ten-page weekly. She certainly deserved to move on up to more challenging territory.

Angel had been his first crush. He couldn't send Toni back to Iowa, but he could make sure she wasn't visible all over town. If his theory about the White Rose Killer was correct. He didn't feel the least bit of guilt for encouraging Angela not to hire her.

Maybe he should call Pastor Glenn and share his theory and fears with him. Several prayer chains and Bible studies at Tabor Christian had made the White Rose Killer a focus of concern, just because Police Chief Ray Cooper was a member. This hadn't become personal yet. The Napolitanos had attended the church during their short stay in town, and Curt had a chilling mental image of Toni's casket at the front of the church during the funeral service, just like Angel's had been.

~~~~~

Toni stepped through the side door into her kitchen with her arms full of groceries. She saw the light flashing on her answering machine, sitting in the wide window seat. After her interview this morning, she had gone on a shopping spree, picking up things like curtains, throw rugs, cleaning supplies and food. After all the work she had put in yesterday, getting unpacked and settled, she had decided to splurge and celebrate in anticipation. Sometimes, acting like she had already succeeded had made all the difference. If she acted like she had the job at the *Picayune*, then maybe she could make it real.

Toni planned to turn on the TV, curl up on her two-seater couch to eat Chinese, and go through her *Star Wars* DVD collection until she went unconscious. Unless she had to start work the very next day. Then she would get a good night's sleep. She actually debated ignoring the message
~~~~~

on the answering machine until she had unpacked all her shopping bags. Anticipation was always the best part of any good news.

Curiosity won out. It always did. She put her bag from the Green Dragon on the window seat, pressed the play button, then stepped across the tiny kitchen to fill the refrigerator.

"This is Angela Coffelt at the *Tabor Picayune*, calling for Toni Napolitano."

Toni dashed back across the room to the window seat. She laughed at herself. As if being on top of the machine would affect the message?

"I'm just calling to say I'm sorry, your credits and your reporting skills are topnotch, but we simply don't have the need for another reporter on our staff. There are a handful of other community newspapers you might try, even the *Cleveland Plain Dealer* or the *Akron Beacon Journal*, if you want to move up to the dailies. Thank you for applying to work with us, but again, we simply can't add anyone else to our staff at this time."

Toni snatched up the first thing she could reach, which turned out to be her hot and sour soup. The splat on the forest green tile floor came nowhere near adequately expressing how she felt and filled the air with the mouthwatering aromas of Chinese food. Toni wasn't hungry. She stared through tears at the red light on the answering machine.

No. She knuckled her eyes until they were dry again. She couldn't cry, not yet. Not until Angel's murderer was caught. Not until she knew any other potential targets were safe.

"What am I going to do?" she whispered and sank down to the floor.

Maybe she was wrong to try to do this alone, but who could she ask for help? She had to find someone who remembered her sister, who cared about what happened twenty years ago.

"Time to take some risks," she told her quiet kitchen. She glared at the answering machine. "You're going to hire me, Angela Coffelt. You just don't know it yet."

~~~~~

He sat in the darkness and cold outside the Harper house and watched Sam Conrad's car pull up and Katrina climb out. His hands clenched around his steering wheel, watching the two of them say goodbye. Katrina leaned in the open window, swaying her backside a little. In the overhead interior light of the car, he saw her face light up at something Sam said, and the two of them laughed.

The news had trickled through town for the past two days, but he had refused to believe it. Sam Conrad claimed that he and Katrina had been dating casually for the last two months. They hadn't been serious about each other until the White Rose made his claim on her. Some of the fools in town had laughed when they talked about Sam and Katrina's whirlwind romance. That would send the White Rose running. Who
~~~~~

would mess with Sam Conrad when he was ready to fight for his girl?

"Whore," he growled, watching Katrina walk backward away from the car, waving to Sam as he drove away into the night. "You're mine. I told you that you're mine. He doesn't have any right to you."

He waited until Katrina climbed the front porch steps and went inside her parents' house. His fingers tightened on the steering wheel, almost cutting through the vinyl cover. How could they stand having a filthy liar living in the house with them? He had thought she was his angel because she looked like a good girl, still living at home with her parents, protected and pure.

He was wrong. Again. She would have to be punished.

But first, he had to deal with Sam.

Without turning on his headlights, he pulled out of the shadows of the trees in the empty lot and headed down the street in the direction Sam had gone. He knew everybody in town, every street, every business. He knew where Sam lived, and the route he would take to go home.

Twenty minutes later, he pulled into the parking lot by the swimming hole in the Metroparks, parking his car behind the bathhouse, which was locked up for the winter. He watched until he saw the blue-tinted headlights coming down the park road. That was Sam's car. He had followed Sam to a stop at Heinke's Grocery and waited until he saw him standing in the checkout line. Then he drove away to get ahead of him on the route home.

He had a bucket of glass shards in his trunk, and it was a matter of moments to strew pieces of broken bottles across the park road. Then he ducked behind the bathhouse and waited until he heard the satisfying screeching of Sam's brakes locking up, the *thud-bump* of the car sliding off the road onto the berm. He pressed his gloved hands over his mouth, muffling his laughter, as Sam climbed out of the car, surveyed the damage, then pulled out his cell phone and called for help. He calculated he had maybe fifteen minutes before Sam's roommate got to that spot in the park.

Plenty of time to teach a filthy poacher like Sam Conrad to leave another man's woman alone.

He had a baseball bat in his trunk, saved to deal with that self-righteous jerk, Mark Donovan, but it would work just as well on Sam.

~~~~~

"Angela." Chief Ray Cooper wasn't surprised to see the editor of the *Picayune* come into the waiting room across the hall from Sam Conrad's hospital room.

Her sense of responsibility for the entire community had drawn him to her, even before he discovered their mutual interest in horses. Her need for a new stable for her horse had been icing on the cake and gave him all the opportunities he could wish for to spend time with her without the
~~~~~

entire town speculating on their relationship.

That had been five years now. How did time go by so quickly?

"How is he?" She tipped her head toward the hospital room, the door still closed while the doctors conferred with Sam's older sister and her husband.

"Lucky to be alive." He heard the footsteps coming down the hall and stopped himself from reaching for her hands. "Yes, Evans?"

Officer Duane Evans leaned into the room, braced on the doorframe. "Everything okay in here, Chief?"

"Fine. You're not on duty. Go on home." He held up a hand, stopping the young man. "You did a good job, Evans. Sam's going to live to thank you for being there."

"If I hadn't been running late, heading home..." Evans shuddered. "Who'd do that to a guy?" He glanced at Angela. "Ma'am? I can stay if you need to talk to me."

"The story can wait for the next edition," Angela said. "Curt will probably catch up with you tomorrow to ask, though. Thanks."

"Yes, Ma'am." He nodded to them and left.

"What exactly did the White Rose do?" Angela asked, sinking down into one of the waiting room couches, a remnant from the sixties with chrome and black vinyl cushions, flat and promising backaches.

"Nobody said it was the White Rose." He sank down next to her and took hold of her hand without thinking.

"Ray..." Her mouth quirked up just a little. "Everybody knows Sam Conrad claims Katrina is his girl, and anybody who knows Sam knows he's doing it just to protect her from the White Rose. The only person who would have any reason to hurt him is the White Rose. So what did he do?"

"Covered the park road with glass, and when Sam stopped with two flat tires, ambushed him from behind with a baseball bat, then hung him by his knees from the nearest tree." Cooper swallowed hard. "Evans found the baseball bat covered in blood, and in two pieces." He watched her eyes widen and she winced. "Angie... we have to do something. I just don't know what yet."

"Dad and I agree, whatever approach you choose on this, we're behind you. If you want to keep it low-key, if you want to make it a media circus to drive him out from cover, we'll do it."

"Sometimes when you're doing those election interviews, it seems like you can read the minds of the candidates. I don't suppose you can manage that now?"

"Sorry." She shook her head. A hint of blush touched her cheeks when he raised her hand and brushed his lips over two knuckles.

That was all they had before the door across the hall opened and the doctors came out, followed by Leslie Hancock and her husband. All they ever had were moments, other than those rare free afternoons when they could go riding together, but Cooper didn't let it discourage him.

Friday, November 8

"No, sorry, Angela is in the bathroom." The gravelly voice of Myrna Calhoun blared down the hall from the front desk to the newsroom.

Curt felt the other editorial staff flinch. They all hated it when Myrna worked the receptionist desk, but on delivery days, the newspaper needed at least two people answering the phones. Myrna was in her seventies, a former gym teacher, and claimed she had danced in Vegas when she was younger. Thanks to that story and a flapper costume she wore every Halloween, the former circulation manager had dubbed her "Bubbles." On days like this, when Myrna didn't have the sense to keep people's private business private, Curt swore the bubbles were in her head.

Sighing, he got up and walked to the front of the newspaper office to rescue whoever was at the counter. Angela was expecting Xander Finley for an interview to talk about the new branch office Common Grounds Legal Clinic planned to open in Tabor Heights. Even a trial lawyer might not be able to stand up against Myrna's interrogation tactics. Curt hurried down the long hallway, past the advertising office, past circulation, past the storage room that held office supplies and the morgue, to the front of the office where Max Randolph worked on copy and the ever-changing staff manned the switchboard. Annalee Gray typed the stringer's stories and helped out on the phones when things got really bad, and Curt saw her hanging up a phone as he walked past her desk. She gave him an apologetic little smile. Curt winked and shook his head. Obviously, Myrna had more important things to do than answer the phone today, so Annalee had to step in, leaving the oblivious old woman to embarrass Angela and the *Tabor Picayune* yet again.

"Can I help you with something?" Curt asked, holding out his hand to the woman standing in front of the counter, still giving Myrna an *I can't believe you said that* look. Then he got a good look and wished he had stayed in the back and let Myrna drive her away.

He had been foolish to hope Toni Napolitano would give up after one failure. She wouldn't have been the good, detail-oriented reporter he saw in her clips if she gave up that easily. He should have expected her to come back and try again.

"I was in here yesterday to interview for a job," Toni said. She stretched out her hand to shake Curt's. Her puzzled little frown when he withdrew his hand was almost comical.

He remembered the way she had stared, her eyes big and stunned, when he gave her parents the news about Angel. Then Toni had let out a little scream and ran from the room. He could still hear the sound of her sneakers slapping on the wooden steps as she fled upstairs, and the slam of her door. And her wracking sobs that echoed through the whole house.

"I know. I also know the editor called you and said there wasn't an opening for you." Curt braced his hands on the edge of the counter. Usually he could intimidate people by leaning in close to them. It helped that he was taller than most of the people who came through the newspaper's doors. Little sparks lit up Toni's eyes, but she didn't back away.

"There's more going on here than just a job."

"Like what?"

"I don't think that's any of your business."

"Considering I'm assistant editor, and if you do manage to bull your way in here I'll be stuck working with you, yes, it is my business."

Toni's face went white. Curt almost laughed at this hint she knew who was the assistant editor, and she remembered him. He had been a scrawny kid, four inches shorter than Angel, back in seventh grade. Now he towered over everyone in Tabor Heights, except maybe Pastor Wally and a few men in the fire department.

"Curt, it's been a long time." She mustered up a smile. "You probably don't remember me, from when we were kids."

The total silence hit Curt like a hammer blow. He looked to his left. Myrna sat up straight at her desk, eyes wide, greedy glee stretching her orange-lipsticked mouth in a wide smile. She lived for gossip and warped everything she heard.

"Old home week, I guess." Curt forced a smile, caught hold of Toni's arm, and stepped around the counter. She didn't resist as he led her to the front door and out onto the sidewalk in front of the newspaper office. Snow had started falling again. "If you're trying to impress the boss with your persistence, you get ten points for that, but you lose ten on timing."

"You don't understand."

"I think I do. I think you're here because of Angel." Curt hated himself when he saw the shock in those big, dark eyes, the hurt mixed with the relief. He hated the proof that she had come here looking for Angel's killer and hated the suspicion that he had just encouraged her.

He wanted to throw her over his shoulder, drive her to the airport and put her on the first plane back to Iowa. Curt let go of her hand and gripped both her shoulders to turn her around.

"Go home, Antoinette. Leave the crime-fighting to the police."

"I have to do this."

"Does anybody tell you how much you look like Angel?" He flinched when a car drove down the street between the newspaper's building and the shopping plaza it faced. The driver didn't look at him. He could only imagine how it looked for him to stand out here in his shirtsleeves with more snow threatening in the horizontal wind.

"No. We don't talk about Angel." Her mouth flattened and the anger lighting her eyes turned into that old pain Curt had seen in his dreams, ever since the White Rose's first "true love" turned up dead.

"You look a lot like her. If I see the resemblance, I bet the White Rose will, too. What do you think will happen if he sees you and thinks you're Angel, come back from the dead?"

"You think that's exactly what's happening, don't you? You think it's the same boy who killed Angel." Toni grasped his arms and shook him once. "Curt, you have to help me with this."

"Help you get killed? Angela has a sign over her door. Maybe you missed it when you came in. It says we report the news, we don't become part of it."

"I'll make you a deal." She leaned closer and Curt caught the scent of peppermint on her breath. "I'm only going to stay as long as it takes to catch the White Rose. Then I'm gone. This town has only bad memories for me. So, we work together, and the faster we catch this guy, the faster I'm gone and out of your hair. Deal?" She released him and stepped back, holding out her gloved hand.

"I don't make stupid deals." Something writhed inside his gut when that hopeful gleam in her eyes died, crushed by his growled words. Curt sighed, knowing he was going to hate this. "By now, Angela probably knows you came back. I'll tell her what you want and we'll get back to you, okay?"

"Why not tell me now?" Angela said.

Curt groaned and turned around to see her framed in the doorway, her big, dark eyes bright with something that wasn't exactly amusement. He could just imagine what kind of warped story Myrna had told her.

"Max warned me there was somebody who needed rescuing from Myrna," Angela said. "I have the feeling I'm rescuing Miss Napolitano from you, instead."

"How much did you hear?" he had to ask.

"More than should be discussed out here on the sidewalk." She beckoned for him and Toni to follow her back into the office.

Myrna was busy on the phone, lecturing someone about the history of Tabor Heights, with her back to the door. Annalee stood at Max's desk, leaning over her shoulder and studying the screen. Max met Curt's gaze and gave him an eye-roll. Curt didn't know if he should laugh or feel guilty for making a scene. Once they reached Angela's office, she closed the door, made sure it latched, and tugged the curtain over the porthole window. Angela perched on the front of her desk while Curt and Toni took the seats in front of her.

"I'm just catching up on the back-story," Angela said as she crossed her arms. "I should apologize for not recognizing your name, Miss Napolitano. Your sister's murder was the first story I helped write, when I started working for my father." She took a deep breath, exhaled loudly, and tried to smile. "I remember Angel. I was in ninth grade when she was in seventh. She used to bring in the ads your father placed."

"If I had told you I wanted the job because I needed an excuse to come back and hunt Angel's murderer, would you have hired me?" Toni spoke softly, with a world of exhaustion in her voice.

"I honestly don't know." Angela tipped her head to one side, like a bird studying something before it pounced. Curt knew that look didn't bode well for him, since her gaze focused on him now. "Something tells me you knew when she was here yesterday. Want to tell me why you didn't say anything?"

"I figured she was safer working somewhere else, if we couldn't get her to leave town," Curt said with a shrug.

"No matter what you decide, I'm staying," Toni said.

"I could tell Chief Cooper you're going to be a hindrance to his investigation," Angela said softly. Her lips flattened into a grim smile. "But I won't do that. Because quite honestly, linking Angel's murder to the White Rose never occurred to Ray or to me, or anyone else working the investigation, that I know of. How long have you had the theory, Curt?"

He felt like a kid being raked over the coals in school when Angela looked at him that way.

"A week or two. I don't know where the idea came from, but all of a sudden it just hit me that Gretchen and Katrina both look like Angel, if she'd grown up. The white roses and the notes reminded me of the notes her parents found. It sounded too similar for a coincidence, but maybe I was hoping that's all it was." He shrugged. "I wanted some more evidence before I wasted the chief's time with my theories."

"Let's hope you don't get any more evidence," Toni muttered.

"Amen," Angela said. "Let's make a deal, Miss Napolitano—"

"Please, call me Toni. If we're going to be working together."

Chapter Three

"That's a pretty big 'if' right now." Angela nodded. "I will go to Chief Cooper and tell him your and Curt's theory, and that you want to help. I assume you and Curt were arguing about you staying out of trouble, and trying to convince you to leave town."

"We were." Curt had the sinking feeling he had just stepped into a mess too large to be cleaned up.

"No matter what Ray decides, can I have your promise of full cooperation whenever the police need it?"

Curt wondered if Toni realized how rare it was for the newspaper and the police department to be able to speak for each other. Chief Ray Cooper and Angela Coffelt were good friends. She boarded her horse at the stables his daughter managed, on the edge of the Metroparks, and it wasn't unusual to see the two of them riding together on the weekends. On the rare occasion Chief Cooper needed silence from the media, because of a delicate situation, the *Tabor Picayune* always cooperated. In return, the newspaper always had the inside scoop on anything newsworthy involving the police in Tabor. It made for less trouble investigating stories and keeping the facts out in the open, less grumbling and feuding between the authorities and the media.

"Full cooperation," Toni said. "But he'll agree with me, I know it. You need my help."

Curt had the awful feeling Toni was right. It would be much easier on everyone having her right there, sharing everything she remembered. He had hesitated to voice his theory because eventually, Chief Cooper would need to contact Angel's parents and plumb their memories.

"Hey, do your parents know what you're up to?" he blurted.

"No." Toni closed her eyes and swallowed hard. "They don't talk about Angel. It's like she never existed. Don't contact them. It would tear them apart."

~~~~~

He watched Katrina leave the hospital room, tears gleaming in her eyes. He might have believed those tears, might have felt sorry for her, but he knew better.

She didn't cry in pity for the man lying in the hospital bed. Sam Conrad deserved the punishment he received for trying to claim the woman another man loved. She cried because she knew her punishment
~~~~~

waited. She cried because soon the whole world would know she wasn't an angel, pure and loyal and worthy of love. She deserved to die.

He followed her to the elevators. He knew better than to wait where she could see him, or to ride down in the same elevator. When she got on the elevator, smiling politely at all those innocent people who didn't know what she was, he took the stairs down to the first floor. He reached the lobby before her and waited just outside the range of the electric eye that opened the doors. When she stepped outside, she looked up at the half-moon in the chilly, clear sky and shivered. He wondered if she sensed justice waiting in the shadows.

Her car waited in the corner of the parking lot, furthest from the lights. That was a sure sign that she unconsciously submitted to her justified punishment. He stood on the other side of her car, hidden in darkness, waiting for that moment. Her cry of dismay, the sob that escaped her when she discovered the white rose he left on her windshield, was pure music to his soul.

"Oh, please!" She turned and flung the white rose away and staggered backward to sag against the side of her car. "When is this going to end?"

"Don't worry," he said, staying in the shadows. "It's almost over. You won't be bothered anymore."

"Who's—" The relief that brightened her face when she saw his borrowed hospital security uniform was almost comical. "You have no idea how glad I am to see you."

He almost corrected her, that she didn't really see him at all. She hadn't seen his face. His true love would never see his face until she had proven she was worthy of his love.

She pulled her keys out of her purse and turned her back to him, to unlock her car. "I have to call this in. Chief Cooper said to call him or Donovan, whenever anything happened. Or do you want to write up the report, since you're here?"

He crept up behind her. He ripped open the sealed bag with the chloroform cloth and slapped it over her face while she was still talking. He wrapped his other arm around her chest to pull her off her feet and pin her arms to her sides. She struggled, kicking, her cries muffled by the cloth. Then she collapsed like a limp rag against him.

"Why do you have to be such a liar? Don't you know liars get sent straight to Hell?"

He took her keys, unlocked the car and tossed her into the back seat. Ten minutes later, he reached the spot at the bend in the river in the Metroparks where he hid his car. It was an easy hike through the park to the woods that backed up to the hospital. He transferred her into the trunk of his car after taping her mouth, ankles, and wrists, then wiped down her car to remove all fingerprints. For good measure, he left the doors and trunk open. It was supposed to sleet tonight, turning to snow near morning. By the time anyone found his treacherous angel's car, any clues left behind would be wiped away by the weather and animals.

Sunday, November 10

He tucked the first white rose in the newspaper in the slot under her mailbox. After a week of watching, he knew his precious angel's habits. She was a good girl, shy and quiet and obedient. At precisely seven a.m., she stepped outside, just like she did every morning. She would fetch the newspaper for her father to read before church.

Today she wore a green dress and her hair hung around her face in a sable curtain. He would have to tell her she was so much lovelier that way, not like he usually saw her with her hair pulled back in a simple ponytail and wearing slacks.

She looked around the neighborhood as she walked down the short driveway and retrieved the newspaper from the box. She wouldn't see him. Until he was ready to claim her love, his angel would never see him.

He laughed when she didn't look at the paper, didn't see the white rose peering out of the orange plastic sleeve that protected the paper from the falling snow. He watched her walk up the steps, wipe her boots on the mat, and step inside, to take the newspaper to her father.

She was a good girl, taking care of her parents, working hard at the newspaper to help people, kind to everyone she met. He was proud to know she was his, proud that even the criminals coming through the police station were polite to her. Her purity kept her safe. She was his angel. What was it people said about the third time being the charm? He had found her this time, the third time. His angel. He would never let anyone hurt her. She belonged to him, and he would love her forever.

~~~~~

"There has got to be some place better than this," Curt muttered.

He wished he hadn't left his gloves in his car, and his car half a mile back in a parking slot near the waterfowl refuge. For the sake of his story, he had hiked down the curving Metroparks road to get to the par course in search of his story. The homeless people allegedly camping in the Metroparks wouldn't come anywhere near someone in a car. Curt wondered if he would have to dress in Salvation Army castoffs before he could get someone to come out of hiding or at least let him approach.

He blew on his cold fingers one more time and jammed his fists into the inadequate pockets of his jacket. At least he had the sense to pull on his stocking cap when he got out of the car. The snow seemed to fall a little
~~~~~

thicker, catching on his lashes. He bowed his head and hunched his shoulders and trudged on. Maybe someone would be lurking around the bathrooms up near the leg lift station of the par course.

The muffled clops of horses' hooves came to him from the right. Curt turned, searching the white horizon. For two in the afternoon, the park was pretty deserted otherwise. He waited a little longer, and two horses appeared around the bend in the park road where it vanished into the trees, plodding steadily along through the snowy grass between the road and the asphalt jogging trail. Curt decided he would walk over to where he would meet up with the riders, check if they had seen anybody remotely resembling vagabonds, and then call it a day.

He certainly hadn't expected to be tramping around through the snow when he got dressed for church this morning. That chance remark he overheard in the fellowship hall when he snagged a cup of coffee between the service and Singles class was too good a tip to pass up.

"Somehow, I just can't picture you as the type to take a picturesque stroll through the snow," Angela called, when the horses were close enough for Curt to make out details.

"Just looking for those squatters we've been hearing rumors about." He grinned and stepped off the trail to wait.

The other rider was Chief Cooper. He wondered idly if he would ever meet up with Cooper's daughter, Diana. She had come to live with him three years ago, after some showdown with her mother and stepfather. He didn't talk much about her, and Angela was pretty tight-lipped, too. Curt only knew his boss got along with the girl because of their mutual love of horses. The Coopers' stables had a good reputation and a waiting list of people who wanted to board their horses with them.

"If you're bucking for a promotion," Cooper said, "you might as well give up. The only step up is to take over as editor, and I have it on good authority she's years away from retiring."

"Boredom, not ambition," Curt hurried to say, holding up his hands in surrender, which made Angela and Cooper both laugh.

A cell phone chirped, making all three dig in their pockets. Chief Cooper was the loser. He rolled his eyes and grimaced as he listened to whoever was on the other end of the line. His grimace turned into a frown of concentration. Then he muttered something, closed his eyes, and shook his head once, sharply.

Angela reached over and grasped his arm. Curt watched the chief, wishing the person on the other end of the line would talk louder. From the man's reaction, it was police business. Couldn't they even leave him alone for a few hours on Sunday?

Then a hunch gave him a dropping sensation in his stomach and a cold chill of premonition that made the icy wind seem balmy by comparison.

"I'm in the park right now, coming up from the ford toward the swimming hole," Cooper said. He listened for a few more seconds, nodding. "All right. Tell Donovan he's in charge down there, and I'll be in my office to talk to her parents in maybe ten minutes, tops." He turned off the phone, looked at it sitting in his gloved palm for a few seconds, then shoved it in his pocket. To Curt, he looked ten years older and exhausted. "Can I ask you to lead Reno back to the stables for me, Angela? I need to head up to the station to meet... Well, you probably heard enough to guess."

"Off the record?" Angela asked.

"Thanks. Unfortunately, there's been enough squawking on the police scanners by now, half the state knows." Cooper rubbed his face with his gloved hands and sighed. He looked tired, when he had been alert and in good humor just a few minutes ago. "Katrina Harper's parents just got back from vacation and panicked when they found Saturday's and today's papers sitting on the porch. She isn't answering her phone."

Curt groaned. He had hoped it wasn't news about the White Rose's current target.

"Nathan Lewis called in an abandoned car he just found in the park, down off Westmore Road," the chief continued. "It looks like it could be hers." He and Angela nodded farewell to Curt and nudged their mounts into a trot, then a gallop, and in a few moments vanished around a curve in the park road, behind a stand of trees.

Curt hurried up the jogging trail back to his car and drove up to the police station, arriving just as Angela was heading out of the police department parking lot, leading the chief's horse. She nodded to him as he drove past her.

When he got inside the station, Joe and Katie Harper, Katrina's parents, were just coming in the main entrance. Curt knew Joe Harper from the Recreation Department. He hated intruding at a time like this, but he had to do his job as a reporter. And maybe it would help the Harpers to have a familiar face with them.

The chief tried to be encouraging but didn't offer false hope. Curt could respect the man for taking that difficult stand. As the afternoon wore on and they retraced Katrina's steps, they pieced together what had happened. There was little to work from.

Katrina had visited Sam Conrad at the hospital. Since the big, friendly mechanical engineering student had been attacked, she had camped out at the hospital. The friendship that started in a chivalrous gesture seemed on the verge of turning into a romance. Mrs. Harper laughed brokenly through her tears when she related her last phone call with her daughter, Friday night, when Katrina was leaving Sam's hospital room. She said

Sam had asked her to go to a movie with him when he was released from the hospital. According to the duty nurse, Katrina had stayed until visiting hours were over.

That was the last anyone saw of her. No neighbors noticed if there were lights on in the house Friday night and Saturday, and the drifts of snow on the front porch prevented anyone from seeing that papers were piling up.

"But she wouldn't go through the park on her way home from the hospital," Joe said, when the news came that the abandoned car was positively identified as Katrina's. "It's too long and roundabout."

Curt knew what had happened, even before Donovan came in and presented his theories. The White Rose had caught Katrina somewhere between the hospital and home and abandoned her car in a densely wooded section of the park where no one would have seen the car right away. The heavy snowfall Friday night and Saturday only helped hide the car. Ranger Nathan Lewis had only seen the car when he was helping some cross-country skiers who had slipped off the trail and became lost.

Monday, November 11

Angela left a message for Curt Sunday night, asking him to gather the staff for a meeting as soon as she got into the office Monday morning. He knew it would be about whatever she and Chief Cooper had decided to do about the media's approach to the White Rose's activities. He couldn't stop wondering if Katrina Harper was still alive or if her body had been deposited somewhere in the park and no one had found it yet because of the snow. Would it be near the spot where he had found Angel all those years ago?

If Katrina was dead, did two murders make the White Rose a serial killer?

Even more important: had the man chosen his third target already?

Curt thought of Toni, how much she looked like Angel all grown up, the determination and the grief in her eyes. Was it possible the White Rose had seen her, and decided to get Katrina out of his way so he could go after his true love?

"You're a sick man," he muttered, heading down the hallway to the editorial room.

"Problem?" Ted Gruber paused in the doorway of the sales office.

"Rough weekend." Curt watched Ted pull off his overcoat and muffler and slapped his beret onto the metal coat rack standing in the corner. He wondered if that white stuff falling off the beret was snowflakes or dandruff. "We're having a staff meeting as soon as Angela gets here," he said quickly, trying to deflect more private griping about Ted's inconsistent grooming habits.

"Meeting?" Loni stopped in the hallway behind him, leaned against the wall, and yanked her snow boots off. "What about?"

"For now, everything is strictly confidential." Curt waited until both of them nodded. "The White Rose."

"Who did he beat up this time?" She tucked a few loose strands of platinum blonde hair behind her ears and rubbed at her cold-reddened nose with the back of her hand. "No... not Katrina."

"We don't know anything yet. Angela's probably coming from the station. Just don't go talking about any of this until we get the word, okay?"

"It's not funny anymore, y'know?" Ted said mournfully. He dropped into his swivel desk chair and pulled open the deep, bottom drawer of his desk. It was crammed full of donut and chip bags. "I could use some pepping up. Breakfast, anybody?" He pulled out a bag of donuts, took two for himself, then offered the bag to Loni and Curt.

"I just read a report on how many empty calories are in that junk." Loni finished putting her loafers on and stepped back, shuddering, as if those calories would cross five feet of empty air and land on her hips.

"That's why they call it junk food." He waited a few seconds, and when Curt didn't take him up on his offer, tossed the donut bag onto the corner of his desk and took a big bite. "Hey, at least I enjoy what I eat," he said, managing to only spray a few crumbs.

"Yeah, if you like horror movies," Loni muttered, and moved down the hall.

"Something wrong with a girl so strict on the health food mumbo jumbo," he mumbled through a few more crumbs.

"Good morning!" Andrew Coffelt called, scooting down the hall with twice the energy and enthusiasm Curt felt. "Gather round, people, I have good news." He tapped on Angela's closed office door, then continued to the lunchroom where the main coat rack hung on the wall.

"Good news about what?" Curt followed him. Andrew obviously didn't know about Angela's meeting.

"The *Picayune* is sponsoring two baseball teams this spring, and I'm going to need help deciding on their names. Let's have a contest, shall we? The people who pick the two best names get an evening on the town as a prize." He peeled off his fur cap, leather greatcoat, and neon red scarf as he spoke, not quite paying attention as he hung them up on the rack.

Curt smiled, despite the concerns on his mind, and bent to pick up the two coats and set of gloves Andrew had knocked off the rack without noticing. That was Andrew, always excited about something, offering support and making things interesting for everyone around him. He had always been white-haired, stocky and involved in twenty different projects at the same time. Andrew was in his eighties, but if not for his white hair, he might have passed himself off as being in his fifties. Curt supposed it was a sign of Andrew's energy and enthusiasm for life that he had persuaded Angela's mother to marry him and start a family when most men were settling down to play grandfather.

"Look out below!" Max called as she came into the lunchroom. "You know those rumors that DDT is remodeling and coming back under a new name?"

"I thought we got rid of that bar," Sherwood Gaynes said, coming in on her heels.

"There's a big sign on the downstairs entrance." Max hooked a thumb over her shoulder, through the back window that looked over a sloping roof and the equally sloped parking lot.

The newspaper office took the street-level floor of the building, with a dance bar below them. It had been named Dancing Danny Twilight, in hopes of attracting the college crowd, but the name had been shortened to DDT when the beer-and-billiards crowd dominated the scene. The mistake, Curt supposed, was keeping the pool tables and pinball machines that had been left behind from the last bar that occupied the space. The original crowd just came back and ignored the change in décor.

"It says 'Under New Management,' but the fine print has the same names as DDT's owners," Max continued as she stowed her lunch bag in the refrigerator. "There are a bunch of guys moving lumber and construction tools inside. So we're going to have some competition."

Curt groaned with the others. During the last renovation of the space downstairs, the noise level had been a constant problem. Every time he tried to conduct a phone interview, invariably some loud machinery would start up. When they weren't in use, someone had a radio set at chop-and-liquefy volume.

Chapter Four

"Fine print?" Loni asked, sticking her head out of the photography lab, which lay between Angela's office and the men's bathroom. "Who reads the fine print on those signs?"

"With all the contracts I have to sign, for Dad's theater and my own books, you better believe I read the fine print all the time." Max offered them a grin and hurried up to the front of the office. Curt heard the sound of the phone ringing. Annalee had phone duty until Simon, the Monday receptionist, got in from his first period class. Why wasn't Annalee answering the phone?

"My friends," Andrew said with a heavy sigh, "I think it's time we start looking at new quarters. Preferably our own building." He nodded for emphasis and strode out of the lunchroom and into Angela's office.

The nice thing about Andrew Coffelt was that he had the money to back proposals like that. Curt didn't doubt the *Picayune*'s owner would spend the entire day on the phone, tracking down every piece of commercial property for lease or sale in Tabor.

On the plus side, he wouldn't be wandering the office, helping everyone. Most of the time, Andrew's observations and bits of advice were useful, but sometimes he had a magical talent for tangling the simplest story or causing a time-consuming breakdown in the system.

Angela came in just when Curt wondered if something had gone wrong over at the police department. He saw her white beret and scarf come through the front door and started to turn, to alert everyone to get ready for the meeting. Then he took a second look. Angela walked in with Annalee and had her arm around the girl's shoulders. Instead of bouncing through the door with a smile for everyone, Annalee walked with her head down. Curt could have sworn Angela was guiding her. As if Annalee didn't want to come to work.

When had that ever happened?

All right, so Annalee had been close to quitting in tears after that first week of answering the phones. All the lunatics in the surrounding four towns had decided to call in one day. That crazy on Prague Road threatened to beat her face in with a tire iron because his paper was late. Angela switched her over to typing duties and gathering the police blotter news, and Annalee loved her job now. What had changed?

Curt walked up to the front of the office, careful to avoid the spot in the middle where the floorboards squeaked. He flinched when a radio blared downstairs in the bar, evidence of the remodeling going full steam, just as Max had warned. He stayed at the end of the hall, watching Angela talk with Max and Annalee. Max's mouth dropped open, then she jumped out of her chair and hugged Annalee. Curt didn't like the shiver of warning going down his back any more than the hard set to Angela's mouth when she turned around and headed down the hall to her office.

"Problem?" he murmured, when she passed him and he fell into step behind her.

"Wait for the meeting," Angela said.

She didn't even flinch or ask for an explanation when the shriek of a drill going into wood resounded from downstairs. Curt walked around the office, first the newsroom, then the advertising and circulation offices, to gather everyone for the meeting. They all settled down in the newsroom, bringing chairs in from the other offices, and turned to face Angela's office. Curt supposed everyone caught the tightening of the atmosphere because the usual pre-meeting banter was missing. Angela waited in her office until Andrew finished his call, and father and daughter held hands as they came out into the newsroom.

"Chief Cooper has asked for our help in keeping everything pertaining to the White Rose confidential. Please don't talk about it among yourselves, even in the office." Angela glanced down the hallway to the front of the office for a moment. "I trust most of our switchboard people, and the paper carriers, but it will be easier to just leave them out of the loop. I don't want to have to track down who overheard something they shouldn't have and then spread exaggerations or leaked sensitive information." She looked around the gathered staff, meeting everyone's eyes, before continuing. "There's going to be a press conference at City Hall in about an hour. Curt, you and I will both be attending."

Curt nodded. He could just imagine the media circus that was building up, ready to explode.

"Katrina Harper has been missing since Friday night," Angela continued after a moment. Her voice didn't waver, but Curt noticed the dark smears of strain almost visibly growing under her eyes. The sounds and expressions of dismay from everyone on the staff warmed him. "Her car was found abandoned in the park yesterday afternoon. More important—" She closed her eyes a moment. Andrew murmured encouragement and patted her shoulder. "I'm asking all of you to be discrete and I'm depending on your support in this." She took another deep breath. "Annalee received a white rose yesterday morning."

Curt felt as if someone had thumped him in the gut with a basketball. He was glad he had taken his usual position leaning against the wall. He needed something to hold him upright.

"Please—" Angela held up her hand, as if everyone was about to leap from their chairs and mob the front of the office and Annalee. "She's requested that we all go on as if nothing has happened. Chief Cooper wants to keep this as quiet as possible. He's hoping that keeping the media attention off her will keep her safe. We don't need any vigilantes getting involved or someone else playing hero like Sam Conrad. From now on, Annalee will never be left alone. I want someone to go with her when she collects the police blotter news, and I want someone to wait with her until her father picks her up from work, and to meet her at the door in the morning. The chief is increasing patrols in her neighborhood and around the office. Maybe somebody will notice someone who shouldn't be here, or we'll pick up a pattern to help us identify the White Rose. It's our aim to make Annalee the White Rose's *last* target."

Angela gave no one any opportunity for questions before she turned the meeting to the general Monday morning newspaper business. In less than twenty minutes, she dismissed the staff to get back to work and beckoned Curt into her office. Andrew didn't accompany them. Curt settled into his usual chair and waited while she sat at her desk, pressed the heels of her hands against her eyes, and took a few deep breaths. He imagined she fought both tears and fury. Angela took care of her staff, considered them her family, even the oblivious and irritating ones. Annalee was a sweet, quiet girl who certainly didn't deserve what the White Rose would soon put her through, if he followed the pattern established with Gretchen and Katrina.

"I'm going to give Toni Napolitano the job," Angela said, before she raised her head from her hands. "Ray agrees with me. We need her insight and memories, and we'd both feel better having her where we can keep an eye on her."

"Makes sense," was all Curt could offer. He wasn't surprised. Now that Angela put it that way, he agreed with her. Better to keep Toni busy during the day, tracking down stories, filling her head with something other than finding the lunatic who had killed her sister.

"I sensed some antagonism between the two of you. Will that be a problem if I have you work with her?"

"No. I was mostly angry that she'd put herself in a position to get hurt. Maybe you don't remember, but I'm the one—"

"Who found Angel's body." Angela nodded. Her eyes were bright, but no tears trembled on her lashes. "I dug through the archives last night, after Ray and I had our meeting, just to brush up on the details. The memories those old papers raised... You knew Toni and Angel, spent enough time with the family to be considered a friend?"

"As much as anyone in Tabor back then, I guess. Mr. Napolitano and my dad were sort of friendly business rivals." Curt shrugged. "Why are you asking?"

"I want to add some insurance to what we're doing already. I want you to spend so much time with Toni, away from the office, people think you're serious about each other."

"Do you think that will really stop the White Rose, if he decides she doesn't just resemble Angel, she *is* Angel?"

"All we can do is try."

Tuesday, November 12

"Enter at your own risk," Max said, meeting Curt at the door of the *Picayune* as he came back from lunch and she was exiting. She had Annalee with her, and to his relief, they both smiled. They also wore coats and carried purses. "Stoplight just came in. He's shrieking for Sherwood and Myrna is giving him a lecture on the programming of stoplights, which is all wrong, of course, and neither one of them is listening to the other."

"Did you warn Sherwood?" Curt turned and walked across the street with them, heading for the shopping plaza.

"Loni grabbed him and dragged him into her workroom with her," Annalee said with a little giggle. Curt loved hearing that sound. He had been afraid she would never smile again, let alone laugh. "Now, why do you call that smelly old man Stoplight, and why does he need to talk to Sherwood?"

"I'm not sure what his real name is," Max said. She tugged the collar of her pea coat higher around her neck and hunched her shoulders as a blast of icy wet air slapped them from behind. "They've been calling him Stoplight since before I started working here."

"He thinks the stoplights in town are programmed to change when pedestrians are halfway across the street, so they'll get run down by traffic," Curt said. "That only happens when his medication runs low and he doesn't want to refill the prescription right away. Happens regular as clockwork, every two months."

"Why does he need Sherwood? He does school sports." Annalee shook her head. The three of them reached the front door of Heinke's grocery.

"Sherwood's first day on the job, he made the mistake of being sympathetic. Stoplight hates me because he keeps insisting I do a full expose and I keep telling him I need documentation," Curt said. "Stoplight thinks Sherwood is the only real reporter on the staff, and he lets me know it, at full volume, every time he sees me."

"And he gets so excited, he spits when he talks," Max added, making a disgusted face. "I figured, let Myrna handle him until he runs out of steam, and we could run across and get some lunch."

"And saved my sorry—" Curt grimaced when his cell phone vibrated in his back pocket. He gestured for Max and Annalee to go on ahead of him while he pulled his phone out. He froze, recognizing Officer Mark Donovan's direct number on the display. Part of the new arrangements for handling the White Rose Killer story was that all communications between the *Picayune* and the authorities would pass between Donovan and Curt. "Good news?" he said, as soon as the line connected.

"If only." Donovan pitched his voice low. Curt wondered who was close at hand whom the officer didn't want to hear the conversation. "They found Katrina Harper's body. The cross-country ski club from the middle school meets on Tuesday nights, and the woman in charge of the rentals went out early to the cabin to set things up. Nora Parker and her son, Ron. Thank goodness it was them. They knew to keep it quiet. The idiot who found Gretchen's body notified every TV station in the state before he called us." He sighed, sounding tired. "In this temperature, it's hard to tell how long she's been there, or how long she's been dead."

"No tracks, because of all the snow," Curt muttered.

"And no sign of forced entry. Whoever did it had keys."

"Or he's a locksmith."

"The chief wants me to call the Harpers' pastor before he goes over to their house with the news. Do you know what church they go to?"

"St. Ambrose, I think." Curt stared unseeing at the light traffic in the grocery store around him. Far on the other side of the store, in the produce section, Max and Annalee chatted across the salad bar as they filled their plastic bowls. Curt thought of Donovan having to make that call to Annalee's parents and Pastor Glenn someday. *It's not going to happen*, he vowed.

~~~~~

Angela had to get away. She was no use to the *Picayune* with her head full of the present tragedy and shadows from the past, fighting each other for her attention. It didn't help that she was friends with Nora Parker, and they both had served on the Sandstone Festival committee with Katrina's mother. The connection just made today's news more personal and tragic. As soon as she could, when every responsibility for the coming edition of the paper had been either handled or delegated, she told Curt she was taking off a little early.

She waited until Myrna was on the phone, deep in conversation, before she left the office. Angela laughed at herself for taking that precaution, as she opened her trunk for the change of clothes she kept there for emergencies. It made no sense. Why should she care if Myrna made a fuss over her leaving work early? Nothing the woman could say about her would do any damage. Myrna thought she was a mover-and-
~~~~~

shaker in Tabor Heights, just because she belonged to the historical, genealogical and a dozen other societies. Angela certainly wasn't answerable to the interfering, nosy old woman. Still, it was easier to get along with Myrna by ignoring her and being careful what was said in her hearing.

For ten seconds, as she waited at the light to turn onto Main and head for Coopers' stables, Angela looked up the slope of the street to the intersection where the post office sat. Just to the left was Tabor Christian. Maybe instead of going riding to let off some of the day's pressure, she should go talk to Pastor Glenn. Or just sit in the prayer chapel, bathed in light from the stained glass windows, and beg for some peace and wisdom?

The light changed and she turned without thinking. Old habits died hard. Once she had it in her head to go riding, nothing would stop her. She sometimes speculated she could drive to the stables with her eyes closed, although Ray Cooper might take exception to such reckless behavior.

"Sometimes I swear, the only reason you won't let me tell people you're my girlfriend," he had teased her more than once, "is because you know everyone would be watching how you drive. The chief's girlfriend can't get tickets or fudge the parking rules."

"Girlfriend," she always responded with a snort. "You and I are far too... mature... for terms like boyfriend and girlfriend."

"Being mature is overrated," was his usual response.

Followed by a soft, sweet, long kiss. Usually in the presence of their horses, in a shadowy spot in the woods where no one could spy on them.

Angela wasn't sure what she was afraid of, why she wouldn't let Ray make their relationship public knowledge. Other than the political in-fighting in Tabor Heights and the surrounding communities, and the scorching other public figures had endured when their relationships became public knowledge. The general public had long memories, and a tendency to ignore dates and facts and figures that didn't support what they wanted to believe. One Ohio senator had given up his shares in a community newspaper elsewhere in Cuyahoga County long before he ran for public office, but according to his detractors, he dictated the slant of the stories. Angela didn't want those kinds of accusations tainting the *Tabor Picayune*'s stand. Maybe if Judge Foggarty ever left office, she might change her mind...

"Leave it for later," she whispered. The coils of tension in her gut and shoulders and neck gradually released with every mile she put between herself and the newspaper office, and every mile closer to the stables.

Ray drove up while she was unwinding by brushing her horse. Angela knew the particular low-pitched rattle-hum of his Jeep anywhere.

She smiled when her heart gave a little flutter and kept on working.

"Great minds think alike," Ray said, when the crunching of his boots on the gravel of the driveway stopped. His shadow stretched down the long aisle between the rows of stalls.

"I muted my phone. I know you didn't." She didn't turn around. Her horse grunted when she pressed a little harder with her strokes.

"I'd hear it if I left it at the station." He sighed and his shadow grew shorter as he moved closer to her. "How bad was it, with Nora and her son?"

"You'd think that knowing the people involved would be helpful to someone." Angela fumbled the brush and Ray reached around her to catch it. "Her son dated Katrina a few years ago, before he met Dana, his fiancée." Her voice caught.

Here it comes. She was almost relieved to know she had reached the shattering point. She couldn't take this pressure and weight home with her. Not when she refused to tell her father about Curt and Toni's theory. Andrew would scold Toni for risking her safety in the hunt for her sister's killer, and then he would feel duty-bound to call her parents.

"Angie..." Ray grasped her shoulders to turn her to face him. The aching weariness in his face broke her more than her sorrow for the Harpers. She buried her face in his jacket and didn't even care that his zipper would leave a pressure mark on her cheek as she let the tears flow. Just for a few minutes, she could hide from the world in the warmth of his arms. The fact that these moments of closeness and shelter were so rare made them so much more precious.

Sometimes, late at night, she played with the idea that she kept their relationship clandestine, not because of the political enemies who would attack, but because she didn't want it to become everyday, ordinary, and expected.

Other times, like right now, Angela wanted to tell the world to go hang itself, and give up all her responsibilities, her heritage as a Coffelt newspaper woman, to be able to cross the yard from the stables to the Coopers' house, and know she could stay for the rest of her life.

Friday, November 15

Toni planned to walk to work when the weather improved. Right now, the prospect of the ten-minute walk from her cottage to the newspaper office seemed like a trudge to the North Pole. There was no time for the heater in her SUV to start churning out warm air, much less heat, by the time she pulled into the parking lot that sloped down to the riverbank, next to and behind the newspaper office's building. Curt had warned her about the construction on the bar downstairs, so she made sure to park far away from that doorway. Her truck had survived six winters in Iowa, with combines and other farm equipment pulling into traffic without any warning, and she didn't want to ruin her record with some falling two-by-fours smashing into the roof or broken glass shredding her nearly new tires.

A scurrying, chubby figure in a long, plaid, hooded coat nearly ran into Toni when she reached the sidewalk and turned left to walk to the office door. A burst of laughter and a muffled apology greeted her, then the figure hurried on ahead, grabbed the doorknob, and held the door open for her.

"Sorry about that. Bundled up like this, I just can't see anything," the stranger said, and hurried into the office after Toni.

"That's okay. It's cold enough to make a polar bear run for cover." Toni muffled laughter when she realized what she mistook for a wide outline was actually a backpack covered in a blanket, held close to the body.

"Hi, I'm Loni Schuster." She yanked her hood down, revealing platinum blond hair and red cheeks and layers of scarves, six inches thick around her face, which explained the previously muffled voice. "I'm the staff photographer. I'm guessing you're Toni?"

"New kid." Toni waited until Loni had yanked off two layers of mittens and leather gloves before they shook hands.

"Come on back. From the looks of the parking lot, I think we beat almost everyone else. The coffee isn't even ready yet. One of my few vices. Coffee isn't really that good for you, despite all the new reports about lowering cholesterol and all that, but... what can you do when it's cold?"

"Drink green tea," a young woman said, appearing from the hallway to the back of the office. She carefully watched the contents of a jumbo-sized mug that steamed and trailed two tea bag strings and tags. Toni vaguely remembered seeing her the last time she was in the office. "Hi, you have got to be Toni. Welcome. I'm Max, the bane of your existence."

Chapter Five

"She's the copyeditor," Loni explained, as she gestured for Toni to follow her into the back of the office. "How late were you up last night, Max?"

"Try early. As in, two a.m. Tony is a slave master!" Max wailed as she slid into the desk tucked into the corner of the front of the office. For punctuation, she slapped the power button on her computer. "This Tony is a guy, so don't let me confuse you," she added over her shoulder, and offered Toni a grin and a wave before turning back to her computer.

"Max is working on the script for this year's Christmas pageant at church, and Tony is her writing partner who volunteered them at the last minute. It's gotta be love. I'd have killed the guy for doing that to me," Loni offered cheerfully. She laughed when Toni gave her a confused look. "Don't worry. You'll catch on to who is related to whom and what they do soon enough." She waved at a curtain pulled shut across a doorway. "My domain. The general rule is, if it's just the curtain, it's okay to come in. If the sliding door is pulled shut, knock and do not enter, because I'm working on something delicate and will cheerfully take your head off at the shoulders if you interrupt."

"Okay. Duly warned." Toni laughed, deciding she liked Loni. She watched with interest as Loni quickly unpacked her backpack, which held mostly blankets wrapped around two very elaborate cameras, one digital and one a traditional 35mm. That explained the blanket outside the backpack, for padding and insulation against the dry, biting cold.

By the time the rest of the newspaper staff started trickling in, Loni had showed her the lunchroom and the supply room behind it, where she could outfit herself with pens and notepads and anything else she needed. She also pointed out the desk that had been cleared off for Toni and furnished with an old computer taken out of storage, for her use. She wondered if it was by chance or choice that she was put at the desk that faced Curt's. Loni left it to the others to introduce themselves to Toni as they came in. She was glad she had snagged a notepad and pen, because she needed to take notes to keep track of who covered what territory. Sherwood laughed when he saw the cipher Toni used, a combination of shorthand and conceding defeat to her own bad handwriting.

"If I had my own alphabet in high school, nobody ever would have cheated off me by stealing my notes. Teach me that, will you? There are a couple lazy sports reporters for other papers who try to read over my shoulder instead of writing their own stories."

Toni agreed to try. She found two notes waiting on her desk. Angela had taken a personal day and wouldn't be in the office until Monday, and Toni was to spend the whole day with Curt. The second note was from Curt, warning that he would be a little late because he had to stop at the police station before coming into the office. Toni sat down slowly and silently laughed at herself for the hollow, dropping sensation that came with that note. In the thrill of being the new kid in the office, she had actually forgotten she was here for a specific reason. Curt was the go-between on the newspaper's side of the partnership with the police.

The story to explain Toni's presence in the office was that she would be sharing the city beat with Curt while he expanded his duties, doing more people-focused stories. They would work together as a team for the next week or two, until Toni learned names and faces and where everybody fit and functioned in Tabor's government and the community. She needed to meet with the leaders of the prominent organizations such as the historical society, business groups, churches, and clubs. It helped that with the holidays coming on, there was much more to write about in Tabor, all the activities, charity functions, community holiday offerings and more.

Toni considered how long they could justify her presence, when the workload dropped off after the holidays were over. She wasn't so optimistic to think that they would catch the White Rose in just a week or two, now that she had come to town to offer her memories and assistance.

Just how long could Annalee hold on as his newest "true love"? Toni contrasted her sister's quiet delight in having a boyfriend to the terror Annalee had to be feeling right now. She had her doubts that keeping the identity of target number three out of the media would help Annalee in the long run.

Maybe that was the thing to do—just pick up and run.

But if Annalee fled for her life, would the White Rose follow her and try to bring her back? Would he punish her? Or would he simply write her off as a bad choice and find someone else to target?

"Deep thoughts?"

Curt's voice and his hand on her shoulder startled a yelp out of Toni. She closed her eyes, pressed her cold hands to her suddenly hot face, and prayed everyone was so busy they didn't hear her totally unprofessional reaction. Curt squeezed her shoulder and she looked up to see his face managed to remain somber, but there was a suspicious twitching in his lips. A sputter escaped her, turning into laughter.

"Yeah, a thousand miles away from here. Sorry." She glanced over her shoulder and was relieved to see that of the four other people in the newsroom, all were either on the phone or deep in their own conversations. "Okay, boss-man, what's first on the list?"

"City Hall. I'll walk you around, let the front desk people know who you are, get you your media pass. Then I thought we'd hit Stay-a-While for lunch."

"Is this a date or business-related?" Toni wondered if her face was still red enough from her first gaff, so Curt wouldn't notice her new blush. Where had that chirpy little comment come from?

"We'll figure that out when we're done." He didn't scowl at her. If anything, that amused sparkle in his eyes grew a little brighter.

Toni wondered if she had just thrown down a gauntlet of challenge to him, and he was going to give back just as good as he got.

"We'll write it off as a business lunch," he continued as she stood up, "if we run into anybody important in town that you need to meet."

"And if we don't?"

"Then we talk about our plans for this weekend."

Toni definitely heard the click of a phone slamming into a cradle and a sudden drop in background noise. She looked over Curt's shoulder, which required going up on her toes. Sure enough, three people were now looking toward her and Curt's desks, and then exchanging glances.

The notion that she and Curt were interested in each other was going to spread through Tabor pretty quickly. Which was just what Angela wanted. Pretending to have a semi-serious relationship with Curt was part of the deal, after all. So why did Toni feel a little throb of disappointment that the deception was getting off to such a strong start?

~~~~~

Toni took careful notes and wished she had borrowed one of Loni's cameras, because her head was reeling by the time she and Curt walked up the street from City Hall to Stay-A-While for lunch. She had expected a large jump in the number of government officials from tiny Calumet, Iowa, to Tabor Heights, Ohio, but obviously she hadn't calculated large enough. Some secretaries had their own secretaries and figuring out who answered to whom might take longer than her hunt for the White Rose Killer. She wondered if she should even try to get everything clear in her head. After all, it wasn't as if she was going to stay, once Angel's killer was finally brought to justice.

Still, her first day on the job wasn't as bad as she had feared. Curt didn't seem to resent her presence. He seemed comfortable with her tagging along. Toni would have preferred if he *enjoyed* having her around. Maybe in a week or two he would be able to kid around with her like he did the people in the office and in City Hall. Everyone seemed to like Curt. Quite a few people gave them raised eyebrows when they saw him rest a hand on her shoulder or link his arm through hers to lead her to a new
~~~~~

office. Obviously, he wasn't a tactile sort of person, so any physical contact was unusual enough to be noticed.

She felt like her brain was tied in knots, wondering what she wanted, trying to remember names, who was pleasant to Curt and who was merely civil, and marking them down in her mental inventory as either allies or potential problems. When he called a break for lunch, she was relieved, until three police officers walked down the street along with them. One she recognized as the officer who had stopped by while she was unloading her trailer. They were all polite, wanting to be introduced, but nobody seemed unduly interested in meeting her, particularly. Which meant they weren't intent on scoping out Curt's new girlfriend.

Darn. There goes my ego. She muffled a tiny snort of laughter by changing it into a cough.

Then they were inside Stay-A-While. Toni had vague memories of this particular section of the shopping plaza being a drugstore and a drycleaner. She was glad to see the place looked busy and prosperous. It had a dozen two-seater tables, a handful of tables that seated four, five booths tucked along the back wall, and couches arranged along the other walls with coffee tables and lots of newspapers and magazines spread on them. Toni laughed out loud when she realized that was exactly what the name of the coffee shop implied: people were invited to stay a while. She looked at the display of muffins, cookies, gooey, rich cheesecakes and other desserts, and the menu of different hot and cold drinks, along with the sandwich platters and soups, and suspected that people didn't need much encouragement to linger.

The three officers picked up soup and sandwiches to go and hurried out again. Curt watched them go, and his pleasant expression turned a little more somber, what Toni had decided indicated deep thoughts.

"Something about them in particular?" she asked, when the college-age girl at the counter took their orders and stepped away.

"Hmm?" Curt glanced at her, then out the door again. "Not really, but... it just occurred to me that all three of them are homeboys."

"Grew up here?" she guessed. "They were around when—"

"When you and your folks lived here, yeah."

"They didn't react to my name, when you introduced us. Evans stopped by that first day when I was unloading my truck, so we've met. He certainly didn't make the connection."

"Might take a while for anyone to remember you were here before. Especially the police. They have a lot on their minds, lately." He gestured at a two-seater table tucked into a corner where two big windows would let them see anyone who came in the main door. "Let's take a seat until our food's ready."

"Do you think they might remember something from... back then?"

Toni glanced at the dozen other people in the café, the remains of the lunch rush.

"Might be good to check. That's what we can do this weekend. Dig through yearbooks, make a list of everyone who was in school with us." He grinned as he dropped into the closer chair. "I don't suppose you brought your yearbooks with you?"

"I don't know if my folks held onto anything from when we lived here." She congratulated herself on not hesitating every time she referred to that brief time in Tabor, when Angel died. "They got rid of so much when we moved, and they certainly never refer to our home or friends here. It's like two years just got sliced out of our lives."

"Well..." Curt squeezed her hands, waking her to the fact she had her hands clenched together, almost painfully tight. "It's a good thing my folks got fed up enough with the clutter to make me take everything when I moved out." He tipped his head to one side and studied her a moment. His grin got wider, and more crooked. "You don't mind helping me rid out my attic this weekend while we're at it, do you?"

Toni laughed, which, she decided later, was exactly what Curt had wanted.

And she was grateful.

~~~~~

Curt was glad to get back to the office, and not ashamed to admit, even if just to himself, that being alone with Toni bothered him. He couldn't stop thinking about Angel whenever she got that sad, introspective look in her eyes. Still, he was glad to get back to the office, even though he knew every time he looked up from his work, she would be there, right in front of him. Just having people around and work to keep Toni busy and away from him would be a reprieve.

There's something seriously wrong with you, he scolded himself on the walk back to the office from Stay-A-While.

When they went to the lunchroom to hang up their coats, Loni stood at the hatch window, tossing what looked like chunks of dried bread out onto the sloping roof. Curt ignored her, but Toni stopped short and did a double-take.

"What are you doing?"

"Feeding the squirrels." Loni dusted off her hands and shut the window, then wrapped her arms around herself and shivered.

"Um, don't the squirrels hibernate most of the time in the winter?" Toni stepped over to the coat rack.

"Maybe in Iowa they do, but the squirrels are crazy around here," Curt offered. He thought Loni was a little crazy herself, but if being a health nut and nature fanatic were her only vices, she was a lot better off than most people he ran into. "You can hear them running around on the
~~~~~

roof all the time, day and night."

"Are you sure those aren't rats, instead?" She gestured out the window, where the bread scraps and whatever else Loni had brought for today's offering lay like black spatters of ink against the glistening snow.

"Nope, squirrels. I see them all the time. We have three different kinds. I'm positive if I wait long enough, I'll see a new variety out there one day," Loni said.

"Yeah, a mutant." Curt laughed when his remark earned a scowl from Loni and a grin from Toni.

"Um, don't you think all that food will just attract rats?" Toni said.

"Good!" Loni nodded for emphasis and headed down the hall to her workroom. "If we get enough rats, maybe it'll drive the bar out for good."

As if someone downstairs heard her, the scream of power drills started up again. Curt and Toni exchanged grins and headed for the newsroom together. Just inside the doorway, she let out a little yelp and skipped sideways, almost running into the rack holding the file server.

"Something hit my foot." She pointed at a spot two feet to the right of where Curt had stopped.

He opened his mouth to tell her there was nothing down there, when a vibration buzzed through the floor, getting stronger with each second. Curt could have sworn the carpeting moved. He bent down to touch it, then thought better of it. And the vibration got stronger under his feet.

"Oh, heck," Sherwood said, coming over from his desk on the other side of the room. "We're being invaded."

"What?" Andrew demanded, coming out of Angela's office.

Then something black protruded through the now-visible lump in the carpet. The scream of the power drills got louder and he understood what Sherwood meant. The workmen doing the renovations had drilled up through their ceiling, through the floor of the office. Curt ran for the phone on his desk, not quite sure who to call. Then he laughed as a totally evil thought came to him.

"Is Myrna on duty?" He didn't wait for an answer but hurried down the hall to the front of the office.

Ten minutes later, he settled in at his desk, trying to ignore the boom of someone's radio blaring downstairs. Andrew had hurried downstairs to let the workmen know what they had done, and they had promised to stop drilling for now. Myrna was busy on the phone, trying to track down who to complain to. She boasted she knew everyone who was anyone in Tabor and Stoughton and the surrounding towns, so now was the time to put her alleged connections to good use. It didn't matter if she spent the rest of the afternoon on the phone. It would keep her out of trouble and so busy, she wouldn't interfere with anything else going on in the office.

Saturday, November 16

Curt had a loft apartment over the Main Street Café. When he teased Toni about helping to clean out his attic, she learned, he had actually been referring to the enormous, dusty storage room that ran along the back of the loft, where the roof sloped down at a forty-five-degree angle.

Nothing in the world could compel her to admit to him she had been nervous about coming to his apartment. It was bad enough she was nearly late because she changed her clothes twice. Sweatpants and a baggy sweatshirt were definitely too casual. And sloppy. Cords and a button-down shirt and matching coral sweater were too dressy. Especially if he hadn't been teasing about working in the attic. Toni finally settled on jeans and her brand-new Butler-Williams University sweatshirt, which she had bought last night when she ran to Heinke's to find something for dinner she didn't have to cook. A group of college students had a table set up in the front of the store, selling sweatshirts for a fundraiser. Toni bought it on a whim, telling herself she needed a souvenir, and maybe something that would make her feel like she belonged a little bit more.

"You don't quite look like a native yet," Curt said, when he had commented on the sweatshirt and she admitted her reasoning. "You need some faded spots and maybe some paint on the cuffs. And wear it pushed up above your elbows." He frowned as he looked her up and down a few times. Then he grinned and turned back to the first box he had pulled out of the storage room. Toni groaned, realizing he had been teasing her.

Still, it was nice to be teased. Curt couldn't tease her if he still resented her presence, right?

Toni had arrived at his apartment just after one, and they dug through yearbooks, newspaper clippings, and other school memorabilia until after six. Then they drove the two blocks to the *Picayune* office rather than walking, because of the icy wind, to photocopy everything they had decided to pull out as reference material for their research. Toni was suitably impressed with how tall a stack it made, even after just the relevant pages were copied.

Unfortunately, feeling impressed didn't last very long, when they went to her cottage to continue the work, for a change of scenery. Every likely suspect who had been attending school with Angel had to be tracked down. First, she and Curt had to determine if those schoolmates had grown up and were living in Tabor or surrounding cities. Then they had to determine if they had any police records or any other records to indicate mental or emotional trouble. Then they had to determine if any of those men had any routine that would have led to them crossing paths with Gretchen and Katrina and Annalee.

"This would have been a lot easier in Calumet," Toni remarked over pizza, sitting on the area rug in her stark living room. Her hearth served as the picnic table, and she only wished she had thought to get some wood so she could have a fire going.

It was going on eight now, and she and Curt had reached a plateau in their work. Either they were both too tired to think much further along, or they had come to a stopping point in their preparation. Time to stop preparing and start hunting.

"How would it be easier?" Curt mumbled through a mouthful of mushroom-onion-green pepper.

"Calumet is a small town."

"So is Tabor."

"If Tabor is a small town, Calumet is microscopic. In Calumet, if a stranger comes into town or someone starts acting strangely, eventually, everybody knows."

"Hey, we watch out for our own in Tabor." Curt didn't look or sound offended. If anything, he acted as if her comments were a joke.

"But a lot of strangers pass through town every day, and I bet most of them are ignored. Especially if they come through regularly." Toni chalked up a point for herself when Curt stopped chewing and his eyes went distant and he visibly thought over what she said.

"And if someone is used to seeing the same face all the time, even if he doesn't know the name that goes with the face, that face becomes invisible." He slouched back against the hearth. "Boy, do I hate missing something that obvious."

"I guess you need my input after all." She offered a thin smile. Funny, but the triumph didn't taste half as good as she had imagined.

She suspected she hated being necessary because the situation was so dire.

Chapter Six

"I'll mention what you said to the chief tomorrow. If not at church, then at the funeral."

"Funeral? Oh, Katrina's." Toni shivered.

"Maybe you'd better come." He leaned over the box and looked inside. This would be his fourth piece and Toni was only on her second. She reflected that she had never seen a man eat so quickly, with so little noise and splatter, and it was a good thing he had insisted on buying dinner.

"Ah, I don't think a funeral is the place to bring a date."

"Not a date." Curt glanced sideways at her. "If you and I go as representatives of the paper, doing a story on people's reactions to the White Rose, then nobody will think twice if you ask more questions later."

"Don't you hate having to always be thinking ahead?"

"You get used to it. And you've been doing a lot of thinking ahead yourself. Kind of unavoidable, from where we're both sitting." He picked up his slice of pizza and just looked at it. "Sometimes, I can't stop thinking about it."

"Curt... are you blaming yourself? For what happened to Angel, I mean," she hurried to add, when he turned sharply to look at her.

"Why? There was nothing I could have done."

"You found her. You were still trying to get her interested in you when other boys were saying some pretty nasty things about her, from sour grapes."

"Did you ever think that difference makes me a likely suspect?"

Toni gasped and jerked away, but Curt dropped his pizza and grabbed hold of her hand, keeping her close. Idly, she noticed that he smeared pizza sauce on the cuff of her sweatshirt.

"You did think it might be me, didn't you?" he pressed.

"Not... not consciously. I had a dream the other night. While I was waiting for the chief to think over Angela's proposition. I barely even remembered it when I woke up, but you were in it and you were yelling at Angel and trying to blame so many people. And I thought, it's always the people who make the most noise who end up being the guilty ones. You know what I mean?"

"The more noise they make, the more dirt they can toss onto other people, the less they think anybody will blame them." He nodded. "But that was just your dream, right?"

"Just my dream. And I know you couldn't be to blame."

"How do you know?" He stared into her eyes, until finally she had to look away without being able to come up with an answer. "A good reporter follows his gut instinct when he's tracking down a story. Doesn't mean he should rely on his gut when his life is at stake." He finally let go of her wrist. "But thanks for your vote of confidence."

When Curt finally left for the night, Toni felt too tired to be able to fall asleep. She would have laughed at the contradiction, but her head hurt and her muscles tried to tie themselves into knots with tension. She settled for scrubbing out her tub a second time and then taking a long, hot bath with scented bath salts. Toni turned on her stereo loud enough to be heard in the bathroom and reflected on the benefits of having a house rather than an apartment. There were so many things she could do, like play the stereo loudly, that she couldn't when she had to worry about thin walls and people living on either side of her.

But if you need to scream for help, who will hear you?

She snarled at herself, sat up fast enough to splash water on the floor, and turned the tap to the hottest to add to the water.

Toni wondered if she should blame Curt for that bit of paranoia that seemed to be looking over her shoulder now. She honestly hadn't thought of herself being in danger, when she first came up with her plan to identify the White Rose. Now, though, she worried. What if he was at the funeral tomorrow? What if he recognized her and decided she was a better substitute for Angel, and abandoned Annalee? That would be good for Annalee, and Toni felt confident in her ability to avoid trouble. She would just have to take those self-defense lessons Curt insisted on. And learn not to inhale every time something startled her. Both girls had been found reeking of chloroform. So when the White Rose grabbed her and slapped a rag of chloroform over her face, she just wouldn't breathe.

"Don't be a total moron," she muttered.

The fact of the matter was, if the White Rose stuck to his pattern, he wouldn't come after her. All three girls lived with their parents and didn't date. She was on her own, and Curt made sure everyone knew they were together, a couple interested in each other from the moment she arrived in Tabor.

And that made her feel just a little safer.

At least, while Curt was around.

Toni looked around her bathroom and shivered despite the scented steam rising from the water. She got up, wrapped her new bath towel around herself, and left a trail of droplets through the house as she ran around checking the doors and windows, one more time. She just wasn't used to the sounds of her cottage, late at night. Nothing to worry about.

No one trying to break in. And besides, if she had any kind of trouble, she was across the street from the police station. Toni had full confidence in her lung capacity, and if need be, she could scream loud enough to wake the entire neighborhood and bring a dozen cops running.

Back in her bathroom again, the water had cooled too much. She finished drying off, put on her thickest flannel pajamas and her terrycloth robe. Then she settled in at the kitchen table with a mug of hot chocolate and the stack of photocopied pages to study and hopefully trigger memories. Maybe if she studied until she couldn't see straight, everything would be so heavy in her mind she would dream and those dreams would awaken more memories.

Toni looked at the first yearbook page on the stack, and shivered. It was the choir photo. Angel had been in seventh grade choir and the girls ensemble and the Concert Chorale. Had her secret boyfriend been in the choir, or had he just been up at the school when choir rehearsal let out? Toni studied the picture of the smiling, innocent seventh and eighth graders standing on the choir risers and wondered if she looked at the face of a murderer. Angel's diary only said that her boyfriend walked her home from choir practice. She never named him, not even initials. Toni felt colder, remembering the places in Angel's diary where her sister wrote about the promise of secrecy they both had made. Why had she felt it necessary to keep things secret even in her diary? Secrecy was the first sign of a predator, but who had known that twenty years ago?

She promised herself, when she went to visit her parents at Christmas, she would find an excuse and dig through the attic until she found the yearbooks and anything else that might help her remember. What had her parents done with Angel's diaries and her sketchbooks and that box full of notes from her boyfriend? Had the police ever returned them? If so, had her parents kept them, or burned them?

Curt was right, when he said a reporter couldn't rely on gut instinct all the time, and the same rule was true for human memory. That part of her life was indelibly stamped into her mind, but Toni knew better than to trust only memories of those horrid, shocking days. She needed Angel's words, Angel's diaries, and her boyfriend's promises, written down in front of her.

Until then, until Christmas, she and Curt would go through these photos and track down Angel's classmates and investigate their lives since then, one by one, until something snapped into place.

"Until the White Rose snaps," she whispered. In the utter stillness of the night, her voice seemed to echo off the tile floor and Formica countertops and wooden doors.

Toni shivered and looked around her little kitchen. When she finally filled it with towels and dishes, decorations and rugs, would it feel more like a home and less like an anonymous hotel room where she was just passing through? If she made this kitchen her place, put her stamp on it, would she feel like she had finally found a place where she belonged?

Sunday, November 17

Curt felt a twinge of guilt as he led Toni around the funeral home, introducing her to people, pretending he didn't see the speculative looks on some faces. He hadn't told her the whole truth of why he wanted her to come to the visitation for Katrina Harper.

The cliché of the guilty party always returning to the scene of the crime was a cliché *because* it was true. He was betting on the White Rose coming to Katrina's viewing. Whether the sick mind wanted to gloat over the pain he had caused others, or to reassure himself that Katrina had deserved death for being unfaithful, or for some other, unfathomable reason, the murderer could be there. Right now. Offering comfort and encouragement to Katrina's parents. Curt couldn't risk wasting a chance to catch the White Rose's reaction when he saw Toni, even if he didn't know that was the White Rose until later. Would he be upset, delighted, just plain startled and confused when he saw Angel's sister? Would he recognize her as Angel's sister, or think, as Curt had done in a few unguarded moments, that Angel had come back from the dead?

Curt wanted to catch that reaction. He made note of anyone who gave Toni a second look, anyone who had an "oh, yeah" reaction when he introduced her and gave her last name.

He felt a little guilty over Toni's discomfort. She was right, and several people thought they were there as a couple, dating, not a team of reporters covering a story that was painful for the whole community. Just like any community, there were the hypocrites who would latch onto the worst possible interpretation of any scene or event. Which of those people would decide Toni was being gauche by intruding into a funeral for someone she didn't know? Which ones would punish her for it later on?

That was assuming, of course, that Toni stayed in Tabor after the White Rose was caught. Why would she want to? The town only held painful memories for her.

All in all, by the time he and Toni left at the end of visitation, Curt had a headache from frustration and his stomach had a few new knots that weren't there when he got up that morning. They had a chance to talk to Chief Cooper and report on their progress and new theories. Curt felt good about that. But otherwise, had the afternoon been wasted?

Only time would tell.

~~~~~
~~~~~

He watched Curt and Toni leave the funeral home, and he felt a warm glow of approval. It was only right that Angel's sister be taken care of. She was a good girl. She deserved someone who watched over her, like Curt did. He liked Curt, always there to make sure the truth was told.

Curt had been there the day Angel died. He remembered hiding in the woods, just out of sight of Angel's body, emptying his stomach, choking on the sorrow that stayed silent and hot inside him. Curt had come running down the abandoned park road, to the dead end where the deer had broken down the barbed wire fencing years ago. He found Angel and he had shouted for help, then ran back up the park road, to come back later with a ranger, and the police had followed.

He had liked Curt way back when they were boys, both trying to get Angel to like them. All the boys had wanted Angel, but Curt hadn't been nasty. He was persistent and polite, and he had stayed Angel's friend when she rejected him. Curt had punched one of the boys who told nasty stories about Angel.

That made him one of the good guys.

The funeral home door creaked open and he took a step back into the shadows. Chief Cooper and Angela Coffelt came down the wooden steps together. The chief reached out to loop his arm through hers, steadying her on the icy steps. She smiled at him and reached up with her other hand to rest it on his.

He stayed in the shadows, watching them walk down the long driveway to the street, where cars were parked. Angela leaned her head against Chief Cooper's shoulder, and he felt sorry for her. She always had so much work to do. Dealing with the story of Katrina's disloyalty, the revelation of her deception and her filthy soul, had to be exhausting. He remembered how they had all been in school together: he, Angel, Curt, Angela. The two girls had been friends, despite the difference in their ages, and made a game out of answering for each other when their names were called in the school hallways or the cafeteria.

Monday, November 18

Toni thought the newspaper customers in Calumet were odd, but Tabor Heights had them beat. Part of it might have been that everyone knew everyone where she used to live, and people didn't let others get away with too much garbage or weirdness. Here in Tabor, as she had discussed with Curt, it was impossible to know everyone so well to deal with or head off strangeness. Or maybe she just didn't expect some of the utter stupidity that people exhibited.

She came back to work from the historical society, after picking up a selection of pictures for the Thanksgiving week feature, to find a disheveled man stomping through the door into the office just ahead of her. Toni stopped short when she saw the row of V-rack boxes in front of the newspaper office lying on their sides. Some had dents in them. She couldn't be sure those dents weren't there when she left an hour ago.

"Now what are you going to do about it?" the man shrieked, as Toni came through the door.

He stood in front of the counter that separated the reception area from the rest of the *Picayune*'s office, legs spread and feet planted, as if he expected to be tackled at any moment. He waved the unraveling end of a long scarf in the air.

A bespectacled young East Indian man slowly stood up from the switchboard desk and approached the counter with visible hesitation. Toni reflected that it was a good thing a gate kept people from just walking past the counter into the office. Not that the four-foot-high barrier would do much good against someone who really wanted to commit violence, but it did make most invaders stop and think. And just having the barrier there kept them from excusing themselves later by saying they didn't know they weren't allowed beyond that point.

"I'm sorry, but what did you say?" the young man finally said. He looked at Toni and offered an apologetic smile. "If you'll wait just a minute—"

"I was here first!" the man with the torn scarf bellowed.

"And if you bothered to listen, he was telling me he'd get to me in a minute," Toni said. "There's this new invention called politeness. Ever heard of it?"

She slapped the folder of photos down on the counter and prepared to wait. Common sense told her now was not a good time to announce she worked here. Experience had taught her if she pretended to be a disinterested third party, she could slap this man's rudeness back in his face and he wouldn't be able to punish this young man for it. Toni didn't recognize him, and he hadn't been at the switchboard when she left, which meant he was one of the many college students who worked for the paper. Max had warned her it was like a revolving door at the switchboard position.

The irate customer glared at her a moment, then his scowl softened a little and she knew she had broken through enough to make him realize he was being an idiot. From this point, either he would back down and they could talk some sense into him, or he would just get nastier to avoid admitting he might be in the wrong.

"Why didn't you listen when I told you what happened?"

"Because you were shouting when you came in and talking too fast and I was on the phone when you came through the door?" The young switchboard operator shrugged and gestured at the phone.

"I said, I stopped to buy a paper from one of your boxes and my scarf got caught in it and I had to cut it off to get free. This was a forty-dollar scarf and your paper boxes are defective. I want a replacement. Now what are you going to do about it?" He slapped his hands down on the counter.

"Um, excuse me." Toni gestured at the three-tiered rack of the latest issue of the *Tabor Picayune* sitting next to the counter. "Why would the paper have a dispenser box of newspapers outside when people can come in here and buy them? And not worry about having exact change, either."

"I don't think any of those boxes out there are ours," the college student said. He shot Toni a look of gratitude.

"They're on your property. That makes you responsible," the man retorted. His volume and his frown both decreased by half.

"This is rental property," Max offered, coming up the hall from the back. "That makes it our landlord's responsibility, because he's the one who gave permission for the boxes to be there. Mr. Carr, did you get your scarf caught again?"

"Oh. Hi, Maxine." The now-named Carr seemed to shrink in on himself.

"What you need to do is call the landlord — Toby, can you get him the number? — and tell him what happened. Or, you can get the number of the owner off the box that caught your scarf and ask for a replacement. I figure, you have plenty of evidence, with your scarf still caught inside it. Do you want some paper and a pen to write it down?" Max stepped up to the counter, rested her elbows on it, and smiled politely.

"Uh... thanks. I think I have paper." He patted his overcoat pockets as he turned and shuffled out the door.

Toni waited until the door was closed and she saw his coat flutter out of sight, going down the sidewalk. Something told her he wasn't going to stop and get the information off the box. "Why do I get the feeling he does that a lot?"

"Not here, but yeah, he's done that at other places." Max snorted. "Forty-dollar scarf. Yeah, and I'm up for an Oscar this year. I saw him buy a whole handful of scarves for about a dollar each at Penny Pincher two months ago. He won't call the box owner, because the damage he did to the box is more than the scarf's worth."

"Thanks for your help." Toby grinned wider and wiped imaginary sweat off his forehead. "What can I do for you?"

"Nice to meet you, Toby. I'm Toni Napolitano. I just started working here." Toni reached over the gate and pulled the latch to open it, then slid the folder of photos off the counter. "How many of you are there on switchboard?"

"Last count?" Max said, when Toby just shrugged. "Twelve who come in between classes. Then we have some part-timers like Myrna, who work on delivery day or when someone is sick and fill in during exams week or when the BWU kids are on break or home for the holidays or whatever."

"Does that happen a lot?" She gestured over her shoulder, in the direction of the now-vanished Mr. Carr.

"Loonies in general?" Max settled down at her desk and swiveled her chair around to face Toni as she headed for the hallway. "Depends on the weather, the phases of the moon, and delivery day. I don't know if it's better that we only come out twice a week, or worse. I sure wouldn't want to work at a daily paper, thanks very much."

Toni laughed with her. She felt sorry for Toby and the others who had duty at the front counter, the first line of defense between the *Picayune*'s staff and the loonies who inhabited Tabor. She had dealt with her share of crackpots and just plain unhappy people who wanted everyone else to take the blame for their problems.

Tuesday, November 19

"Hey, can we reschedule tonight?" Max said, coming around the corner into the newsroom. Toni and Curt were the only ones left. Most of the reporters left early on paper delivery days to make up for staying late the night before.

"Reschedule?" Toni looked at Curt, a little confused, because it seemed Max was looking at both of them and she had no idea what the copyeditor was talking about.

"Oh, yeah, Christmas play story." Curt held up his hand, one finger in the air signaling them to wait a moment. He tapped a few more words into his computer. "What's up?"

"Mom says to bring you two for dinner. Joe and Jeremy are both out with their friends, so it'll be safe," Max said with a roll of her eyes.

"Miss Emily's cooking? You better believe we'll be there." He turned to Toni and laughed. "What's that look for?"

"I'm about two steps behind. Okay, I know Max is writing the Christmas play for your church," Toni said slowly. "Are we doing a story on it? And why so early? Wouldn't it be better running in December?"

Chapter Seven

"It's a community outreach thingy," Max said with a shrug. "A fundraiser for the Mission, so it's not exactly a church story. And the play is running for two weeks, and we're hoping the story'll get picked up by some of the other locals and maybe even the PD, so the earlier it runs, the better the chances lots of people will hear about it and want tickets."

"The Mission. That's where Eloise Elementary used to be?" She pressed her knuckles against her temples, pretending a headache. "I went there. It makes me feel old, knowing my old school isn't a school anymore."

"You and me, both," Curt said.

"There's a daycare and after school programs and a senior center, right? Your church runs it and you hope to open up a food pantry and clothes closet and maybe some housing for the homeless. So the Christmas play is a fundraiser. What else do you do for fundraising?"

"Well, they're talking about Firesong doing a concert one of these days." Max shrugged. "So, can I tell Mom you're coming?"

"Are you free?" Curt looked at Toni. She nodded. It wasn't like she had anyone waiting for her at home. Not even a goldfish or a potted plant that needed watering. "We're good."

"Great. Mom says come on over any time. Which means I have to call Tony and make sure he didn't get caught up in something. He's so excited about the West Coast proposal, he'd forget his head if it wasn't attached." Max scurried around the corner.

"West Coast?" Toni had to ask.

"Okay, Max and Tony write novels. Romances, mostly. Don't ask," Curt said, holding up a hand to stop her. "Save it for the interview. Anyway, he just got approached to do a writer-in-residence thing in the LA area. I can't remember if it's UCLA or USC or some other big school."

She took her cue from him and started turning off her computer. "Last question. At least, until we get to the Randolphs'. Who or what is Firesong? I assume they're a band?"

"Local rock group. Pretty good. Good enough to do youth festivals and sell a bunch of indie CDs. They really need an agent. Remind me to introduce you to Dani and Andy and the rest of them some time." Curt snatched up a notepad and his ever-present tape recorder. "Ready?"

"How about a coat?" Toni laughed at his look of disgust, and the next moment felt a strange little half-pang, half-thrill. She got along with Curt far better than she could have hoped, almost as if they had been friends for years. It was going to hurt when she kept her word and left town.

~~~~~

Toni thought she was prepared for just about anything, but meeting the actress she had watched on the midnight movie last night was not on her list.

Emily Keeler-Randolph greeted Toni like an old friend who had come back to town, and hugged Curt when she met them at the door. She welcomed them inside and invited them to join her in the kitchen while she finished up dinner. Toni wisely kept quiet and let Curt and Emily chat about the children's Christmas production at Homespun Theater, which was attached to the Randolph home, and the upcoming season at the community theater.

Visiting Homespun Theater was on Toni's list of things to do. Somehow, she had never connected Joel Randolph with Max, who worked at the paper with her. It was even more discomfiting to realize that Max and her writing partner, Tony Martin, wrote under the pen name of one of her favorite new authors, Antonia Maxwell.

Concentrating on untangling the relationships and who did what helped Toni get over the fact that the star of the Civil War movie she had cried over when she should have been sleeping now stood in front of a stove, five feet away. Whatever she was doing with the green beans in the stir fry pan smelled heavenly, but didn't interfere with the mouthwatering aroma of garlic and roast beef seeping from the oven.

"How long have you been here in Tabor?" Toni asked, when the conversation slowed down and both Emily and Curt looked at her, trying to include her. "I'm trying to remember if you came to town before my folks moved away."

"Just about twenty years. Joel had a rental house when he first came here to teach at the university. Max and I joined him, and we started working on his idea for Homespun almost from the start. We moved into the firehouse while I was pregnant with Joe." Emily laughed and slid the green beans out of their pan and into a casserole, which she covered. "What a time that was. Joel was positive we could hitch together an old barn and a firehouse and turn them into a home and a theater. I swear, most of our neighbors thought we were crazy and it was only my very advanced pregnancy that kept them from running us out of town." She looked around the kitchen and gestured, taking in the entire complex of buildings all melded together into a cohesive whole. "Somehow, it all worked out, and we've been part of Tabor ever since." She winked at Toni. "If you have some time to kill, ask Joel for a guided tour and the long version of how it all came together."
~~~~~

"I heard that," Joel Randolph said, coming through the swinging door from the living room, which, from the desks and makeup tables, costumes lying all over and storage cabinets up to the roof, evidently served as the Green Room for the theater. "Some people don't know how good they have it." His words raised laughter from Curt and Emily, so Toni decided to laugh with them.

Max obviously took after her father, with her dark hair and eyes, rather than Emily's light eyes and golden hair and heart-shaped face. Toni wondered what the story was behind Joel Randolph, how he had met and married former Hollywood starlet Emily Keeler, and what made them decide to set up a community theater in Tabor Heights. There had to be more to the story than just the fact he came here to teach theater tech at Butler-Williams.

Dinner was filled with laughter and talk, and Toni soon felt right at home. She and Tony Martin laughed about the confusion caused by two people with the same-sounding names. Even when it was obvious who was being addressed or referred to, they deliberately confused the issue by answering or reacting to whatever was meant for the other. Toni thought about the years of silence in her house after Angel's death, and fleeing Tabor Heights and the memories in their big old house. She envied the Randolph family, even though both Joel and Emily readily talked about the lean years when they had to feed three children and pay for repairs to the building, didn't have health, car or building insurance, and disaster of one kind or another struck. She envied them their ability to look back and laugh and look to the future with hope and anticipation. She shivered when they talked openly about times when they had to go on faith, but they were too angry with God for seemingly failing them to keep praying, let alone choose the right path instead of the easy one.

The reminiscences about the theater devolved into the upcoming season for Homespun and then the Christmas production fundraiser for the Mission. Toni gritted her teeth in embarrassment when she looked up and saw Curt had pulled out his trusty tape recorder. There hadn't been time for him to criticize her technique as a reporter, but she could imagine the lecture she would get in the morning. She pulled out her notepad and pen, and blushed when Max grinned and winked at her. Soon, though, the laughter and teasing and grumbling between Max and Tony made her forget her lapse.

It was nearly ten when she and Curt put on their coats and headed for the door. Toni wished she could have stayed longer. She wondered if she would be around long enough to attend at least one production at Homespun. Here was something else she would miss when she had to leave.

Part of her was almost angry with Curt, because of that promise to leave when Angel's murderer was identified and captured. If he hadn't been so stubborn and angry when she first arrived, Toni wouldn't have made her rash promise to leave when the mystery was solved. She loved Tabor, just as much as she had loved it as a child, and she hadn't even been back two weeks. How would she feel when she had made friends and a place for herself? It would hurt like tearing open a wound when she had to leave.

Then the kitchen door slammed open, letting in a gust of cold air and two boys. Toni guessed from their blond hair and their resemblance to Emily that these were Joe and Jeremy, Max's brothers. Joe was a junior in high school and Jeremy was nearly fourteen.

"Hey, Curt! Can I bum a ride with you next Saturday?" Jeremy yelped.

"Saturday?" Curt glanced at Toni, as if she knew what the boy was talking about.

"*Starship Defiance*? The convention?" The boy rolled his eyes in disgust. "It's just the biggest convention to come anywhere close. You're going, aren't you?"

"That's the one in Akron, just off the Turnpike?" Toni asked. "I read about that. So you're into the whole *Defiance* fandom scene?" She laughed when Curt's mouth dropped open and he stared at her. Joe groaned and stomped away after barely acknowledging the introductions Max made.

"Don't tell me you're into all that," Curt said.

"Okay, I won't." She winked at Jeremy. "If you need a ride, I might just go down. I've never been to a con, and it'd be nice to have someone to go with. It's a good way to avoid all the post-Thanksgiving shopping rush, anyway."

"You'll be sorry," Max said. "When Jeremy talks about needing a ride, he probably means his whole crew."

"Crew?"

"Yeah," Curt said. "I can give you and two of your space-jockey friends a ride in my car." He gave Toni a challenging grin, visibly daring her to back down. "How many can you fit into your car?"

"Three more." Toni felt like she was playing mental catch-up. "So, you have a club, you're that serious about the whole thing?"

"Club? How about a bunch of kids on the verge of turning into a cult?" Tony ruffled Jeremy's hair, earning a scowl from the younger boy. "They're rabid. Almost as bad as those Trekkies who caused so much trouble a couple years ago. Remember the ones who were running a club at the university? Some of them had a contest to turn their dorm rooms into crew quarters from the various series. It wasn't so bad if your roommates were into *Trek*, but it got really nasty when the roommates weren't." He rolled his eyes.

"Enough," Curt said. "I covered that story, remember? And comparing the *Starship Defiance* universe to *Trek* is like comparing a Corvette to a Pinto. They can both get you where you want to go, but the experience is completely different."

"Snob," Toni said, and was delighted to be able to tease. Especially when Curt just grinned at her, and the look in his eyes made her feel warm and included, part of the gang.

They soon had their arrangements for the convention the following Saturday and made their farewells. Toni was glad to sit in silence in Curt's car and let him do the talking, roughing out how they would approach their story. The evening had been full, almost overwhelming with impressions and ideas and the slightly unsettling sensation that she had come back to a place that had been waiting for her.

"You okay?" Curt asked.

Toni looked up and realized they sat in front of her cottage. She must have zoned out during the ride. How much of the plotting had she missed? Well, she hadn't taken notes, and maybe Curt wouldn't mind if she couldn't remember everything in the morning.

"Yeah. Fine. Overwhelmed."

"The Randolphs are great people. I'm glad they like you."

"Really?" Toni silently scolded herself not to read more into the statement than what was on the surface. It didn't matter if she made friends with Curt's friends, because their growing relationship was nothing more than a façade to protect her from the White Rose.

Curt just looked at her for a moment, frowning a little bit. She didn't think he was angry, so much as he had to consider what he would say next. Then again, in the shadows of the car, how could she clearly read his expression?

"You know, Toni, I'm really not an ogre."

"I don't think you are," she hurried to say.

"This is a whole lot more complicated than we bargained for, okay? Just leave it at that."

"I think that's safe." She took a deep breath, decided a strategic retreat was the wise step, and reached for the door handle. "Thanks for driving."

When she got inside, she looked at the clock and silently scolded herself for even thinking about inviting Curt in for some coffee and to talk about the story they would write. It was late, and tomorrow they had another paper to put together.

Wednesday, November 20

Curt knew immediately something was wrong, as soon as he walked in the door to work that morning. Max wasn't at her desk, but a half-empty mug of tea indicated she was somewhere in the office. She was probably in the back conferring with Angela on a tough headline. Ty Mangione was on phone duty. Curt idly watched him while he riffled through the stacks of pink phone message slips haphazardly tossed into the reporters' box.

The college student wore his habitual sweats with his microscopic headphones hanging around his neck and homework spread across the desk. The acne-scarred boy nodded and tapped his boot-clad feet on the roller mat under the desk while tapping his pen on the edge of the desk in counterpoint. The person on the other end of the phone did all the talking. Curt could hear the voice, but not the words, so the situation hadn't escalated too badly. He glanced at the clock and whistled. An irate caller only ten minutes after the office opened? He tried to remember if there was anything in yesterday's paper that irritated someone enough to call as soon as the newspaper opened. He rested his elbows on the counter and waited for the call to finish. If it was a complaint about a story, he would probably have to handle it anyway.

Ty flinched and inhaled quickly as the buzz of voice from the other end abruptly cut off with a squeak. "I can understand why you're so angry, Ma'am, but like I've already told you, I can't do anything." The boy winced and held the phone away from his ear. Now Curt could hear the high-pitched babbling, but still couldn't make out individual words. It was definitely a woman. He gave Ty a commiserating look. "Ma'am, please-- Like I already told you, this is the *Tabor Picayune*. You said you live in Middleville, and you're supposed to get the *Middleville Torch*, right? You have to talk to the *Torch* to take care of that. We can't."

Curt winced, hearing the definite bang-click of the phone hanging up.

"You could at least say good-bye before you slam the phone in my ear," Ty grumbled. He forced a smile as he hung up the phone. "Well, at least she didn't demand to know my name and home phone number like that psycho last week."

"Middleville? Where is that?" Curt had to laugh. The only alternative was to scream in frustration at the stupidity of people.

"Far enough away for her to shriek, 'Where the heck is Tabor?' before she hung up."

Then Curt realized what was wrong with the office. "Hey, where's Annalee?"

"She looked kind of upset. Max took her in the back. Something going on?"

"The usual," Curt muttered, and hurried through the gate. He was relieved that Annalee was at work, but his gut twisted with apprehension.

He found Annalee in Angela's office, sitting in one of the conference chairs, with Angela sitting in the other and holding her hand. Other than the pallor in her face, she looked fine. A white rose sat on Angela's desk and a note written on that heavy, plain ivory stationery Curt had seen among the growing pile of evidence against the White Rose Killer. Both rose and note were in clear plastic zipper bags.

"You okay now?" Curt asked.

"Unfortunately, this isn't something that can be cured by chocolate," Max announced, coming into the office with a steaming mug of hot chocolate, "but I figure it couldn't hurt."

Annalee sputtered a little laugh and took the mug with a nod of thanks. Her hands weren't shaking, Curt was glad to note.

"Could you get that to Chief Cooper when you walk Annalee over for the police blotter today?" Angela said. "The fewer people who can connect all this with her, the better."

"Maybe if he thinks I'm not afraid, that I'm not telling anyone what he's doing, he'll think I... well, how could anyone *like* him?" Annalee murmured. "But maybe he won't get so insistent, like he was with—" She choked and her hand shook a little.

"The others?" Max said. "If hardly anybody knows, they won't make a fuss and there won't be so many editorials and rabble rousers calling him a sick lunatic. So he won't get all territorial, and so protective and jealous. I'm no psychologist, but it makes sense to me."

"He might think you're encouraging him," Curt had to say. He tried to recall what Toni had told him about the notes from Angel's boyfriend. There had been a consistent theme of loyalty and secrecy. He could understand how his target reacting in fear might irritate the White Rose and push him to more extreme demands, but if a girl didn't tell anybody that he was stalking her, wouldn't that be exactly what Angel's killer had asked of her? Secrecy?

"How could anyone expect love when he won't show his face, won't tell me his name, when he just makes demands? Love isn't like that. Love is open and trusting and giving." Annalee gripped the mug in both hands and took a long drink. Curt admired her self-control, fighting her fear physically as well as intellectually.

The lights went out, the utter darkness punctuated by the click of the furnace suddenly shutting off. Annalee yelped and Curt heard a *thud-splash-crack* that was likely the hot chocolate mug hitting the floor.

"Everybody sit still." He fumbled his way to the door of Angela's office. Opened, weak light spilled through from the lunchroom windows. Not for the first time, Curt griped about the lack of windows anywhere but by the front door and the lunchroom. The designer of the building hadn't been thinking ahead.

He followed the stream of light from the front, down the long hallway, and nearly got run over by Ted Gruber coming out of his office, still wearing his gloves and overcoat. Voices echoed from the circulation office and the newsroom as people fumbled for flashlights. Curt knew the drill. Usually the lights went out in the summer when there was an excessive drain on the city's power from thousands of air conditioning units going full blast. There were some sections of Tabor's infrastructure that hadn't been updated in ninety years, and unfortunately, parts of the power grid were included in that To Do list.

"Street lights are on," Ty reported, coming back into the office. "And the shopping center is still lit up. Nobody else on our side of the street is dark. I think it's just us."

"And it's awful quiet downstairs," Curt growled.

"What happened?" Toni asked, coming in the door at that moment. "Did we forget to pay the electric bill?" She grinned, and he appreciated her attempt at a joke.

"Ty, call the landlord." He waited until the younger man pulled out his cell phone, then gave him the number to call. "I think the geniuses downstairs cut a power line or turned off the wrong breaker box. How well do you see in the dark?" he said to Toni as she opened the gate and stepped past the counter.

"Don't need to." She reached into her voluminous bag that was part briefcase, part purse, and pulled out a flashlight. She pumped it back and forth a few times until the light bulb lit. "Back at the *Cyclone,* we were constantly getting the power knocked out, so it was a survival tactic to always carry a flashlight."

"Good, then you can be my seeing eye dog." Curt winked at her and linked his arm with hers.

"Somehow, I think that was an insult, but I'm not sure exactly how." Toni grinned, so he knew he wasn't in trouble. Or not much. Something told him she knew how to keep score and get even in tiny, creative ways.

He decided he was looking forward to it.

Chapter Eight

By the time Annalee needed to walk over to the police station to get the police blotter information, the lights had been restored. Toni was hard at work on the first draft of the feature story on Max, Tony and the fundraiser for the Mission.

Mark Donovan met Curt and Annalee just outside the main doors leading into the City Hall/Police Department/Municipal Court complex. His uniform jacket hung open and he merely held out his hand for the evidence bag, slipped it into his jacket, nodded to them, and turned to walk around to the back of the building.

"Talk about cloak and dagger," Curt muttered. Annalee's crooked smile encouraged him. As long as she didn't burst into tears or get angry at off-hand remarks like that, she was doing just fine.

Joe Watkins had desk duty that morning. He winked at Annalee and made his usual teasing remark about the confidentiality of the information she would see. She managed a smile as the officer brought up the binder books of reports and put them on the far end of the counter for her.

Joe watched Annalee copy the information from the reports into her notebook for a few moments, then wandered back to the counter where Curt waited. "Is she okay?"

"As well as can be expected, I suppose." Curt didn't like the angry little flicker he felt at the question. He guessed Joe was one of those who didn't know the White Rose had targeted Annalee. If he knew, then he was a callous jerk for asking.

Just how many in the police department knew? Such a thing was impossible to keep quiet, unless of course Chief Cooper decided to handle everything himself with no assistance from anyone. Ordinarily, Curt would trust any member of the Tabor police not to divulge sensitive information to the public, but he had had several unpleasant brushes with officers who were no longer serving in Tabor Heights. Curt knew better than to believe everyone in Tabor Heights was honorable and kind. The White Rose lived in Tabor, after all.

That reminded him. He had to check his personal email account about his first request for information on a former classmate. Toni agreed, they had to work quietly and clandestinely, so the White Rose wouldn't realize they were on his trail. That meant tracking down one suspect at a time, instead of sending out requests for information simultaneously on every single boy who might have given Angel Napolitano a second look. Curt gritted his teeth every time he thought about the slowness of the investigation, but it was necessary.

"She's a sweet kid. So innocent," Joe muttered. "I'd bet my next paycheck, everybody in this office just loves Annalee."

Curt bit back a retort that such a comment wasn't safe. Who knew how the White Rose got his information, how he kept an eye on his "true love," and what made him decide she was unfaithful? There were many different kinds of love in the world, and unfortunately many cruel and perverted people insisted their idea of love was good and valid, no matter how it damaged or even destroyed the objects of that so-called love.

Saturday, November 23

Toni slept late Saturday morning, then ate breakfast at her computer, catching up on email and taking care of the last few chores for completing her move, including giving magazines and credit cards her new address. When she went to the kitchen to put away her dirty dishes, she saw her cell phone sitting on the counter and picked it up to check messages. The insulation was as good as Mandy Gordon said. She hadn't heard her phone ring at the other end of the cottage. She had several messages, and she groaned at the thought of having to catch up with people.

One message was from her parents, checking on how she had settled in so far to her new job. Toni quashed a flash of guilt and was glad she hadn't been available to talk. She had never been very good at lying to her parents, and since she planned to spend the day pursuing research into former classmates in Tabor, it would have been at the top of her mind when she talked with them. Something might have slipped out.

The second call was a salesman wanting to sell her an Internet cable connection at the newspaper office in Iowa. Toni laughed and erased that message. Voicemail and soundproofing definitely had their advantages. She contemplated changing her phone number, so it wouldn't be long-distance for any of her contacts in Tabor Heights and the surrounding communities to call her. Maybe she should just give them her number at the newspaper office? After all, if she was going to move once the White Rose was identified, she would just have to change the number again.

The third call was from Curt. Toni wished she had been available for that call. He wanted her to know he had gotten nowhere on the first name on his list and he was spending the morning in the Metroparks, researching his feature story on the homeless problem. She wondered why he bothered telling her that, just a second before Curt laughed and invited her to join him.

"You are an idiot," Toni told herself as she looked for her clock, which still wasn't hanging on the wall. Curt had given her a list of times he would be at certain places in the park, if she wanted to catch up with him. She had half an hour until the next rendezvous. She could at least get started on her share of the research, and hopefully have something to report when she caught up with him.

Twenty minutes later, she doubted that what she had found could even be called a start. Why did Mike Wilson's name have to belong to at least four hundred other people who were all active or at least mentioned on the Web? Just weeding out the ego spots, like personal Web pages and news releases would take her the rest of the day. What she needed were police records and real estate and school references, to track Wilson's academic career and the places he had called home in the last twenty years. Toni saved and printed out the first dozen pages of links, to use as a master chart she could check off and give her a sense of making some progress. Then she went looking for her boots, which she hadn't taken out of her moving box and put in the closet yet. If she was going to go tramping through the park to look for Curt, she was going to need them. In five minutes, she was in her car and turning into the Metroparks entrance, only a few dozen yards up the street from her cottage.

The place where she hoped to meet up with Curt was on the border of Tabor Heights and Stoughton. Toni played with the idea of telling him his research wasn't valid if the homeless people he found weren't physically in Tabor's section of the Metroparks. She grimaced at the snow dusting her windshield and decided that made a pretty lame joke. She looked for signs of activity as she coasted down the winding Metroparks road. A few families pursued exercise, pulling little children on sleds and walking their dogs. She glimpsed a car parked right next to a sign warning that the ice was dangerous and ice fishing was prohibited at that spot. Toni hoped the car belonged to someone taking a walk, and not a determined fisherman who refused to read.

She reached the parking area, just off a bend in the road before it crossed Pearl Road, five minutes after Curt's message said he would be there. His car wasn't there.

Later, Toni couldn't say why she didn't just assume Curt was running late. She turned around and headed back to the last spot he said he would be, less than half a mile up the road. She saw Curt's snow-covered car — and someone who definitely wasn't Curt opening the door.

All she saw was a mass of dirty denim, scraggly red beard and frightened eyes as she laid on the horn and pulled into the parking slot, close enough to scrape the side of Curt's car. The stranger screamed, flung several objects at her and took off running, floundering through the snow.

"Horror movie survival rule number one: never, ever, go chasing someone into unfamiliar territory," Toni muttered as she pulled out her cell phone. She debated calling 911 rather than dialing the Tabor police department directly, and whether she was going to get into trouble for running down an innocent man because she had mistaken his car for Curt's. "Stupid! Sometimes you are so stupid!"

She dialed the first two numbers and kept her finger on the third as she climbed out of the car, into the dusting of snow in the air. She scrabbled for whatever had hit her car. Odds were good one of them was the keys. She kept looking around at the slightest sound, in case the redhead reclaimed his courage and came back. She found the keys and put them in her pocket, then a cell phone. Or as her father called it, a "dumb phone," not a smartphone. It was the same model as hers, meaning no password protection. She checked the call log. The last number was hers.

"Okay, Curt, where are you?" she muttered. Then her next step dislodged Curt's wallet. That settled it, 911 it was. She punched the final number and prepared her words while she waited for someone to answer.

Then she saw the partially filled footprints in the snow. The redhead had run toward the road, but these footprints led into the woods.

"Hi, my name is Toni Napolitano and I'm in the Metroparks about half a mile down from the restrooms and the par course, heading toward Pearl." Toni stepped over the mounds of snow that covered the railroad ties marking the edges of the parking area. "I just stopped a man who was trying to steal my co-worker's car. He threw the keys and cell phone and wallet at me and fled."

She barely hesitated long enough for the dispatcher to start asking questions.

"I'm okay, but it's snowing and I'm scared my co-worker is injured somewhere out in the woods. Who? Curt Mehdlang, from the *Picayune*."

She kept walking, staying out of Curt's footprints and trying to look in all directions. It was too quiet all of a sudden, as if the entire park held its breath, waiting for something to happen.

"Okay. I'm heading into the woods—no, I will not wait in my car! Curt could be hurt. I don't know how long he's been lying in the snow already. Have you ever seen frostbite, what it does to fingers and toes and faces? I have, and believe me, it is not pretty!"

A siren blared behind her. Toni shrieked. She turned around, almost tripping over her own feet. A Tabor patrol car pulled into the parking slot on the other side of Curt's car. Vaguely, she heard the dispatcher shooting questions at her.

"Um—sorry—yeah, I'm okay. An officer just got here and he scared me. Um—is it okay if I hang up now, since someone's here? Thanks, by the way." Toni didn't wait for an answer but closed her phone. To her relief, the officer slogging through the snow and avoiding Curt's tracks without being told was Mark Donovan.

"I told him these people were a little bit crazy," Donovan said, when Toni repeated her story. He grinned when she got to the part about the carjacker throwing the keys, phone and wallet at her, and handed over all three to him. "Curt's a good, cynical reporter, but he still thinks if you tell someone you want to help, they're automatically cooperative."

Toni flinched when Donovan unsnapped his holster, but he didn't draw his gun, so that reassured her a little. Together, still careful to stay out of Curt's rapidly filling footprints, they headed into the woods.

It was almost an anticlimax to find Curt about twenty yards into the woods, stumbling down the path with a bloodstained glove pressed to the back of his head. Toni scooped up snow into a soft ball and pulled his hand down so she could see his injury. She gulped audibly when she saw the blood, fresh and steaming and turning his pale hair black.

"This'll probably hurt," she warned, as she pressed the snow against the wound.

"Good thing you didn't go into nursing," Curt joked, and hissed when the snow touched his head. "How bad does it look?"

"Probably not as bad as it feels," Donovan said. "Somebody was really serious," he added, and showed them a muddy rock with blood frozen on the dull edge.

"It feels like somebody tried to take the back of my head off."

Curt didn't resist when Donovan linked arms with him, turned him around and headed back to the parking area. He didn't wobble and answered without hesitating when Donovan questioned him about what had happened. Toni had to trot to keep up with them, with their much longer legs, but she was determined to keep the snow pressed against the wound until the blood stopped flowing. Curt laughed, immediately wincing, when Donovan related how Toni had stopped the carjacker.

"Darn, and I was hoping I could use the insurance money to buy a new car." His smile faded only a few heartbeats later. "Thanks. Really. I don't know what I would have done if you hadn't shown up at just the right time."

"Walked up to the station to report a carjacking, for one thing," Donovan said. He opened the passenger side door of his patrol car and guided Curt to sit down. "Let's get a good look at that in some light."

He pressed on Curt's shoulders to make him bend forward. Toni fought a queasy rolling in her stomach as she looked at the bloody snow cupped in her gloved hand. She grimaced and flung it out toward the woods as far as she could. Donovan whistled once he had gently parted the sopping hair and exposed the wound.

"Did you get the guy mad at you?"

"I have no idea." Curt sounded a little breathless, with his ribs pressed into his thighs. "Never saw the guy. I was just walking around, trying to find somebody to talk to. The next thing I knew, I heard someone running up behind me and then—wham—lights out. How bad is it?"

"You'll need stitches. No butterfly strip'll hold this baby together."

Donovan refused to let Curt drive himself to the hospital, just in case the injury turned out to be something serious. Toni agreed to wait until Curt's brother could come get the keys and drive his car home for him.

"Then I'll come up to the hospital and drive you home," she added.

"You don't have to do that." Curt tried to smile, but the pain was making itself visible in dark smears under his eyes.

"Hey, we're partners. Lois Lane and Clark Kent. Although, come to think of it, you're supposed to be invulnerable. Clumsy, but invulnerable."

"Well, you sure have the Lois Lane part down pat, rushing into danger." Curt didn't sound like he was criticizing her. If anything, there was something tender in his voice. Of course, that could have just been the pain making him speak slowly and softly. "It's okay. My folks will probably camp out at the hospital until the doctor tells them I'm not going to need brain surgery or a transfusion or something."

"Hey, can we get going before you bleed all over my car?" Donovan winked at Toni, turning his grousing tone into teasing.

"Yeah, yeah." Curt nodded, barely stopping himself in time. "If you don't mind... yeah, I'd like it if you drive me home. Thanks." Then he shut the door before she could answer. He leaned forward, pressing a handful of fast food napkins against the back of his head.

Not until the patrol car's brake lights vanished into the snow and around the bend in the park road did it occur to Toni that she had no idea how to identify Curt's brother. Ten minutes later, she started her car to get the heater working, and wondered why she hadn't thought to ask how far away Curt's brother lived, or even what his name was.

"Yeah, for being Lois Lane, ace reporter, you're pretty oblivious at exactly the wrong moment," Toni muttered. A flicker of movement in the corner of her eye prompted her to lock the car doors, just in case the redhead decided to come back and take another try at Curt's car. Or take revenge on her for scaring him away.

That flicker of movement turned out to be a Jeep pulling into the spot where Donovan's cruiser had sat. Toni glanced at her watch. Twenty minutes since Curt called his brother. Could she be so lucky? She was just starting to get feeling back in her toes and fingertips, too.

"Hi, Toni?" The voice could have been a near-miss for Curt's, and the face and figure were close enough for them to be twins. But this man who jumped out of the passenger side of the Jeep had pure white, receding hair, and the lines around his mouth and eyes gave away his age. "I'm Dave

Mehdlang, Curt's dad." He caught hold of her hand and held it when she opened her car door. "Can't tell you how much we appreciate you helping out my boy like this."

"Well... we're partners. I mean, that's what friends are for, right?" Toni had no idea if Curt had told his family about her presence in Tabor or her connection to the White Rose investigation.

"Yeah, and I wish my partners were as cute as you," the driver of the Jeep grumbled. He was Curt with an extra thirty pounds, his hair more oak than white-blonde. He winked at Toni. Chuck, if she remembered his name right.

She had to repeat everything that had happened, and when she drove away, her face was still hot from the thanks Curt's father and brother heaped on her. Toni hoped they wouldn't hurry to get to the hospital. If she was lucky, Curt would be examined and stitched up, and she could take him home before his family caught up with them.

To her dismay, Curt's mother and his oldest brother, Mike, had already reached the emergency room. Donovan, the traitor, pointed her out to them before he left. Toni saw Mrs. Mehdlang's face light up and she groaned, silently, when the woman hurried over to meet her. She was a dead ringer for Mrs. Claus, just as sweet and warm without being overbearing. Toni felt embarrassed by her gratitude.

She had to repeat what happened for a third, or was it the fourth time? Curt's mother remembered Toni's parents, because her mother had been in a counted cross stitch class with her. So that meant a recitation of what her parents had been doing since moving away from Tabor Heights.

"Are you going home for Thanksgiving?"

"Umm... no. Kind of far to drive, and I have to work on Friday." Toni bit her lip to keep from saying that she had plans to go to the *Starship Defiance* convention with Curt that Saturday. With his mother holding her hand, Toni didn't think it was smart to give even a hint of more than a working friendship.

"Then you're spending it with us." Mrs. Mehdlang nodded for emphasis.

"Spending what?" her husband asked, coming into the waiting room at that moment. He grinned and nodded when she explained. "Great idea. There's always more than enough."

"But—" Toni began.

"Might as well give up right now," Curt said. "They won't shut up until they get their way." He looked a little green, standing there in the doorway, and he wobbled a little bit. "No, really, I'm okay," he insisted, when his mother took hold of his arm and tried to guide him into a chair. "The doctor says I'm fine. Bad reaction to the anesthetic, can you believe it? No concussion, and I didn't even lose enough blood to be worried."

Toni wondered if he said that just to ward off his anxious family and keep them from smothering him with their concern. Curt had to go through what the doctor said twice before his parents would let her drive him home. She wondered if she should have been worried about how easily they gave in, instead of insisting on taking care of Curt themselves.

"Mom's already planning on what her grandchildren will look like," Curt muttered, when they were nearly to the intersection of Sackley and Main. He hadn't moved or spoken since they made a stop at a drugstore to fill the prescription the doctor gave him. Toni noticed he hadn't mentioned the prescription to his parents.

"What?" She slammed on the brake without thinking. Fortunately, there was no one behind them. Curt gasped and pressed a hand to the back of his head. "Sorry."

"They got you worried already, didn't they?" He managed a sleepy smile, still never opening his eyes.

"Worried about what?"

"Matchmaking. Could see it in Mom's eyes."

"I *thought* they were a little too eager to have a total stranger over for Thanksgiving." Toni managed to laugh a little, though there was a funny twisting sensation in her stomach that took her breath away.

"Not to shoot down your ego, but they usually invite a few kids from BWU for Thanksgiving every year. You won't be the only guest. I don't know if it'll hurt things or help, if I ask you to spend the rest of the afternoon at my place. You know, in case I have a seizure from some brain damage the doc didn't find."

"Ha ha." Toni stepped on the brake, gently this time, and slid up to the stoplight. She glanced sideways at him. Curt still hadn't opened his eyes or moved. She guessed he was pretty miserable, just waiting until he was home and in bed before he took his first pill. "What do you mean by hurting or helping?"

"If you stick around, Mom can't call and grill me about you. But if you stay, they could think we're serious about each other."

"Well, that's what Angela wants, right?"

"To a point."

"Don't worry, Clark Kent, I don't plan on sitting in your place with nothing to do while you sleep off your headache. I have a ton of Web surfing to do before I can make the tiniest dent in all that research you gave me."

"Oh, yeah. That."

Toni wondered if Curt sounded disappointed, or that was just his pain talking.

Chapter Nine

Sunday, November 24

When Toni called her parents Saturday evening, she had Curt's injury and trip to the hospital as an excuse for why she hadn't called back right away. She managed not to mention him by name. After all, Curt's father and her father had been friendly business rivals and they would recognize it. How many Mehdlangs could there be in the state of Ohio? Then her parents would put things together and realize she wasn't living in a suburb of Akron and she would really be in trouble.

Guilt prompted her to tell her parents yes, she had found a nice church to attend. She silently promised God she would attend Tabor Christian. Then it wouldn't be a lie anymore, would it? It seemed like half the people she had met attended there, so why not? It wasn't that she didn't like church, but she had never felt any interest in getting involved any further than attending Sunday morning worship. Toni had the distinct feeling once she walked through the doors of the church, she would have no excuse for being a pew-warmer and nothing more.

Guilt prompted her to walk across the center of town instead of driving the short distance, up the slight hill past the post office, and walk through the doors of Tabor Christian that Sunday morning. Toni had the sense to call ahead and find out when the services were. It was a little daunting to realize there were three. She chose the second service. After all, she didn't feel guilty enough to attend the early service.

Annalee and her parents sat in the pew in front of Toni. She spent most of the service remembering Angel and speculating on how Mr. and Mrs. Gray were handling this threat to their daughter. She thought about Angel walking with her to Sunday school and sitting through long, boring worship services with nothing to do but draw tiny pictures in the margins of the bulletin. Had Angel's boyfriend attended the same church with them, hoping for a chance to meet her and exchange notes or whisper together? Did the White Rose Killer sit somewhere in this sanctuary, watching Annalee, making sure she stayed pure and faithful to him?

When the service ended, Toni hesitated just a few seconds too long before standing and fleeing the pew. Annalee turned around and their gazes met. She smiled and introduced her to her parents, and didn't act at all as if some dark cloud of danger hovered over her life. They talked for a few minutes about shared experiences, being newcomers to Tabor, since the Grays had only moved to the town a few months ago. When the press of people in the aisle had diminished enough to let them out, Annalee walked with Toni.

"I really envy how well you're handling all this," Toni murmured. Then she blushed hot and wished she could have taken the words back. What happened to her tact and sense of timing? Had she lost it yesterday in the snow when she was hunting for Curt?

"Actually, I don't think I am." Annalee gestured around the sanctuary, taking in the whole church. "This is the only place where I feel safe. I can feel him watching me everywhere else, but not here."

Toni hoped Annalee was right, and the White Rose Killer would never walk through the doors of the church.

Wednesday, November 27

Toni walked Annalee to the police station to get the police blotter news and Curt couldn't concentrate on his work the entire time they were gone. He knew he was being ridiculous, worrying that having the two of them together would present a tempting target for the White Rose. Maybe too tempting to resist. The whole purpose of having Toni or him walk with Annalee was to give them a chance to see who tried to approach her, to pick up on patterns, and see who saw Annalee on a regular basis. Even if the White Rose was foolish enough to try to kidnap her in broad daylight, he wouldn't try it while someone accompanied her.

And after last Saturday, Curt knew Toni could take care of herself. He still grinned, picturing the reaction of the man who had attacked him when Toni came barreling in with her car. She knew how to think on her feet and she wasn't afraid to take chances and stand up for someone.

It gave him a strange, tight feeling in his chest when he listened to the 911 tape of her call. Toni had been angry at the suggestion that she hang back and wait until it was safe, rather than look for him. He dared to hope it was more than her innate goodness and concern for a co-worker that motivated her words and actions.

What was he going to do about Toni? Or should he do anything at all? After all, once she had her justice and the White Rose Killer was caught and punished for Angel's death, then she would be gone. Life would go back to normal.

Thursday, November 28

"How's your dad doing?" Mr. Mehdlang asked, startling Toni so she almost dropped the box of Christmas decorations she had brought up from the basement.

One of the many Thanksgiving traditions in the Mehdlang family, along with inviting BWU students to dinner, was to decorate the Christmas tree with the help of their guests. Toni laughed with Curt when he had commented, so his parents could hear, that they started the tradition because it was so much work and they needed help. She had agreed after seeing the enormous tree that scraped the vaulted ceiling of the family room. There were enough decorations for three ordinary Christmas trees. Just hauling all the paraphernalia up from the basement had taken half an hour, between Mr. Mehdlang, his three sons, four BWU students, and Toni.

"My dad?" she asked, after getting a better grip on the box. Was the snow too thick out there, in what felt like the Storm of the Century, for her to run for her life? What had she gotten into, coming here and joining this family for Thanksgiving?

He took the box from her and set it down on the long table where the others were unpacking and spreading out the decorations. "I remember Ben now. He ran that garage down by the tracks. Seems to me, his company brought him in to set it up."

"Yeah, they transferred him in from Columbus." Toni hoped her smile didn't look as tight and fake as it felt. This was the wrong time for Mr. Mehdlang to remember details like that.

"He was a good man, your dad." A snort of laughter escaped him. "There I go, talking about him like he's dead. He isn't, is he?" His grin widened when Toni shook her head. "We used to meet up at Marge's Diner sometimes. We sat at the counter with an empty stool between us, pretending we were fighting over customers. Just started to get to know him and your mom when—well, when that tragedy hit." His eyes narrowed and he tipped his head to one side and Toni felt as if he really saw her for the first time.

"Dad?" Curt came over when the silence between them seemed to ring and the air thickened so Toni thought she wouldn't be able to breathe in another moment. Ridiculous, she knew, but that was how she felt.

"Odd isn't it, that Toni's back in town when we've got all this new trouble?" Mr. Mehdlang looked at his son. Curt didn't flinch so much as he went very still. "Ah, well, today's not the right time for that kind of talk, is it?" He clapped him on the shoulder, stepped around him, and supervised Chuck and Mike, who were setting up a ladder next to the tree.

"Are we in trouble?" Toni whispered.

"No." Curt tried to smile. It was almost as if she could read his thoughts, the unspoken words: *Not yet, anyway.*

She hoped he could talk his father into keeping his suspicions to himself and not cause trouble for them. Toni's conversation with her parents that morning still hung in her mind. Everything had been so innocent, loving, sharing regrets that they couldn't be together for Thanksgiving, but excited over her new job. How much longer could she keep the truth from them? Her mother had asked for her address to pass along to relatives, so they could send her Christmas cards. Toni had fumbled through explaining that the mail delivery wasn't very secure in her apartment building, and she was still in the process of getting a post office box. The lies left a bitter taste in her mouth.

The day passed in a warm, happy blur, much to Toni's surprise. Curt's parents had the extraordinary gift of making total strangers feel like old friends and making everyone who came into their home feel welcome. Everyone ate far too much and the three Mehdlang sons fought over who got to do what in the kitchen when it came time to clean up. Mrs. Mehdlang insisted on sending home enough leftovers with Toni for four more meals. She felt guilty taking food, because the BWU students were limited by what they could fit in their mini refrigerators.

Curt, she discovered, had a good singing voice. Another Thanksgiving tradition was to pull out all the old songbooks and sing Christmas carols around the piano. Mr. Mehdlang played the piano and his wife alternated between the flute and guitar. None of the boys played, and Toni decided to tease Curt later about not inheriting his parents' musical talents. Then she heard him sing. His voice wrapped around her like thick, melted chocolate, warm and rich and soft. She liked it, liked the emotions triggered by his singing, but she was glad when the song time gave way to board games.

"You okay?" Curt asked, when she had made her farewells and headed for the door late in the evening.

Toni laughed at him. She hated to leave the warm, loving house where she felt so at home. She had been partially delighted when the BWU students started packing up to leave, and resentful, because she knew it would look odd if she stayed after they left.

"Fine. It's been a long day, that's all. And we have duty at the office tomorrow. Which, if you think about it, is a blessing. Who really wants all that insanity of shopping and traffic?"

"Yeah, that's true." He nodded slowly but kept studying her face. "Miss your folks?"

"A little." She glanced over his shoulder, back into the living room where everyone else made their last farewells. "Oh, you think being here and not with my folks bugs me?"

"I guess."

"Not really. For so long, it's just been my folks and me. We never felt right going to anyone's house or inviting anyone over." Her throat closed up, resisting the urge to tell him that Thanksgiving had been Angel's favorite holiday. "It's nice being included with a big family for a change." She shifted her heavy basket of leftovers to one arm and dared to reach out and squeeze his wrist. "It was really nice today, Curt. I'm glad I came."

"Yeah. Me, too."

Saturday, November 30

Participating in online chats and reading fan stories online for the *Starship Defiance* series was a vastly different experience from actually going to a convention. Toni thought she had been prepared. After all, she had covered a few science fiction-based conventions when she worked for the *Cyclone*. Participating was a totally different experience from standing on the sidelines and observing.

Her first clue came when Jeremy Randolph and his "crew" showed up with various pieces of costumes and props. A uniform jacket on one, night-vision goggles on another, laser-rifle hanging off the back of another. Everyone wore a T-shirt with the *Starship Defiance* logo on the back and their rank and ship insignia on the front.

"They're going to let you into the convention with that?" she said when Jake, the boy with the rifle, elected to ride in the back seat of her car.

"It's peace bonded." He turned it around to show her what looked like a plastic clip over the trigger and a cap over the muzzle. "Besides," he added with a grin and a shrug, "it's not loaded. I used to fill it with water and food coloring, but it leaks when it's cold out."

"Oh. Good idea."

Well, Curt had warned her that some of Jeremy's crew were hard-core.

They talked eagerly enough, telling her on the drive about things their club did, such as paper drives, volunteering at the local PBS station during telethons, writing their fan magazine and selling it at conventions. Which explained the ten-ream copy paper box Jeremy loaded into the back of Curt's car. Toni decided they were mature enough to tell reality apart from their play universe, and that let her relax and anticipate enjoying the convention. Somehow, though, being warned about the participation drama-slash-war games that would take place all day hadn't been preparation enough.

She was met at the door by a fully costumed alien, what appeared to be half-cat and wearing roller skates, demanding her identification and affiliation. When she just gawked at him, he groaned and called her a "mundane." Then he handed her a small, simple booklet with the rules and order of events for the day, and a map of the various rooms being used by the convention.

"It's okay," Curt said, catching up with her once they were inside and through the registration line. He hooked his arm through hers, and she was glad to hold on. "We're probably the oldest people here, and they'll leave us alone."

"Promise?"

He laughed, and even if he didn't keep a tight hold on her arm all day, he did stay close. Toni was glad of that when the first act of the participation drama came tearing through the main hallway, accompanied by ear-piercing sound effects, strobe lights, swords, and guns that gave off eerie red and green beams of light. She was nearly trampled by a gaggle of squealing, stampeding fans in full uniform who obviously weren't sure they wanted to participate.

Toni let Curt dictate where they went and what panel discussions they sat in on. The food was plentiful, most of her favorite junk food, and cheaper than she had expected. The dealer's room amazed her. Much of the merchandise was quality, sold in retail stores, and what came from private craftsmen was displayed with pride. Jewelry, homemade perfumes and soaps, fan magazines by the score, weaponry, handcrafted textiles, T-shirts, bumper stickers with silly, sometimes rude slogans, music, costumes, and used books. Of the three panel discussions they attended, only one threatened to devolve into a melee of arguing and pushing. Most of the people around them seemed sane, balanced, and there to have fun. It wasn't their entire reason for living, as Toni had often heard said about those in fandom.

"Glad you came?" Curt asked, when they waited at the door for Jeremy and his friends to show up so they could go home.

"It was fun. Weird, but fun." Toni bit back the urge to say that, for a first date, it was exceptional. She didn't want Curt to laugh or be angry, and she didn't want to see that guarded, worried light in his eyes. She wasn't sure herself if she would mean it as a joke.

Curt groaned and dug in his pocket, and Toni realized that chirping she heard was his cell phone ringing. She didn't like that little crease of frown that formed between his eyes when he looked at the number on the display. She liked even less that surprised look on his face when the person on the other end started talking, and the way he shook his head.

"Okay, I'm out with some people," he said, "but I'll be home in about an hour and then I can take off again. No problem. Tell him not to worry about anything. And if he needs anything, call me."

Toni sagged against the wall, feeling a sick little weakness in her knees and in her stomach. It hadn't even occurred to her that something might have happened to Annalee until she heard Curt say "he" and the relief hit her.

"Sherwood got trampled yesterday. Fell down the escalator at the mall and broke his leg," Curt said, when he finally slid the phone back into his pocket.

"Isn't he covering a basketball tournament this weekend?"

"Yeah, that was Loni. She showed up to take pictures and he wasn't anywhere around. Luckily, the schools reporter was able to fill in, and she got the pictures. That's all the parents really care about, seeing their kid in his moment of glory. But I have to fill in for him tomorrow, do the follow-up, catch all the stats."

"Poor Sherwood. What?" she had to ask, when Curt grinned and shook his head.

"Loni says he's just glad for the excuse to sit down for a while. Of course, it could be the pain meds he's on, but he's in a good mood."

Monday, December 2

Curt wasn't sure later what made him turn to look as he pulled out of the parking lot that evening. The shopping center across the street was bright with all its Christmas lights glowing green and gold and red, but he was already jaded from the onslaught of color and holiday cheer. Maybe it was the glimpse of movement when everything seemed so quiet and still, at nearly nine at night. Maybe he was just tired from the long day handling last-minute problems with the paper.

Then he saw them, walking toward the parking lot he had just left. Toni and Annalee held onto each other, sliding on the icy pavement and struggling with several shopping bags each. Curt waited until he saw them approach Toni's SUV. There was no other traffic on the street, so he didn't have to worry about being in someone's way. He watched until he saw Toni open the back door and toss their bags into her car, and Annalee climbed into the passenger seat.

Then snow started falling, and the two women seemed to just vanish among the lights and shadows. Curt swallowed a growl of pure panic and made himself sit until he saw the taillights of Toni's SUV light up, then the reverse lights, then the dark bulk of it backing out of the parking space.

"They were just shopping," he muttered, but his angry, racing heart didn't seem to pay attention.

He should be grateful that Toni and Annalee had made friends, and the younger woman was comfortable enough, felt safe enough to indulge in a little Christmas shopping.

Still, the mental image of a dark shape emerging from the shadows of the parking lot and the falling snow, snatching Annalee and knocking

Toni unconscious, lingered in his mind all the short drive to his apartment. It haunted his dreams when he finally got to sleep.

Tuesday, December 3

"Have a good time last night?" Curt said, when Toni waltzed into the office at five minutes after eight. Her workday didn't officially start until 8:30, and somehow he resented it that she wasn't late and didn't give him an excuse to yell at her for that, too.

"Last night?" Toni put her purse down on her desk and leaned against it to pry off her boots, which she tucked under the desk. "Last night... oh, yeah. I went shopping with Annalee. Just across the street." She stopped, frowned a little. "That was you sitting in the middle of the street? What were you doing, spying on us?"

"You're lucky I was the only one who saw you two out there, that late at night."

"It wasn't late and there were dozens of people still shopping. Half the shops are open until ten now, for the holidays."

"You weren't at the stores." Curt fought to keep his volume down. There were no other reporters in the newsroom, but voices had a way of bouncing off walls so sometimes conversations in the back were audible at the front door. Myrna was on duty today, and even though the plan was for people to believe he and Toni were "together," he didn't need the interfering, know-it-all woman to blow things out of proportion. The way Myrna and her gossipy friends operated, Curt could hear that he was engaged to Toni before they even went on their first real date.

"You were in the parking lot, just the two of you. Nobody around to see if something happened or hear you call for help," he said, trying to sound reasonable. It didn't help that he wanted to grab her and shake her. What was wrong with him?

Chapter Ten

"Nothing happened," Toni said. "And isn't it better if Annalee can go on as normally as possible? Wasn't that the whole idea, making sure she had an escort? Besides, I like her. Why can't I be friends with her?"

"The more time you spend with her, the more the White Rose can see you."

"I won't become his target." Toni finished putting her shoes on and dropped down into her desk chair.

"You don't have any guarantee—"

"For me to become his target," she whispered with the intensity of a shout, "he has to kill Annalee, and that isn't going to happen. We're going to catch him before he can even try to touch her. Aren't we?"

She glared at him, meeting his angry gaze with heat of her own. Suddenly, everything went quiet inside Curt and he felt a little lost. He slowly nodded.

How could he have forgotten what all this meant to Toni? She never forgot. Every time she looked in the mirror, she was reminded of Angel. Every time she looked at Annalee, she remembered her sister.

"Yeah, we are." He nodded and suddenly felt as if he hadn't slept a wink the entire night. "Guess I was kind of stupid, huh?" He offered her a weak smile by way of apology.

"Comes with the territory." Toni's eyes sparkled and her lips twitched as she fought a smile.

The relief he felt made Curt feel lightheaded. Why did her friendship matter so much to him? He was Mr. Untouchable. His friends in the inter-church basketball league claimed he was a founding member of Bachelors-'Til-The-Rapture.

"Yeah? What territory? You mean me being klutzy Clark Kent?"

"Nope." She scooped up her jumbo-sized *Calumet Cyclone* mug, fished two bags of hot chocolate mix from her desk drawer and stood up. "Testosterone poisoning. Causes paranoia along with all that brain damage." She wrinkled up her nose at him and scurried out of the newsroom.

Curt leaned back in his chair. His shoulders shook a little with silent laughter. *I am in a lot of trouble.* The problem was, he couldn't quite figure out where that trouble was leading, only that Toni was part of it.

He owed it to Angel to keep her sister safe. He owed Toni help in tracking down the White Rose Killer and determining if he was the same boy who had killed Angel. Where did friendship and guilt stop, and what he feared was real attraction to Toni as a woman begin?

Wednesday, December 4

Toni was honestly surprised when Curt let her take escort duty with Annalee, to walk to the police station. She refused to admit to him that she hadn't considered any risk to the two of them, shopping so late at night on Monday. The thought that Curt worried about her as much as Annalee bothered her. All right, she and Curt were supposed to pretend to be interested in each other, just to provide her some protection, but wasn't getting angry taking it just a little too far?

For a treat, she talked Annalee into taking a detour on the way back to the office and walked up Span Street to Stay-A-While, to see what bakery was left over from the morning rush. Maggie was sitting on a snowy bench outside the door when they came outside, arms folded across her chest, eyes closed, the image of comfort.

"Shouldn't we let somebody know she's there?" Annalee said, when they had detoured around the crazily dressed old woman and started across the next street. "I mean, won't she freeze?"

"Maggie?" Toni glanced back. Maggie was still sitting on the bench. Funny, but the old woman with her mismatched clothes and iron gray hair didn't seem much different than she had been when Toni was a child. "She'll be fine. She's a lot tougher than anybody in this town, never gets sick, never gets hurt."

She regaled Annalee with some stories of Maggie that had become legend in Tabor, how the old woman talked to squirrels in the park and got them to perform tricks, how she always had quarters to buy ice cream for any child who wanted some, when the ice cream truck trundled down the street. Funny, but it never occurred to her until just that moment that it was rather odd that parents let Maggie buy treats for their children. But Maggie was a fixture. Only outsiders distrusted her. Things were just done differently in Tabor Heights, and Toni was glad of it.

She finished a story about the time Maggie camped out in a life-size Nativity scene in front of St. Ambrose church, just as she and Annalee got back to the office. The younger woman's laughter made Toni feel good. She wished she could make it possible for Annalee to permanently forget about the threat that hung over her.

Annalee slid through the gate at the counter first and stepped over to her desk. Her soft chuckles stopped with a gasp. She stumbled back, dropping her gloves and scarf.

"What?" Toni almost ran into the gate in her hurry to get through. Words clogged in her throat. There was nothing bitter and sharp enough in her vocabulary to express what she felt right that moment.

Two white roses sat on Annalee's desk, tied together with a white ribbon.

"Jackie?" Toni turned to the girl at the switchboard. She waited until the pigtailed college student looked up from her books. "Who was in here after we left?"

"I don't know. A couple dozen people. We had a run on paper sales, and then a bunch of people wanted to place last-minute classifieds, so Ted was up here for a while and you know what a mess he makes of things. Why?" She started to stand up.

"Annalee left some pictures on her desk and they're gone now, that's all." Toni turned to put herself between Jackie and the desk. She scooped up the roses with a tissue, wrapped an arm around Annalee's waist, and hurried her to the back of the office.

Angela's office was empty. Toni settled Annalee in one of the chairs in front of the editor's desk and hurried out into the newsroom, still clutching the roses.

Curt swore, the first time she'd ever heard such words leave his mouth, when he saw the roses. She didn't have to say anything. He followed her back to Angela's office, then detoured into the lunchroom. Angela and Loni followed him back into the office a moment later. Loni closed the door and Angela bent down to wrap Annalee in her arms.

Annalee had been silent and pale and still up until that moment. Then she burst into tears, shaking hard enough Toni feared she would have a seizure.

~~~~~

"He got into the office without anybody seeing him," Toni muttered as Curt came back to the corner of the office holding their desks. She looked up from her notepad filled with scribbles and names that were struck off a list.

He knew what that list was. Jackie had tried to list everyone who had been in the office while Toni and Annalee had been gone. There were several strangers who couldn't be accounted for, along with four politicians who had come to talk with Angela about community charity events the *Picayune* was to cover, three police officers, and more than a dozen people who just wanted to get a paper. In between working on stories for next week's paper, Toni had spent the day trying to track down information on anyone who had come into the office. It didn't help that Jackie had been either busy on the phone and didn't see someone step through the gate and drop the roses on Annalee's desk, or she had stepped away to use the bathroom.
~~~~~

"I think someone did see him, but he had a good reason to be here." Curt rested his hands on her shoulders and whistled when he felt the rock-hard muscles. He squeezed a few times in a token effort to get her to relax, she groaned and slumped forward over her desk.

"I'll give you an hour to stop."

He laughed and looked around. They were the last ones in the office. He shivered a little at the idea that they could do anything without fear of discovery. Not that there was anything illegal or immoral that they would want to do, but... well, what if he decided to experiment, just find out what it was like, and kiss her?

That thought didn't stun him as much as it should have. Curt pushed it away in favor of dealing with a much bigger problem: convincing Annalee that Chief Cooper and Angela were right, and it was time to change their tactics. It wasn't enough to increase police protection around the Grays' house and talk about installing a security camera in the newspaper office. He and Toni agreed that the number of roses and the fact that the stalker was able to get into a public place in daylight to leave them for Annalee meant he was stepping up the pressure on her, and maybe his timetable. How soon until he either decided she was unfaithful and killed her for it, or he took her away to the private paradise he had promised his other two victims?

Sunday, December 8

"We're taking Annalee out to lunch," Curt announced when Toni opened her cottage door only twenty minutes after she returned from church, "and Chief Cooper will just happen to be there."

She blinked several times, and he swore she nearly laughed before sighing and beckoning for him to come inside. "I hope it's not fancy. I don't have the energy to change my clothes, much less make a fashion decision."

"It's a casual place." He swallowed down a comment that he thought she looked great. Mandatory sexual harassment training raised its ugly head, reminding him that commenting on a woman's physical appearance could lead to trouble. But Curt wanted to tell Toni that he always thought she looked nice. He liked sitting across the desk from her, watching her frown over her computer keyboard or chew on her pen cap.

Just to be careful, he looked her over, trying to pay attention to the details, instead of the overall impression. Sweatshirt with embroidery of hummingbirds. Black jeans. Stocking feet. She looked fine to him. Toni bent to pick up a pair of hiking boots from the mat next to the door.

"I used to think all this clandestine meeting and cloak and dagger would be fun." She rolled her eyes as she sat down to put her boots on.

"So, what's the meeting about?"

"Annalee is ready to think about a safe house." Curt grinned at the loud, gusting sigh of relief Toni made.

"You know, I was willing to let things go on as they were, hoping we'd catch him, but when he got into the office without anybody seeing... he could be anybody. The last person we'd suspect." She gestured at the piles of papers spread out on the floor in front of the TV, which still played, the volume turned down. It meant that like him, she had the TV on for company while she worked. "I don't know about you, but my half of the research is getting us nowhere."

"We've crossed ten people off the list, because they're either dead or too far away to be suspects. That's pretty good," he offered.

"Not good enough. I wish we could get the police involved —"

"But there are security issues. Yeah." Curt shivered. "You know, there are ten people in the department who are lifelong residents of Tabor, that I know of. They could all be suspects. And they can all get into the police computer and follow any research into records that's being done."

"Oh, that's really comforting." She sat up and took a deep breath and straightened her shoulders. "So, we casually run into the chief and he makes arrangements to get Annalee out of town. Sounds good. What's on the menu?"

~~~~~

The Magic Time Machine in Stoughton was hopping, crowded, with two groups waiting to be seated when Toni, Curt and Annalee arrived. That was just what Curt had been hoping for. The noise would cover their conversation and make it hard for anyone to spy on them, if they had been followed. Everything was going perfectly, as far as he could tell. No one would think it odd if Chief Cooper sat with them. In a place this crowded, sharing a table only made common sense.

Then he saw Angela walk in with Chief Cooper and a young woman who looked enough like him, she had to be his daughter, Diane. All three were dressed in jeans and riding boots and Angela had her hair pulled back and tucked up under a thick, brimmed felt hat.

"They must have been out riding," Toni said, when she saw where Curt was looking.

"Yeah, probably." He quelled a little flicker of anger. What about all the chief's talk about secrecy and having as few people involved in this as possible?

"Is there anything going on?"

"Going on?" Curt felt totally lost. "Where?"

Toni gestured at Angela and the chief, who still stood in the doorway, looking over the crowd. "Are they an item?" She waggled her eyebrows suggestively.
~~~~~

"No more than we are." Even before her grin dropped off her face, Curt knew that was the wrong answer to give.

On the other hand, it did give him a little boost to think that maybe, under other circumstances, Toni might be interested.

"The chief went through a pretty vicious divorce," he hurried to say. "Things he's let drop, he avoids getting serious about anybody. And from things Angela's said, Diane—that's his daughter with them—she isn't too happy about the chief getting involved with anybody. Guess she was pretty badly hurt in the whole battle."

"Seems like they spend a lot of time together, though," Annalee offered.

"Angela boards her horse at the chief's stables, that's all." Still, Toni and Annalee's observations got him thinking. Did the chief and Angela spend more time together than could be explained by their love of horses?

Then the other three made it through the crowd and joined them in their somewhat sheltered nook in the restaurant's foyer. As planned, Chief Cooper pretended to be surprised to see them there, and suggested they share a table. Curt realized it was ridiculous to be angry with Cooper for including Angela and his daughter. Angela was as much a part of this effort to protect Annalee as anyone else, and if Cooper couldn't trust his daughter, who could he trust? He looked at Diane and wondered how much relief the chief felt, knowing his daughter, being fair-haired, was at least theoretically safe from the White Rose's attention.

They didn't approach the subject of Annalee's safety until they had ordered and the waitress brought their drinks and appetizers. It struck Curt as sad and unfair that while everyone around them laughed and enjoyed their lunch, the six of them had met to deal with so much danger and fear. And anger. If he ever got his hands on the White Rose Killer, Curt didn't know if he could restrain himself. He had twenty years of anger and hurt and guilt to make up for.

Angela reached across the table and took hold of Annalee's hands. "The last few weeks have been hard, but I want you to know how much I admire your courage, staying here and trying to help the police. We will catch the White Rose. I promise you that."

"Hey." Chief Cooper nudged Angela. "I'm the one who's supposed to make promises like that, not you. Newspaper's supposed to be impartial, remember?"

"Since when does impartiality have anything to do with protecting the innocent?" She scowled at him, eyes sparkling in mischief, before turning back to Annalee.

Curt felt something drop in his gut, in reaction to the byplay. Toni couldn't be right, could she? Was there something going on between the chief and Angela, and it had taken the newcomer to the group to recognize it? He studied Diane, but she didn't seem affected either way by the banter between her father and Angela. Either Diane liked Angela and approved, or she didn't notice, or there was no relationship beyond friendship.

He hoped there was something. As Toni had pointed out, Angela fit the profile of the White Rose's targets just as much as she did. So far, he had been picking on girls in their early twenties, but what was to stop him from picking a new target who would be close to the same age as Angel Napolitano, if she had lived? A relationship would protect Angela.

Chief Cooper announced he had approached Hannah Blake in church that morning, to ask for help in finding a safe house for Annalee. Curt wished he had thought of that. Xander Finley and Hannah Blake, who both went to their church, ran Common Grounds Legal Clinic. The Arc Foundation, which sponsored Common Grounds, had shelters for battered women in several states. Curt felt as if a huge weight had fallen off his shoulders, when their group got up to leave the restaurant after lunch. Annalee would soon be safely out of the White Rose's reach.

~~~~~~

"Annalee is as good as out of town already," Curt said, after he and Toni had driven the girl home and watched her walk through the door of her parents' home.

"Mission accomplished, huh?"

"Well, almost." He smiled, but she didn't like the shadows lurking in his eyes.

"Tell you what, let's go do something to celebrate."

"Like what?"

"You haven't started your Christmas shopping yet, have you?"

"Well, no—"

"And if you're like most guys, you'll wait until the last minute and then you'll be in a grump because you can't find anything nice and the prices are so high. And I bet you always call your mother for ideas of what to get your brothers and your dad. Right?"

"Yeah." He smiled at her. Toni chalked that up as a point in her favor.

"Beat the rush, I always say."

"You were one of those smart kids who started working on your term paper at the beginning of the semester, as soon as you got the list of topics, weren't you?" he accused.

"And what's wrong with that?" She flinched when he turned right at the next light instead of turning left, to take her home. "Umm, wrong way?"

"I thought we were going shopping."

"Yeah, but you can take me home and we'll meet at the mall. Then when you get worn out after about an hour, I can keep going and you can go home."
~~~~~~

"If we were dating, there's no way I'd get away with doing that."

"Oh, good grief. There goes the testosterone brain damage again."

"Come on, Toni. Think about it." He squeezed her hand, resting on the console between them, and she hated the way her heart picked up the pace. "We have to work even harder to make people think we're together. Once Annalee vanishes, the White Rose will be looking for a new target. I don't want him aiming at you."

"That's supposed to make me feel better?" She shuddered but didn't twist free of his grip. "I hope Annalee doesn't think of that. Her running away to safety means someone else is in danger now."

"Sorry. Didn't mean to bring that up." Curt sighed. "Just let me be the macho guy taking care of his girl, okay?"

Toni looked up into his worried face and realized that Curt really did care about her. Maybe just as a friend, but he did care, and that was something. Would it be so hard to play along if it made him feel better? Besides, she never really had a boyfriend who wanted to take care of her. In college, she hung around with a big group and had guy friends, but never someone special. She had no idea how to act if the situation ever became serious, so maybe it was better this way, pretending to have something she didn't have? If her emotions weren't engaged, then she could think clearly.

At least, Toni hoped so.

Chapter Eleven

"You think so?" Curt held up a gift set with a coffee grinder, two matching cobalt blue mugs, and two bags of whole bean, flavored coffee. He knew his father lived for his morning coffee, but he had never thought of him as someone who would enjoy flavored beans.

"Trust me. I got something just like this for my parents three years ago and they loved it." Toni held up the shopping basket with three bags of flavored coffee and a metal rack holding four fancy glass jars of flavored creamers. "It makes shopping easier, because you can always get them refills."

"Okay. You've sold me." He liked that half-grin she gave him. "You think this is something a girl would give the parents of the guy she's dating?" he asked, just to be sure.

"We're not..." Toni sighed and closed her eyes for a moment and nodded. "As far as everyone else thinks, we are."

"Does that bother you?" He looked around, relieved to find they were relatively alone in the back corner of the gourmet cook shop. With Christmas carols blaring over the loudspeaker, they could have a private conversation at a normal volume.

"We get along good, don't we?" She didn't look at him but fussed with the items in her basket.

"Yeah. Really good. It's nice. We think alike, but different enough, it helps when we collaborate on stories. We make a good team. Does that bother you?" he had to ask again.

"What if we get too used to this? Can you get too comfortable with something?"

He opened his mouth to tease her, then gut instinct told him now was not the time to use humor. "Okay, let's be honest about this."

"You mean, you haven't been?" She tried to smile, but Curt noticed she also didn't meet his gaze.

"I like working with you. I like spending time with you. What little time we do spend together that we aren't working or trying to put the puzzle together, y'know? Heck, I even like getting mad at you when it feels like you take stupid risks." He rested a hand on her shoulder, which made her flinch. "I didn't expect that. I thought we'd be sniping at each other from the moment you sat down at your desk. The thing is, with everything happening—"

"There might be nothing once the whole thing works out. Yeah. That's what I was thinking. So don't push what we might just be imagining, because then somebody'll get hurt once the bad guy is caught and the case file is closed." Toni nodded and backed up, so he had to either take his hand off her shoulder or walk along with her. Curt chose to lift his hand.

"For now, though, people expect us to be together, and there'd be a lot of weird questions if I gave people presents that didn't have your name on them, too."

"How does anyone survive dating? There are so many rules. Is there a book somewhere that you can use to help you keep up?"

He laughed, and somehow that helped. She met his gaze and didn't look away this time, and she laughed with him.

"Make you a deal," he said and held out his hand to shake and seal it.

"Uh oh. The last time you made me a deal, we got turned into Lois and Clark."

"Not so bad, was it?" Curt barely waited for her to shake her head, with a little half-smile. "We keep playing the game, let people think what they want, and avoid a lot of awkward questions by telling everybody we're taking it really, really slow. And who knows?" He shrugged, tried to look nonchalant, but his heart skipped a few beats. "When things settle down, maybe we'll want to keep going."

"Yeah. Who knows?" She looked into his eyes a few seconds longer, then slowly slipped her hand into his grip and shook, sealing the deal.

Monday, December 9

Ray Cooper waited until Hannah at Common Grounds Legal Clinic reported some progress on the hunt for a safe house for Annalee before he made his phone call. It was almost amusing, how much he hated to hear that someone else was waiting for an answer, even when that was the safe, neutral response he used most of the time, when people wanted answers or progress reports from him. He needed to let Annalee know that something was being done, that there was some follow-up on their dinner conversation from yesterday. How the frail-looking, sweet girl could stand up under all this pressure and uncertainty and the fear, he couldn't imagine. He admired her greatly.

Annalee's mother answered the phone. Her voice grew more cheerful when he identified himself, and he wished he had better news, as in definite arrangements to get her daughter out of town and out of danger.

"Hannah promised we'd have an answer by tomorrow morning. What's slowing down the final decision is that the foundation has to protect the safety and anonymity of the women already in the safe houses.

They keep the numbers down, so neighbors don't notice all the traffic, the turnover, and talk about it. It's more complicated than even I ever considered, but the Arc Foundation and its friends have a good track record of protecting women in all sorts of dire situations. In fact, Hannah told me that Mrs. Carter, at Quarry Hall, said Annalee could come stay there if nothing came through right away. Tomorrow morning, either way, your little girl is leaving Tabor Heights and she'll be safe."

He liked saying that. When he hung up a few minutes later, he was satisfied that he had managed to cheer up and encourage the Gray family.

Ray prayed this was the last time he would have to make a phone call like that. If not the last call like that in his career, then at least the last one having to do with the White Rose Killer.

"Please, Lord, let this be over with soon," he whispered as he looked around his cluttered office.

As they often did since the details of this sick man with his sick ideas of love came to haunt Tabor Heights, Ray's thoughts turned to Angela Coffelt. He loved her, and he knew she loved him, but it bothered him more as time went on that they didn't have the courage to reveal it in the light of day. He used to have his daughter's wounded heart as an excuse, but Diane had let him know months ago that she liked Angela and wished the two of them would take their relationship into something more serious. That blessing from his daughter was more than he had ever let himself hope for.

The problem was that now Angela was the one holding tight to excuses not to let anyone else know how they felt about each other. The corrupt former administration had been cleared out of City Hall years ago, so there was no one left to point fingers and make baseless accusations. True, Judge Foggarty and his crony, lawyer Arthur Montgomery, wouldn't hesitate to raise questions of ethics, but Ray knew he could handle them, and Angela could make mincemeat out of them in public opinion without breaking a sweat. He had seen her do it to nastier individuals.

The fun of a clandestine romantic relationship lost its luster when Ray detected some comparison between them, and what the White Rose Killer demanded of his alleged "true loves." Real love, healthy and strong, didn't need secrecy and tests and proof.

So what did it say about his and Angela's commitment to each other, that they wouldn't or couldn't admit to their friends and co-workers that they were a couple, that they were ready for the long haul, and nothing could separate them?

"Maybe because she isn't sure about me?" he whispered.

A knock on the door startled him. He sat up and barked for the person outside to come in. Evans leaned halfway in through the door, just letting him know he had signed in and was heading out on patrol. Ray thanked him and held onto his official smile until the young patrolman pulled the door closed and walked away.

He liked Evans, and he regretted keeping him and so many other concerned, dedicated officers out of the loop when it came to the White Rose Killer investigation. Evans had volunteered for extra duty, even unpaid time to watch over the previous two victims. He had been stunned and even a little hurt when Ray and Donovan made the decision to keep new details between them, after Katrina had been killed. The White Rose had been able to evade too many precautions and patrols, and Ray feared the police department had a leak.

"Please, God..." He sighed and levered himself out of his desk chair. Ray wanted to call Angela and update her on the progress in getting Annalee out of town, but he wanted to discuss things outside the investigation. That meant he had to get out of the station and use his cell phone. There was no telling when someone might walk in on him or overhear the wrong thing.

And he worried that if he pressed her again about letting go of the secrecy surrounding them, they might argue for the first time in years.

~~~~~

He yanked the tape from the cassette player clipped to his belt and crushed it in his fist without intending to. He nearly tossed the fragments, the filmy twists of tangled brown tape into the snow, but caution stopped him. He put the broken pieces into his pocket and kept walking.

His angel was betraying him. She told lies about him, told people that he frightened her. That was the only explanation. Chief Cooper was a good man. He wouldn't plot to take a man's true love away from him unless someone lied to him. She lied to him. She was lying to everyone she met when she smiled and pretended to be sweet and innocent and afraid.

Sunset spilled crimson and gold across the snow piled around the dormitory parking lot as he stalked up the sidewalk. He walked to work off his anger, the surging waves of pain that made him want to scream and smash things to pieces.

How could the chief have betrayed him like that? He nearly wept, grateful that he knew how to set up wiretaps and record phone conversations. All of City Hall was set up for recording, for security purposes, so it had been ridiculously easy. He taped all Chief Cooper's and Mark Donovan's phone conversations now, because they weren't telling anyone about the hunt for the White Rose.

How could his angel have betrayed him like that? How could she go to the police and tell those lies, saying he frightened her?

No, she had never been his angel. She had deceived him, lied to him, played games with him, broke his heart. Just like the others.
~~~~~

"Tracy, wait up!" Laughter rang against the dormitory walls and the icy parking lot and bounced off the Mission building across the street.

He turned and saw the college girl standing on the steps of the dormitory, waiting to go inside. She stood in a puddle of sunset, wearing jeans and white boots, a green sweater and blue down vest. As he watched, she swept her blue stocking cap off and laughed at the girls hurrying to catch up with her. Long, dark hair fell down almost to her waist and she turned her face to the setting sun, so it painted her pale, oval face in gold.

"Angel," he whispered, and the sharp pain filling his chest softened. He watched her laughing with her friends as they hurried up the steps and into the dormitory.

He smiled and turned to go back the way he had come. How could he have missed her all this time? She was here, right under his nose. He walked this path a dozen times a week.

His angel. She had been waiting for him to find her. And now that he was no longer blinded by his false angel, he could see her now.

She was the one. He had waited so long for her to return to him.

Tuesday, December 10

The Grays lived in the old Shipley house. He used to play here, and knew how to get inside without using the doors. The big old half-dead apple tree in the back yard offered thick, steady branches up to the roof, like a natural stairway. The same pines that sheltered the tree from the snow, so the wood was dry and safe for climbing, also cast the entire back yard into shadow. No one could have seen him even if they stood underneath the tree and looked up as he climbed.

It was a matter of moments to step up onto the roof and then climb down the slope to the dormer window of Annalee's bedroom. The slimjim that let him open locked cars made it easy to unlock her old-fashioned sash window so he could raise it and climb inside her bedroom. He waited, hidden in her closet, and watched her prepare for bed. He wept silently, watching her brush her hair and rub cream across her face and hands and elbows. She was so beautiful, and so faithless. Why hadn't she obeyed him? Why had she lied to the police and asked for help to run away from him, when she knew he loved her?

No, he used to love her. Not anymore. Not since he realized she was false, a liar, deliberately blinding him to the existence of his true angel.

His tears dried, abruptly stopped when she folded her hands and bowed her head and prayed. He watched her lips move and he raged. God wouldn't listen to her. She wasn't pure and faithful. She deserved to die.

She had no right to pray.

He waited as she read her Bible and climbed into bed and turned off the light. He waited, listening to the sounds of the TV playing downstairs, punctuated by snores from both her parents. He pulled out the zipper bag holding the chloroform-soaked rag and opened it, then stepped from the closet.

She stirred just a little, startled halfway out of her sleep when he slapped the chloroform rag across her face and held it there. Her eyes fluttered just for a moment, but never opened.

When he was sure she slept, unable to awaken, he wrapped her in a dark blanket, flung her over his shoulder and climbed out the window. He almost left the window open, but eventually the cold air would creep down through the house and alert her parents that something was wrong. He refused to disturb their sleep. They didn't deserve to be punished for the sins of their daughter.

~~~~~

A storm descended across Tabor when he had finished his task, strangling her and dressing her in the white robe. He took her to the old house on Main Street because he had heard her tell someone once that she would like to live there someday. She dreamed of taking old houses and restoring them and making them beautiful.

She had betrayed him, but he proved how much he loved her by leaving her body in the house where she wanted to live someday.

Wednesday, December 11

"Where's Annalee?" Max said, scurrying into the newsroom. Curt was the only one there so far. He glanced at the clock. 8:20. Usually Annalee was there by 8:15.

"She's okay." He smiled and felt a last few tense muscles in his back relax.

"You talked to her folks?" She reached for the phone. Curt stopped her, catching her hand before she lifted the receiver.

"Hannah Blake was calling around yesterday, finding a place for her at one of Arc's shelters. I'm guessing they left last night or even this morning."

"Thank You, God," Max sighed, and dropped into the chair of Toni's desk. "She was really shook up last week."

"She wasn't the only one."

Angela didn't ask about Annalee when she came in, and Curt felt a little flicker of resentment that she knew the arrangements had come through and she hadn't said anything to him. It made him wonder again
~~~~~

about Toni's suggestion that there was something more than friendship between Chief Cooper and Angela. He didn't admit that to Toni, though, when she came in later, after an interview.

"So she's safe," Toni murmured, glancing around the newsroom at the other reporters hard at work. "When did she go?"

"Don't know." Curt grinned at her scowl. "Nobody tells me anything around here. Tell you what, though. I'll ask when I go over to the station."

"Why would you go?"

"Somebody has to get the police blotter news."

Later, Curt kicked himself when he realized how trusting they had all been, everyone assuming someone else knew what was going on.

Donovan was crossing to Chief Cooper's office door when Curt walked up to the desk to ask for the log books. He stopped short and gave Curt an odd, frowning look that sent chills up the reporter's back. Curt waved to the desk sergeant and continued across the room to meet up with Donovan.

"What's up?"

That odd, confused look deepened. Donovan signaled him to silence and opened the door, gesturing for Curt to go in ahead of him.

Mr. and Mrs. Gray sat on the couch, and Taylor Dunlop, who worked as dispatcher and counselor, knelt in front of the couch, holding their hands. Curt took one look at their drawn, teary faces and he knew, with a sickening, dropping sensation in his gut. Angry words caught in his throat, but he wasn't sure who to yell at. Donovan, for not telling him when Annalee's parents came into the station? Chief Cooper, for not having gotten Annalee away from Tabor sooner? Himself, for assuming she was safe and not checking with anyone?

Chief Cooper came over to the door and the three men conferred, leaving Taylor to minister to the shocked parents.

The Grays hadn't seen Annalee since she went to bed the night before. Both of them had fallen asleep watching TV. They heard nothing. They had both slept until after ten because Annalee usually woke up her father to drive her to work. When they woke and realized how late in the morning it was, they had panicked, tearing the house apart. Then they came to the station, hoping they were wrong. After all, even if she had gotten the call in the middle of the night and someone came to pick her up, Annalee would never have left the house without telling her parents or at least leaving a note.

Curt lingered at the station, trying to concentrate long enough to pick up the police blotter news. In all his years of reporting, he had never been so shattered by a tragedy as he felt right that moment. Chief Cooper wanted everything kept as quiet as possible, so he couldn't even gripe with some of his friends on the force, get their feedback, air some of his anger and helplessness.

He could call Toni. She would understand. She would cry in his arms, if she didn't scream and trash the room. Curt thought maybe he would like comforting Toni. He would feel like he was some use to someone today, at least.

McGuire answered the phone when Xander Finley called. Curt was waiting at the counter when he saw the senior officer stiffen and turn sharply to look at Chief Cooper's office door. The stern look that took over the man's normally friendly, weather-beaten face, alerted Curt. He listened and nodded a couple times, then said he was patching the caller through directly to Chief Cooper.

"What's up?" Curt asked in an undertone. He had that same chill he felt when he saw Annalee's weeping parents.

"Xander Finley, that lawyer moving in up where Kiddie Time used to have their store." McGuire looked around the front office area, as if afraid of being overheard. "He's checking out his new office and finds a body in the back room. Asked specifically for the chief. Hey, you okay?" He reached out and gripped Curt's arm, steadying him when a wave of sickness and anger made him dizzy for a few moments.

"No." Curt slammed a fist down on the desk, making the logbook jump. Maybe he could cry in Toni's arms, and she wouldn't laugh at him? "It's Annalee. She vanished last night."

McGuire's face got a little redder and his eyes glistened with furious tears. He gripped Curt's arm a little tighter and swallowed audibly a couple times. Neither one of them could move, just stared into each other's eyes and shared the anger.

Chapter Twelve

When Chief Cooper and Donovan stalked out of the station five minutes later, Curt followed them. He knew better than to ask if he could hitch a ride in the cruiser, but he bet himself that he could jog up Main Street to the converted old house almost as quickly as the two officers could get to the car and drive around the back of the municipal building and up the street.

The car with Donovan driving passed him when Curt was two side streets away from Xander's new offices. Neither man seemed to notice him. Curt could understand that. He still felt as if he'd been slapped between the eyes with a two-by-four. He wasn't going to tell anyone at the *Picayune* until he got all the details and had something concrete to give them. The sudden plummet from relief to grief was something to only be faced once, not again and again as more details came in.

Curt didn't slow his steps as he watched the police cruiser park in front of the old blue house and the two officers got out and walked up to the porch. Both men carried those black bags of police equipment that he hated seeing brought onto a scene. Usually, it involved a crime that was particularly deadly or painful or grisly. He was close enough to see them walk in without waiting.

He reached the bottom of the porch steps just as Donovan reached back and shoved the door halfway closed. He caught a glimpse of Xander with his homely, friendly face composed in somber lines, just as the lawyer reached to push the door closed. Xander must have seen him, because he pulled the door open again just before Curt opened his mouth to shout and let him know he was there.

"Sorry," Curt gasped as he vaulted the steps. "I hope you guys don't mind, but I was picking up the police blotter news at the station when the call came in and..." He shrugged and waved his reporter's notepad for explanation. It had never felt so lame and mercenary before. "It's my job." He raked a gloved hand through his mop of windblown hair and offered an uneasy grin when he saw Hannah sitting on the deep windowsill.

He felt sick when he remembered with a jolt that Hannah knew exactly how close they had come to getting Annalee to safety. For all he knew, she had found a place for her last night and was going to contact Chief Cooper this morning with the news.

Xander managed a half-hearted smile and stepped back into the room to the left of the entryway. Curt nodded to Hannah before looking down the hall. A flash of light indicated the two officers had started their work.

"Maybe if I get the questions out of the way, you won't have to repeat yourselves too much," Curt murmured. He settled down in the wide window seat with his back to the alley. He pulled out his recorder to avoid looking at Hannah. "Coroner'll be here in maybe half an hour. They can't move the body until then."

"I can't believe she's dead," Hannah whispered.

Xander sat down in the window seat and wrapped his arm around her shoulders. Hannah leaned into him.

Annalee was dead. Who had the White Rose found for his next target? Curt nearly leaped to his feet to run down the street to the newspaper office. Better yet, go to Toni's house. What if there was a white rose and note waiting for her when she got home, claiming her as the property of a madman who wouldn't show his face?

The three of them talked, easing into the subject. Curt knew he was babbling, but he wanted to erase that shocked, pale look from Hannah's face. And he admitted that talking made it harder to think. At least for a while. He was relieved when Chief Cooper came out of the back room and started asking Xander and Hannah questions, what they had seen and done, and then talked to Hannah about what she had seen last night. She lived only two doors down from the building, and might have noticed something last night, despite the falling snow.

Curt took notes, and from the glance Cooper gave his tape recorder, he knew the man was going to ask for a copy of the tape. He listened and shuddered once, imagining Xander and Hannah inspecting their new offices, and the shock of finding the body lying there.

"Found out a few things," Donovan announced as he rejoined them. He finished putting his camera away in its case as he talked. "The murder took place someplace else. Someplace wet, judging by the condition of her hair. She was strangled with some thick wire just like the first two, because of abrasions on her throat. The skin was broken and bled in several places, but the bleeding stopped before he put her in the robe. And," he paused dramatically, "he broke a window to get in here last night."

"How do you know that?" Curt asked. He offered a sheepish smile when both police officers frowned at him. Had he been so quiet they actually forgot he was there for a few minutes?

"The killer took the time to replace the window he broke with a plastic pane, meaning he was prepared. Meaning he planned to dump her here, it wasn't just spur of the moment. He cleaned up after himself, but not good enough." Donovan nodded and held out a few evidence bags. Shards of glass glinted in one of them when Chief Cooper took them. "I found spots on the floor where snow melted on the dust and then dried. Probably someone can calculate how long ago that was, factoring in the heat of the house and how big the puddle mark is. But not me. I wouldn't have known the pane was plastic, but the wind's strong enough to knock a tree branch against the window and there's a different sound between plastic and glass."

"But it's good enough to fool the eye," Xander said. "Who has the money for that kind of plastic?"

"Another clue," Chief Cooper said, nodding.

"One that doesn't go in the paper?" Curt asked, before the man could turn to him and open his mouth. "You forget, I have a stake in finding out who this guy is."

"What's that supposed to mean?" Hannah asked, her voice breaking again.

"I have a theory, that's all. Somebody I knew, who was killed when I was a kid, was probably the first real victim. Kind of personal," he added with a shrug.

Angel had been strangled by fencing wire, left in the park from an old farm fence. Curt wondered if it was the same kind of fencing wire or the White Rose broke from tradition. He wasn't going to ask, though. Not in front of Hannah.

~~~~~

It was ridiculously easy to get into the dormitory during the day, while the students were out at classes or studying in the library or the dozens of things college students did. He found it even easier to get hold of the keys for the dormitory, so he could avoid the front door and use the back entrance, opening directly into the stairwell.

The ease in getting those keys was a sign. It was proof. A gift to reward him for his endurance and patience and faith. This girl was his angel, the one he had been waiting for. The first three were filthy whores who deserved to die for distracting him, lying to him, deceiving him into thinking they were each his one true love.

Her dormitory room door was locked, but he jimmied it with only a few twists of the lock picks he carried in his jacket. Her blue down vest lay across the bed on the right side of the room, showing him which side was hers. He picked it up and buried his face in the slippery material, inhaling her scent. She even smelled pure and clean. Innocent. His angel.

But if her coat was here, that meant she was in the building. Now wasn't the right time to meet face-to-face. He quickly put down the rose he had brought for her, nestled in her jacket, and went back down the stairs, out the side door. Then he stood for half an hour in the shadows of the big pine trees outside the dormitory, watching her window. Would she see the rose and know why he had left it there? Would she come to the
~~~~~

window and look for him? Would she open the window and call to him, sensing he waited in the shadows, watching and protecting her?

After half an hour, he knew he couldn't stay there any longer. Someone would get suspicious. There were many innocent people in Tabor, but the evil ones, the liars, would accuse him of committing crimes if he stayed here to watch over his angel. But he promised her, and he promised himself, he would return, as often as possible.

~~~~~

Angela called a meeting of the entire office at the end of the day, just when Toni had built up a full head of steam and the courage to back Curt into a corner and demand some answers. Especially the details on when Annalee had been able to leave for the safe house. He had avoided her all day, either tapping like mad at his computer or holed up in Angela's office. Toni knew something had happened, just from the somber looks they wore whenever they weren't talking in hushed voices behind the closed office door. Toni wasn't ashamed to admit that she stood outside the door, as close to it as she could without actually pressing her ear to the crack, trying to hear something.

"I have some painful news and thought it wise to leave for the end of the day so it wouldn't interfere with our jobs," Angela began. She looked at no one as she spoke, staring at some spot in the middle of the newsroom, where everyone had gathered. "There's going to be a news conference this evening, and I wanted you all to know to spare you the shock. Some of you asked where Annalee was. I'm sorry to say we lied when we said there were family problems." She swallowed hard, looked down at her clasped hands, and flinched when her father stepped up next to her and put an arm around her shoulders.

Toni caught her breath, suddenly chilled with a sense of what Angela was about to say. She looked at Curt and for the first time all day, he met her eyes. She muffled a sob in her hand when she saw the pain in his eyes.

"We thought Annalee didn't come in this morning because Chief Cooper had found her a safe house. Unfortunately, we learned that the White Rose kidnapped her right out of her bedroom last night. Her body was found this morning in one of the rental offices on Main. The funeral is Saturday, and I hope all of you will give your support to her parents and—" Her voice broke with a sob. "I'm sorry," she gasped, and hurried back into her office.

"No," Toni whispered. She huddled in her chair, arms wrapped tight around herself, and ignored the talk among all the others.

"I'm sorry," Curt said.

She jerked her head up and glared at him. She wanted to launch herself at him and punch and pound and work off the jagged, tearing fury that filled her stomach and made her lungs burn. Then she saw the hurt,
~~~~~

the shadows in his eyes.

"Wouldn't have been—any use to anyone—today, huh?" she managed to say without letting loose the sobs filling her throat.

"Come on." He yanked her to her feet and moved her aside so he could get to her computer.

She didn't protest as he shut down the stories she was working on and logged her out. She let him put her purse in her hands, and lead her out of the newsroom, to the coat rack in the lunchroom. Toni obediently put on her coat when he gave it to her and let him lead her out of the office. She didn't protest and try to get in her car when he bundled her into his car and drove the short distance to her cottage.

Toni barely got her coat off before Curt wrapped his arms around her. She gasped, feeling as if something had been torn open inside her. They stood there in the kitchen, holding each other, while the tears came and she shuddered and clung to him. Curt didn't say anything. He just rubbed her back slowly and swayed from side to side a little bit.

It was dark in her kitchen when she finally raised her head from his shoulder and looked around. Light from the street spilled through the window over the sink but illuminated little.

"Doesn't help much, does it?" Curt said.

"When is this going to end?" Toni almost laughed at the way her voice cracked. She doubted she could ever laugh again. The sound of Annalee's laughter, the fear and the determination in her eyes, her courage in cooperating with the police when she should have fled the town, filled Toni's thoughts.

"He knew she was trying to run away. That's the only answer."

Toni didn't need to ask who he referred to.

"The chief is tightening things up even more. No more phone calls or entering information in his computer. All that security, sometimes it just seems to make it easier for people to hack in and find out anything they want."

"He thinks the White Rose hacked into his computer?" Toni shuddered, thinking of all the work she had been doing, trying to track down the White Rose from a long list of boys who had wanted Angel for their girlfriend twenty years ago. If he could get into the police computers, he could get into hers with no trouble.

"It's either that, or he tapped some phones. The chief said he only told three of his men that he was hoping to get Annalee away, because they were watching her house last night. He talked with Hannah Blake on the phone about the safe house, and he noted it in his case files on his computer. What else could it be?" Curt groaned when a loud rumbling in his stomach punctuated his words.

Toni gasped laughter and realized that she was still held tight and close in his arms. Not that she was complaining. She liked the warmth, the strength of him. It occurred to her that her sweater was just as wet as the front of his shirt had to be. It hurt a little when she stepped back and he let her move out of his arms. She reached back and found the light switch. Her eyes hurt in the sudden light filling the kitchen, but she still saw Curt wiping the tears off his face with his fists. It gave her a warm feeling to know he was able to cry. Maybe he had needed to hold her, as much as she needed to be held?

"Well, if we're going to hold a war council, maybe I should get us something to eat." It occurred to her that she hadn't seen Curt eat all day, and he usually downed more junk food in an eight-hour period than she consumed in an entire week. Toni kicked herself for not noticing that aberration. It should have warned her, more than anything else, that something was very wrong. She yanked the refrigerator door open, encouraged when she got a snort from him. It wasn't laughter, but it was a step toward healing.

"War council, huh?" He sat down at the table tucked into the corner. "Think it'll do any good?"

"Doesn't matter. We have to try something. If he's following his pattern—" She gasped, startled at the sudden pain in her chest, and wrapped her arms around herself.

"He's already contacted his next target." Curt raked his long, lean fingers through his hair. "We can't help Annalee, but we have to keep trying to help the next one."

"Besides," she offered, "I don't think you want to be alone tonight any more than I do."

"You got that right."

Saturday, December 14

Toni was gratified to see how many people attended Annalee's funeral. The Gray family hadn't been in Tabor very long, but the sanctuary was more than half-full for the service at Tabor Christian. She couldn't stay for the luncheon afterwards in the church fellowship hall, despite Mr. and Mrs. Gray's earnest invitation. She nearly burst into tears when Annalee's mother hugged her and told her how much her daughter had enjoyed Toni's friendship.

There was only one place Toni could go after that. Only one person who wouldn't condemn her for breaking her vow that the White Rose wouldn't hurt anyone else.

The daisies and carnations she had brought yesterday were still on Angel's grave, shriveled a little by the cold air, but still bright. Toni stood a long time, arms wrapped around herself, trying to frame in words the questions that burned deep inside. The worst part of this painful new inability to verbalize what was inside her head and heart was the sense that if she could just bring this elusive idea to her conscious mind, she would have the answer to the puzzle, she would know what to do to get the White Rose to identify himself and stop causing so much pain. She barely heard the footsteps approaching from behind her and didn't look up when she saw the shadow move across the snow. It was hard enough to fight the tears without having to look at people and see the sympathy or even the questions in their eyes.

"No matter what we do, it's never enough, is it?" Angela said.

Toni looked up, startled. She had somehow expected Curt to follow her from the church. Her face warmed at that thought. She glanced around and saw Chief Cooper stood at the edge of the asphalt cemetery road, head bowed, hands jammed in the pockets of his long coat, his gaze distant. She wondered what he saw when he looked at her sister's grave.

"We have to keep praying, and keep trying, and trust that we will find the answer," Angela continued. She hooked her arm through Toni's and patted her arm with her other hand. "Annalee is safe now. She won't be afraid or hurt anymore. We have to remember that."

"It's not enough." Toni swallowed hard. Her voice rasped like she had gargled with sand. "She shouldn't have to find her peace here. Angel shouldn't be here, either."

"We'll catch him," Chief Cooper said. He sounded tired.

"When? How many more girls have to be scared for their lives? How many more have to die before we catch him and make him pay?" She shook her head and tugged her arm free of Angela's hold. It wasn't done as gently as she could have wished, but she needed to get away from all that useless sympathy.

"We can never make him pay," he said, finally raising his gaze from Angel's grave. "There's nothing in the world that can pay back the lives he took. But we can stop him and make our town safe again. I'll be thankful for that much."

Toni nodded, unsure she could speak and not spew all the questions and anger and frustration that twisted inside her. She wished she had told Curt where she was going, maybe asked him to drive her here. Maybe the warmth and caring and comfort he had wrapped around her on Wednesday had been an aberration, a result of the strain and pain that had drowned them both, but she missed his arms around her and knowing he understood what she felt. The longer she stayed here in Tabor, the more she was going to want that warmth and closeness to become permanent.

She had to find the White Rose and expose him and get out of here. It was ironic that to heal one pain, she might have to endure another.

Sunday, December 15

He watched and waited until the girls in the dormitory were downstairs in the lounge, having their Christmas party, then he went up the back stairs and left another rose and a Christmas card for his angel on her bed. He smiled as he crept down the back stairs, and dreamed of the day he would approach her and she would see his face and know him, and willingly give her love to him. She was pure and good and innocent. She was his angel.

Monday, December 16

The window display at the Treasure Chest caught his attention that night as he walked past after his dinner break. The angel stared at him from the top shelf of the display done in white and silver. Light danced off the cut glass edges, shattering into prisms that filled the display window.

Angel had had earrings of crystals that made rainbows dance in his eyes. He remembered how she laughed and turned her head from side to side to let the sun catch in the tiny, multiple splinters of diamond brightness.

It was another sign that the right Angel had returned to him.

He bought the angel, paying cash, and had the clerk wrap it for him. He had to hurry to give it to his angel before she went home for Christmas. He imagined her joy, imagined the angel as her favorite present and most treasured possession. He imagined her eager and impatient to come back to school, so they could be closer together.

Chapter Thirteen

Tuesday, December 17

When he drove past the dormitory that afternoon, to ensure the safety of his angel, he saw her come out the door, suitcases in her hands. She hurried to her car and tossed the suitcases in the back seat, then hurried back inside, but left the car door hanging open.

He frowned, confused. He was positive she didn't plan to head home until tomorrow. He had heard her talking with her friends about her plans. She wanted to relax for one more night after she finished her exams and go caroling with her friends in the choir.

Something was wrong. Or maybe she had just changed her mind.

Yes, something had to be wrong at home. Why would she want to leave Tabor any sooner than she had to, and leave him? She was a good girl, hurrying home and giving up her fun with her friends because her family needed her.

He parked his car far down the street, but close enough he could still keep an eye on her car and make sure nobody stole anything. Just before he passed the big, dark pines that stood in front of the dormitory, the door banged open and two more girls hurried down the steps, carrying boxes. They put the boxes in the trunk of her car. He frowned, even more confused. Why were they putting all those things in his angel's car?

Maybe she was driving someone home. Yes, that was it. That was probably why she was leaving early. To help someone. His angel would do something like that, even if it took her away from him.

He waited until the girls went back inside the dormitory, then looked in all directions before he approached her car. There was room in the back seat. This was yet another sign his Angel had come back to him as she promised. The timing was perfect. He had her present in the car with him, to safeguard it. Now, he tucked the package in between her suitcases and pulled the car blanket around the box to protect it. He whistled a Christmas carol as he walked back down the sidewalk to his car. He wished he could be there when his angel found the present. She would laugh at how he had managed to sneak it in among her belongings without her seeing.

Friday, December 20

Toni was in the circulation office, chatting with Marty Sykes, when she heard a crash from the newsroom. She hurried down the hall, her heart in her throat. One of these days, her overactive imagination was going to get her in trouble. For just a second, she had a clear image of a man dressed all in black, breaking into the newspaper office through the back window and attacking everyone, to punish them for the stories they had written about the White Rose Killer.

Curt was alone and there was a new dent in the side of the filing cabinet standing at the end of their desks. He hunched over, but his face showed anger more than pain.

"What did the filing cabinet do this time?" she blurted.

Curt stared at her a moment, but he didn't laugh. He swore, making Toni jump.

"What happened?" Gut instinct guided her to reach for his hand. It wouldn't be safe to wrap her arms around him, but touching would help, wouldn't it?

"You just heard, didn't you?" Angela said, coming out of her office. The angry sparks in her eyes matched Curt's fury. The three of them were the only reporters left in the office. Toni had the feeling she was going to be glad for that in a minute.

"Okay, could someone let me know what's going on?" she demanded.

"Hannah Blake got a white rose yesterday," she answered after a long pause. Curt sank into his desk chair and raised his fist for a moment as if he would pound something else.

"No." Toni thought she would throw up but settled for finding her own chair and sitting down.

"Donovan thinks it's a copycat," Curt said.

"What?"

It took very little time for Angela and Curt, taking turns, to tell Toni about the Butler-Williams University student who had received several white roses and kept silent, fleeing home in terror. Then they compared what little the police and university officials knew to what had happened when Hannah and Xander came to the police station with the white rose and threatening note she had received. But in that short time, Toni felt as if everything had been turned sideways.

"Why would someone be so sick as to play a game like this? Not the White Rose," she hurried to clarify. "Pretending to be him. That guy is even more sick. I hope it's a copycat going after Hannah."

"Why?" Angela settled down on the edge of Sherwood's desk, which sat against the opposite wall.

"Because if the college girl is the White Rose's target, he won't realize she's gone until January. That's a few weeks the next girl is safe from him."

"And that's more time for us to narrow down who the White Rose could be," Curt said, nodding. He managed a tired smile. "But until then, we have to worry what the copycat might do next to Hannah."

"I don't suppose she could go away to a safe house?"

"No." Angela shook her head. "Hannah isn't the type of girl to give up and take the easy way out."

"Tell me about it." Curt's smile warmed a little. "She's been waiting years for Xander to wake up and see she's there. She hasn't given up on him, so why run away when some loony is sending her nasty love notes?"

"I think I'd like to meet Hannah," Toni mused.

Monday, December 23

Toni's weekend passed in one long struggle with her computer, trying to untangle all the threads of leads on the list of suspects and find out where they were right at that moment. Several times, she wished she could turn everything over to the police, to use their connections to the personal records of anyone who had ever lived in Tabor. She reminded herself the White Rose had killed Annalee because he must have heard she was trying to escape him. If the police department couldn't keep information secret enough to protect one girl, how could they keep a full-scale records search secret? The White Rose could even be one of the officers who handled all their data searches and records.

She was happy to get up and go to work Monday morning, both to escape from her self-appointed hunt and to report to Curt that four more men had been deleted from the list of suspects. The general mood in the office was better than it had been last week, even though it wasn't up to the levels usually expected two days before Christmas.

"I have a present for you two," Angela said, calling them into her office after she got back from dinner.

Everyone was working late because they had to put together both the Christmas Eve and the day after Christmas editions. With a choice of working until nearly midnight tonight or coming in on Christmas day to put together Thursday's paper, there was no real choice.

"How would you like to write a story to help us smoke out the White Rose?" She smiled when Toni and Curt both stared at her and slowly sank down into the chairs in front of her desk.

"Speaking of smoke..." Curt's smile turned fierce. "Does this have anything to do with the fire over at Xander and Hannah's new office?"

"The suspect turned himself in." She waited a moment, but neither Toni nor Curt asked any questions. "He was blackmailed into setting the fire and didn't realize it was their office. And he was told to leave white roses for Hannah."

"Definitely the copycat," Toni whispered. Part of the tightness in her chest evaporated. Christmas wouldn't be tainted for one girl, at least. She hoped the college girl, Tracy, would have a good Christmas, knowing she was safe and her records had been sealed so no one could follow her home.

"The arsonist didn't know the name of who hired him. We have our suspicions, but..." Angela shrugged. "We're in agreement, it's being done to stop Common Grounds from setting up their branch office here."

"We?" Curt asked.

"Chief Cooper, Donovan and me. We need a story to lure Xander's enemy out into the open, to contact the boy he forced to do his dirty work. And... we're going to do a full-blown retrospective on everything the White Rose has done. Maybe we can make him angry enough, calling him what he is, he'll make mistakes. We need to warn the women of our town so they don't mistakenly believe they're getting love notes from someone they know. The first time he makes contact with his next victim, we want her to come to the police and get protection."

"Not very nice reading for the day after Christmas," Toni mused. "And do you think anybody'll actually be reading the paper, with all the holiday activities going on?"

"There's that." Angela nodded and settled back in her chair.

"Maybe if we really want to lure him out, we should do a story about Angel, how she was the first victim," she ventured.

"No." Curt clutched her arm, resting on the arm of the chair. "That'll just get him angry, maybe focus his attention on you. I don't want him coming after you."

"It might make someone who was here at the time remember something that would help. The boy who got beat up. What was his name? He might remember something, might at least remember who was strong enough to ambush him and hang him in a tree."

"And anybody that strong could do the same thing to you. He *did* do that to Sam Conrad. No. And I think we shouldn't put our names on the story about the White Rose. Give him no real target, except the paper."

"He'll come after Angela," Toni retorted. "She's the editor." A gasp of nervous laughter escaped her when Curt flinched at that argument and turned to stare at Angela.

"We've already considered that. Chief Cooper has promised extra protection." Angela sounded confident enough, calm enough, Toni had to accept her word for it.

"Still," she pressed, "the story about Angel could be the best weapon we have. We're taking too long narrowing down the list of suspects."

"The story about Angel is too dangerous," Curt said, gripping her arm tighter. "You reveal his past, let him know we have more clues to his identity, he'll come after you. You know too much."

"We'll only do that as a last resort," Angela said, with that firm tone of voice that meant there would be no arguing with her.

Toni decided not to argue at all. She would simply write the story and have it ready.

Tuesday, December 24

Curt tried to concentrate on the Christmas Eve service, but his thoughts kept slipping to Toni. By this time in the evening, depending on the weather in Indiana, she should be with her parents, enjoying her own Christmas Eve. He thought about the things she had let slip, how quiet the holidays were for her family. Those thoughts led to how much fun she seemed to have on Thanksgiving with his family.

He smiled and glanced sideways at his parents, sitting to his right, in the middle of the pew. Even though he and his brothers were all grown up and living on their own, they turned into little boys when it came to Christmas, everyone dressed in their best, sitting with their parents for the service. Someday there would be daughters-in-law to sit in the row with them, and after that, grandchildren. His mother longed for grandchildren, and he was grateful she didn't nag.

His mother especially liked Toni. She wasn't the first girl he had brought home for Thanksgiving. Then again, he hadn't really brought her home, because his mother had done the inviting. Still, it was understood she was there as his guest.

Curt wondered if Toni would have willingly sat with his family for Christmas Eve service, if she hadn't gone home. His parents would have welcomed her as if she was family.

His face warmed. He mentally slapped himself to try to get his attention back on the short sermon. What was wrong with him? He knew. He spent most of his workday looking at Toni and conferring with her over stories, and then they spent a few hours together every other evening, working on their research to find the White Rose. She was a part of his life now. She was one of the few people he could talk to about the topics that seemed to consume most of his waking moments.

And what happens when the White Rose is caught and we don't have anything in common anymore? Curt asked himself.

If he wasn't brutally honest with himself sitting in a packed church sanctuary on Christmas Eve, when could he be?

All right, total honesty. When the White Rose Killer was caught and the mystery of Angel's death finally resolved, Toni would leave town, just like she promised. They might stay friends, but there was no reason for her to stay in Tabor. She might make a place for herself at the newspaper by then, and Angela might ask her to stay, but then again, maybe not.

Deal with it when the time comes, Curt told himself, and yet again tried to focus his thoughts on Pastor Glenn's sermon as it drew to a close.

Problem: Curt had the sneaking suspicion he was being an idiot and a coward, by putting the whole question off.

~~~~~

"Merry Christmas, Angel," he whispered as he stared at the city's brightly lit tree that towered over the Civil War monument and the gazebo. His breath puffed out in a white cloud that rose to the sky. He smiled, remembering how his aunt had told him that the clouds were angels carrying his Christmas prayers to God.

The strains of organ music filtered through the frosty air. On the other side of the Triangle, up the street by the post office, the Christmas Eve service was starting at the church. Hannah's church. He frowned, thinking of Hannah.

Something was wrong. Someone was trying to frighten Hannah. Ever since they found Annalee's body in Hannah's office, everybody had been so secretive. He couldn't find out anything. Nobody was talking to anyone.

He regretted putting Annalee's body in Hannah's office. He wouldn't do that to Hannah. She was nice to him. She didn't deserve to be scared.

Annalee didn't matter anymore. His angel was safe at home with her parents, far away. In another week, the students would come back to the university and he would see her walking around campus. He could watch over her again, keep her safe and pure for him.

"Merry Christmas, Angel," he repeated, and started down the street. He had to watch over the whole town, to make sure it was worthy of his angel when she came back to him.

Wednesday, December 25

"What are you doing up there, dear?" Mrs. Napolitano called, her voice echoing off the steep stairs to the attic. Toni started to stand up and banged her head on the joists of the attic. She muffled a hiss of pain, rubbed her head and went back down to her knees in front of the fifty-gallon plastic storage bin. At least she had missed the nails sticking through the plywood.

"Just checking if there's anything I forgot when I moved out, Mom!" Toni groaned as she looked at all the yearbooks and scrapbooks and other pieces of memorabilia she had pulled out of the box.
~~~~~

She could almost cry. For a while, Toni had been sure she was mistaken and her parents hadn't destroyed everything that reminded them of those two short years in Tabor Heights. Now, she couldn't even find the yearbook that Angel had refused to let anyone look at. She had hoped against hope that she would find a love note from the mysterious boyfriend, and maybe she could compare it with the yearbooks Curt had been able to scrounge from people in the classes before and after the grade he and Angel shared. With that bit of handwriting to compare, it might help them identify the White Rose.

But no such luck.

"Face it, kid," she muttered as she piled all the books and papers back into the bin. "Lucky breaks like this only happen in the movies."

"I'm going to pack you something to eat on the way, is that all right?" her mother called up the attic stairs again.

"Sounds good!" Toni looked around the attic once more.

The narrow, chilly space wasn't as neatly arranged as her parents had kept it. Then again, it wasn't nearly as dust-covered as it had been. She swore she had ransacked every single box and crate. She hadn't had to lie too much to her parents, fortunately, because she had found a few things she wanted to take back to Tabor Heights for her cottage. Some dishes, a framed photo collage, an old table she could fit into her SUV once the legs were taken off. The bits she had found to help in the search for the White Rose Killer wouldn't be noticed among all the other things she had taken.

She dreaded the six-hour drive back to Tabor, yet at the same time, she couldn't wait to get on the road. It wasn't that she wanted to get away from her parents, but that she couldn't wait to see Curt again.

"Just to compare notes. Just to show him what I found," she told the dusty attic, and emphasized her words by snapping the lid shut on the plastic bin.

Toni refused to be silly and pathetic and hope for some connection between her and Curt, once the White Rose had been caught and unmasked. She had promised to leave town once they finally had justice, for Angel, Annalee, Tracy, and the other girls the White Rose had terrorized. The satisfaction they felt would probably be the only emotion she and Curt would ever share. They would be friends, yes, but Toni had heard people talk about Curt, and she knew she was better off not hoping. He was a confirmed bachelor, too busy with his job as a reporter and helping with summer youth sports to have much of a personal life. Of the three Mehdlang brothers, he was the least likely to ever pursue a girl, much less ask her to marry him.

"Don't be stupid," she scolded herself under her breath, as she stopped at the top of the steps and pulled the attic door shut. "If you even think the M-word, he'll know it and take off running."

"What was that, baby?" her father asked, appearing in the doorway at the bottom of the stairs.

"Thinking out loud, Daddy." Toni forced a bright smile when she reached the bottom of the steps.

"Talking to yourself is a sign you've been working too hard." Mr. Napolitano nodded slowly. He raked a gnarled hand through his thinning strands of still-black hair, then shoved his glasses up higher on his nose. "Wish you didn't have to head back to work so soon."

"If I want to get back to my place before it gets dark, it's actually kind of late." She slid past him and headed for the kitchen to wash her dusty, grimy hands.

As usual, her mother had packed enough food for ten people. Normally, she would have laughed and teased her mother about it, but today she looked at the plastic containers and the mini-cooler and blinked back tears.

She hated lying to her parents. What were her alternatives? Awaken the pain that still dug poisonous roots into their lives by telling them about the new murders in Tabor Heights and her part in the investigation? Or give up and leave town and let Curt do all the work? She couldn't do that. She needed to dig up the truth and find some justice after all these years.

And she dared to hope that when everything was settled, she could tell her parents what she had done and when they were done crying, they would understand. They might even be proud. Was it too much to hope they would finally have some healing, and peace?

Chapter Fourteen

Thursday, December 26

The newspaper fell to pieces at his feet, but he could still see the words — the lies — branded into the paper.

No, the words themselves weren't lies. He had to remember that. The *Tabor Picayune* wasn't like other newspapers, leaving out facts and twisting the truth to make stories exciting so they could sell papers and make a profit. The *Tabor Picayune* didn't lie. Curt Mehdlang always told the truth. Curt was his friend. But the reporters had to repeat the lies that other people told, so everyone would know there were liars among them.

Someone was pretending to be the White Rose.

That liar was frightening Hannah.

He had to stop the lies. He had to protect Hannah, because she was nice to him. Hannah was nice to everyone.

Who in Tabor didn't like Hannah? That was the person who was frightening her. That was the liar, who pretended to be the White Rose.

No one was allowed to pretend to be the White Rose. He was the White Rose.

White, for purity. For the angel, his new angel, his sweet, young, pure Angel.

He walked away, leaving the torn pieces of newspaper on the damp concrete floor, and concentrated on thoughts of his new angel.

She was the right one, this time. Despite what the paper said, she would come back to him. She belonged to him. She loved him. She would stay true. She had promised to come back from the dead for him, just like Eurydice had come back for Orpheus. She would come back.

Saturday, December 28

"You're right. I should have listened to you before. I think you should meet Hannah," a man said almost before Toni finished mumbling her hello into her bedside phone.

"Um — Curt?" Toni blinked and rolled over and stared at her clock. The luminous blue numbers were blurry, but she thought it was nearly midnight.

"Sorry." Curt laughed. His voice sounded rough, as if he had been yelling. "Guess I should have just waited until tomorrow, huh? But I couldn't be sure you'd be in church tomorrow. You don't seem to go very often."

"Yeah, well, I haven't exactly been on speaking terms with God since Angel..." She sighed, rubbed at her eyes, and tried to get a better grip on the phone. "Actually, that's one of the things I decided had to change. You know how they have you sit really quiet for about ten minutes on Christmas Eve, thinking about the year behind you and all the things you wanted to change, but didn't, and they tell you to resolve now to change going forward, and forget about the past and... well, I realized it's kind of stupid, my attitude."

"Kind of hard not to have it, I'll bet, if your parents share it," he offered softly.

"Yeah." Her throat felt tight and the clock numbers were blurry again. Toni blinked and two warm tears traveled down her cheeks. What was wrong with her, to get so sappy just because a guy understood all the things she didn't say? It wasn't like he really *cared* about her, personally. Curt was that sensitive all the time. That was what made him a great reporter. "Um, what were you saying about Hannah? Hannah Blake?"

"Yeah. I think you should talk to Hannah and get her impression of the whole White Rose situation. And maybe... I don't know... it might help to tell someone else about Angel. I know I feel a lot better talking to you. I think Hannah and Xander will understand."

"Xander? That's the lawyer she works for, right? Why tell him?"

Curt snorted. "Xander doesn't know it, but he and Hannah are a matched set. I guarantee, if you ask to talk to her about the White Rose, Xander will be right there. Besides, until they catch the copycat, she could be in just as much danger."

"Makes sense. I guess. I'm still half asleep," she admitted with a breathy chuckle.

"Oh. Yeah. Sorry. Guess I should let you get back to bed, huh?"

"It's a good idea. Thanks for thinking of it. I'll meet you in church tomorrow, okay?"

Long after she hung up the phone, Toni lay curled on her side and stared at the few stray beams that penetrated her curtains from the streetlights. Would it help to tell someone else about Angel? Maybe. She knew she had felt some relief when Curt and Angela recognized her name and understood her motivation. She still couldn't quite explain the sense of having come in from the cold, when she realized Curt remembered Angel and he had connected the White Rose Killer with Angel's murder.

The more people who knew the truth, the less chance Angel would be forgotten. And maybe remembering her death would help keep another girl alive.

Sunday, December 29

"Xander? Hannah?" Curt grabbed Toni by the wrist and half-dragged her through the crowd to catch up with the two at the back of the sanctuary after the service was dismissed.

Hannah offered them a smile. Curt wondered how much of it was her normal cheerful personality and how much was putting up a brave front. Even though the police were getting closer every day to identifying the copycat, it still had to be nerve-wracking for Hannah. No wonder Xander stuck close to her side at all times. They made quite a pair, Curt decided. Hannah wasn't beautiful, but she always looked nice with her strawberry blond hair and smiling face. Xander was homely enough to just escape being ugly, with his features just slightly out of proportion, but his eyes and his smile were always clear and honest and genuine. Curt was glad Xander was his friend, as well as his lawyer.

"This is Toni Napolitano," he continued, gesturing at her as the two sides sized each other up. "She just joined us over at the paper."

"Welcome to Tabor," Xander said. He held out his hand to shake. The four moved over to the side to get out of the flow of traffic coming down all the aisles to the back of the sanctuary. "New in town?"

"Not really." Toni smiled crookedly. "I used to live here when I was a kid. Curt barely remembers me."

"Yeah, she keeps rubbing it in, every time I give her pointers about getting around town or the history of some of the people," Curt said with a shrug. "Look, could we buy you two lunch? There's something we need to talk about."

"Reporter to source?" Xander asked.

"More like a personal matter," Toni said.

After a little discussion, they ended up picking up their meal at Stay-A-While and then went to Hannah's apartment. Hannah's roommate was out for the day, so they would have plenty of privacy to talk.

"Nice," Toni said, when they had settled in the living room.

Curt stifled a snort of laughter. He shared one of the small sofas with Toni while Xander shared the other with Hannah. They set up their food on TV trays. Now all they needed was to turn the TV on and watch a football game, or maybe play some word game. Any casual observer would think they were two couples on a date.

If he had eaten anything, Curt thought he might have just choked on it at that point. Dating? Him?

But why not? Especially if it was Toni.

"I remember walking by these houses on my way to school, thinking how cool it would be to live in one of them, above a store." Toni's smile grew strained. She glanced at Curt and nodded. He guessed immediately she wanted him to take over the conversation.

"Oh, no you don't, Lois Lane. You're the one who pushed for this meeting. It's your show." Curt nodded for emphasis, then picked up his tuna deluxe and took a big bite.

"Coward." She looked down at her clasped hands for a moment, then picked up her salad fork and fumbled it, nearly dropping it on the floor.

"Curt said he had a theory about the White Rose, about a murder a long time ago," Xander said.

"Yeah." Toni let out a long, gusting sigh. "If he's right... heck, I know he's right. The clues, everything that happened is so similar it gives me chills. Makes me want to string up the guy and use him for target practice, with very dull table knives." She offered a grimace, took another deep breath. "You probably think I'm not quite there."

"Nah," Curt said. "They're used to me, taking off at a completely different angle from everything else. These leaps of intuition, it's an occupational hazard."

Toni groaned and elbowed Curt. He pretended to be deeply wounded and had to bite his lip to hide his grin. He would take a dozen bruises from Toni if it would help keep her from sliding into that darkness hovering at the back of her eyes.

"Could you tell me what you know, your impressions of the White Rose, first?" Toni said. "I've read the police reports that are public, and what Curt put in the paper, and his notes for things that he's agreed not to put in the paper yet. But I'd like to get it from you, too."

Curt was impressed at how logically Hannah arranged the sequence of events, her memories of when she heard the latest bits of news, what she remembered other people saying or their reactions to the stalking and then deaths of the three known victims. Xander offered his ideas but left most of the talking to her. In a sense, it really was Hannah's story more than anyone else's in the room. Curt shivered, wondering what their reactions would be when they heard Toni's side of the story.

"Okay." Toni toyed with her salad as she talked. "If Curt is right, my big sister was the first victim of the White Rose, almost twenty years ago." She paused a moment, took a deep breath, and then a sip from her glass of water. "Angel was ten when we moved to Tabor. I was seven."

"Angel?" Hannah's voice sounded strained.

Curt didn't blame her. He hadn't trusted his first nebulous theories about the White Rose until he actually saw some of the love notes sent to the victims. In several, the murderer referred to them as his angel. After that, the connection was blindingly obvious.

"Angelique, actually. My full name is Antoinette." Toni shrugged.

"Mom was really into fancy names. Anyway... Angel was gorgeous, and shy. She wanted a boyfriend, but the boys in school scared her. It seemed by the time we'd been here a month, every boy in her class, in the neighborhood, even two grades ahead of her, wanted to be her boyfriend. She said no. She wasn't stuck up, like so many of the girls thought. She was just... shy. She didn't know what to do or say. And all these boys who kept coming by and sneaking presents or notes into her desk at school or into her locker, they really scared her."

"And the White Rose was one of those boyfriends she refused?" Hannah guessed.

"The White Rose was her boyfriend, for real," Curt said.

"I missed something." Xander frowned, put down his sandwich, and leaned back and crossed his arms.

"Angel changed, about two weeks before she died. She was happy, she had some great secret that she wouldn't tell me, and she didn't want me to walk home from school with her. When she told me she had a boyfriend, and they were keeping the whole thing secret, I was so jealous I didn't want to know anything about it," Toni said.

The old pain gleaming in her eyes stabbed Curt hard. He reached up and rested a hand on her shoulder and squeezed. He wanted to put an arm around her and hold her, but she might just clobber him instead of crying on his shoulder as she had the day Annalee was found dead.

"Rumors started going around that Angel was meeting boys behind the bathhouse, down at the swimming hole. Some girls were jealous and spread the tales just to be nasty. But we found out one boy in particular was telling everybody that Angel let him kiss her and put his hands under her clothes, just because she wouldn't have anything to do with him. He suspected Angel had a boyfriend, but whoever he was, he wasn't bragging. Later, we figured he told the lies just to get the boyfriend to confront him. Probably so they could fight. How could he beat up Angel's boyfriend and make him give her up, if he didn't know who the guy was?"

"I bet that ticked off all the boys who couldn't get anywhere with her," Xander muttered.

Curt nodded. He remembered how angry and betrayed he felt, when he heard the first rumor. He had bruised knuckles by the time he tracked down some of the rumors to their sources and found out they were just that: rumors, not truth.

"One Saturday, Angel went for a walk. She was going to meet her boyfriend, as far as we could tell." Toni swallowed hard and her eyes glistened. "She didn't come back."

"Strangled with a wire?" Xander said softly.

"Down in the park," Curt said. "There was an old access road, blocked with some old fencing. They found her body there, strangled with the wire from the fence. Everybody hoped it was an accident."

"Curt found her," Toni whispered. "He came to our house to talk with Angel and our parents were starting to get worried because she was late coming home. So he went to look for her and..." She knuckled more tears from her eyes before they could fall, swallowed hard, and sat up straight. Took a deep breath, let it out, and regained her composure. "My parents found dozens of letters from her boyfriend, in her room. He begged her to stay faithful to him. He promised he'd take care of her forever and they'd be together and he'd make her happy. And Angel had written in her diary about him, that he was quiet and smart and they were in love and they swore they'd be together forever. And they weren't telling anyone how they felt about each other because—" Toni's voice broke with a rusty, wry chuckle. "Because everybody in school was so infantile and just wouldn't understand. They swore they'd be together forever, and when they died, they'd come back from the dead to be together, just like Orpheus and Eurydice. Angel was really big into mythology. I used to tease her she'd marry a librarian."

"Makes you shudder, huh?" Curt muttered. He shifted his hand from Toni's shoulder to hold her hand and rub it.

"If I remember right," Xander said, "that particular myth didn't end very happily."

"Angel wrote in her diary that her boyfriend was upset about the nasty stories, and she was angry at him that he wouldn't believe her when she said she never did any of those things," Toni added.

"He thought she was unfaithful to him," Hannah murmured. "So he killed her for it."

"And for a whole week after the funeral, someone kept dropping white roses on her grave," Curt said, taking up the story for Toni. "Every time they took the rose away, a new one appeared. Nobody ever saw who dropped it there. Which at the time was just as freaky as Angel being murdered. At the end of that week, the boy who started the nasty stories about Angel got knocked out and hung by his ankles from a tree in the park. He was beat up pretty bad."

"The same tree that victim number two's fake boyfriend ended up in?" Xander asked.

"We're still trying to determine that. But do you see where we're going?"

"Something set him off." Hannah's voice thickened. Curt wondered if she was trying not to be sick. "Maybe he thinks Angel has come back from the dead and he's trying to find her. Or maybe he's just tired of waiting for her, and he's looking for her."

"Any girl who looks anything like Angel is a possible target," Curt said.

"Have you started checking out anybody who was in school with her?" Xander said.

"It's taking a while," Toni said, her voice raspy with repressed emotion. "First we have to get names of everybody who lived in Tabor and went to the same school, then we have to figure out if they're living here, or just living, period."

"Baxter," Hannah said. "He's a genius with the Internet. He can find information that you'd swear wasn't even on the 'Net. Go to him."

"Baxter." Curt slapped his forehead with the palm of his hand. "Why didn't I think of that?"

"Because you're playing the part of klutzy, oblivious Clark Kent a little too well?" Toni suggested. "Who is this Baxter?"

Curt kicked himself, mentally while Hannah explained about Gold Tone Gym and how Baxter Stemple ran a computer business out of the back of the gym. He had been in there more times than he could remember, laughing at things Baxter found on the Internet, playing video games, just watching the four computer screens flash and work through programs while he sat there with a few others from town, shooting the breeze. He should have thought of Baxter weeks ago, when they first started their background checks.

When they contacted Baxter and gave him a very sketchy explanation of their theory and the work Curt and Toni had been trying to accomplish, he didn't hesitate to agree to help. His sympathy and the angry determination in his eyes had been gratifying. He said he would get to work on the search but warned it could take several days before they saw any results. He would have to go through what they had found so far, just to make sure he wasn't duplicating their efforts.

Having Baxter involved in the search took another heavy weight off his shoulders.

Monday, December 30

"Frank! Just the guy I was looking for," Max called, when Curt walked into the office after lunch. She leaped up from her desk and pulled the gate open, gesturing for him to come through. "I'll be right back, folks," she said, looking around Curt to the couple sitting in two of the four chairs that faced the counter.

Myrna sat at the switchboard, studying a catalog of some kind. Curt saw the concerned look Max shot the woman as she hustled him down the hall. Something was up, and he didn't need to engage his tired brain to realize it had something to do with that couple.

"Why the new name?" he asked, careful to keep his voice down.

"Do you have Toni's cell phone number?"

"Yeah, why?"

"You're the only one who does. Call her and warn her that her parents are here, would you? Just from a couple things I overheard..." Max raked her fingers through her hair and let out a long, exhausted sigh. "They're arguing about something, and I think it has to do with Toni, and they didn't sound really happy when they asked to talk to you."

"Toni's parents?" Curt turned to look behind himself. He stood just around the corner of the editorial room and couldn't look down the hall to the front of the office. What was going on? Why did her parents come here, instead of to her house?

Unless they didn't know where Toni's house was? But that didn't make sense. Wouldn't she have told her parents how to get to her house? Maybe Toni didn't know they were coming to visit? But still, even if she wasn't expecting them, wouldn't she have told them how to find her house?

Unless her parents didn't know she was living in Tabor Heights and working for the paper? But then, how did they know to come to the paper to begin with?

All these questions were giving him a headache.

"How did they get my name, do you know?" he had to ask. The picture coming together in his head wasn't very clear, and a lot of pieces were missing, but he didn't like what he began to suspect.

"Not until after they picked up Thursday's paper and read your name sharing the byline with hers." Max bent forward to look around the corner. "Why do I have the feeling she didn't tell her parents she was working here?"

Chapter Fifteen

"Because you're incredibly intelligent and I'll bet you anything she still hasn't told them she moved to Tabor." Curt laughed, one short bark, when Max gave him an incredulous look. "It's a long story, but basically, Toni lived here a few years when she was a kid. Something pretty awful happened to her family. When she got the job here, I'm guessing she didn't tell her folks because she knew they'd hate it." He dug in his pocket for his cell phone. The stricken look on Max's face stopped him. "What?"

"Thursday, first thing, someone called wanting to talk to Toni about the White Rose story, and Myrna told them she wasn't going to be in until today."

"No, that's *Loni* who was taking the rest of the week off." Curt groaned.

"Anyway, whoever it was had a snit and Myrna said she'd call Toni at her folks' house and pass on the message."

"And Myrna got into the personnel files in Angela's office, against policy, again, to find Toni's emergency number, and called her parents. But she was already in town, just out on a new story before coming in." It wasn't the first time the inexplicable old woman had felt it necessary to violate privacy rules. Why couldn't she have argued with the unhappy reader like she usually did? He reached for the closest horizontal surface, which fortunately happened to be a chair. "The next murder in Tabor isn't going to be the White Rose's fault."

"I'm sorry. Honestly. I told her she was wrong and Toni would be here in like ten more minutes, but Myrna always knows better. Thank you, God, she retired from teaching before I had her in school. She'd be impossible to work with, otherwise."

"She's easy to work with now?" Sherwood chimed in from his seat in the corner. He had his foot propped up on the edge of his filing cabinet. "Hey, Curt, if you're taking up a collection to have Bubbles rubbed out, I'll contribute gladly. Do you know how many people she gave my *unlisted* phone number, when I first broke my leg?"

"Are we talking about Myrna?" Angela stepped out of her office.

"We have a big problem, starting with the fact that Toni's parents are up front and they don't look too happy to be here." Curt gestured back to her office and let her precede him through the door. It took him less than three minutes to explain what Max had said and what he theorized.

"You call Toni and I'll take care of the Napolitanos," Angela said.

Curt would have saluted her if he hadn't been pulling out his cell phone. He wasn't a coward, but he hadn't looked forward to facing Toni's parents. Angela had faced furious politicians who blamed their failure at the polls on the coverage or lack of coverage of their campaigns in the *Picayune*. She had calmed enraged attendees at City Council meetings. Curt looked up at the sign over the office door and thought about that first news story Angela had ever written for the *Picayune*, when she was in high school. He didn't give much credence to Eastern philosophies, but there was a sense of something coming full circle in all this trouble with the White Rose Killer and the Napolitanos coming back to Tabor.

"I am dead," Toni groaned, when Curt got hold of her.

"You didn't tell them, did you?" He honestly sympathized, but some demented part of his tired brain wanted to laugh at her.

"They're probably here to pack me up and drag me back to Indiana with them. No, I did not tell them. Half our photo albums are locked away because they don't want to look at pictures of Angel. What would ever make me think my parents could handle it if I told them not only had I returned to Tabor to work, but I was helping hunt down Angel's murderer?" Her breath hissed through the speaker. "Okay, I'm on my way in. Thanks for the warning. You are the best pal in the world."

"Well, not totally my idea. Max ran interference," he offered with a chuckle. "And Angela's getting to work on fire control."

"I knew I should have gotten her something big for Christmas."

"Just get in here as fast as you can and face it, okay? And remember, you're a legal adult. They can't make you go with them."

"That's what you think. I'm still ten years old, when it comes to my parents. On my way." Toni sighed and cut the connection before Curt could respond.

That was probably the problem, he reflected, as he slid his phone in his back pocket and headed for the front of the office to lend his support to Angela. Time had stopped for the Napolitanos when Angel was killed.

The last time Curt had talked to Toni's parents, it had been in the police station when he had repeated for the investigators exactly what happened the day he found Angel's body in the park. Curt vowed he would convince the Napolitanos that he could protect the one daughter they had left. There was symmetry in here, somewhere, but he was just too tired to figure it out completely.

He stepped out of the corner of the newsroom where he had his desk, grateful that the only person currently present to overhear his half of the conversation was Sherwood. Curt could trust the sports writer not to gossip, although the other man would probably demand an explanation sometime in the near future. He glanced at Angela's office as he started up the hallway to the front, and saw the door was closed. That made sense. She certainly wouldn't confront the Napolitanos at the front of the office where the public, starting with Myrna, could witness what might turn unpleasant. Taking a deep breath and bracing himself for a bad situation, Curt tapped on the door. He didn't wait for Angela to respond, but pushed it open and walked in. All three turned to look at him. Curt couldn't tell from anyone's somber expression if things were getting cleared up or just starting to disintegrate.

"Did you get hold of Toni?" Angela gestured at the closet of her office, where a few extra folding chairs were kept.

"She's on her way in." Curt concentrated on unfolding and setting up the chair and sitting down before he looked Toni's parents in the eye. "Mr. and Mrs. Napolitano, you probably don't remember —"

"Dave Mehdlang's boy." Mr. Napolitano nodded. "You look enough like him, I should have known you the minute you walked in the office. Had me fooled for a few seconds, when that girl up front called you Frank. I hope you pay her what she's worth." He offered Angela a wintry smile. "You're either a saint or a glutton for punishment, having Myrna Calhoun working for you."

"The jury's still out on that one," Angela said. Just a spark of humor brightened her eyes. "Curt, Toni's parents understand that we weren't aware she had lied to them."

"To protect you," Curt hurried to say. He wished he had Joel Randolph's acting ability right that moment, so he could convince these people of his sincerity and trustworthiness. All he could do was meet their eyes, each in turn, and not flinch away from their concern.

"From what? What is she doing here, that she's ashamed to admit?" Mrs. Napolitano asked. Her voice cracked with a mixture of confusion, laughter and worry.

"She's not ashamed of what she's doing," Angela said slowly. "In some ways, your daughter is exceptionally brave. And maybe a little... foolhardy. Certainly stubborn. She didn't want you to worry about her."

Curt realized most of the wrinkles around their eyes and mouths came from confusion, not anger. He slowly shook his head as a new facet of this confrontation dawned on him.

"Max said you looked at the paper and got my name because you saw it next to Toni's." He knew there was only one story in the last paper where they shared a byline. "Did you read the story we wrote together?" Curt wasn't surprised when they shook their heads. He glanced at Angela. She nodded, hopefully meaning she understood what he was thinking.

Toni's parents didn't know about the White Rose Killer.

Curt wished he could laugh at all this because it really was rather ironic. All Toni's efforts to keep her parents from finding out she was involved in the hunt for the White Rose, and they didn't even know what was going on in Tabor.

"I think we'd better leave the rest of the story to Toni, when she gets here," Angela said, standing. "Would you like some coffee while we're waiting?"

She gestured for Curt to go up front, probably to wait for Toni. That suited him just fine. He walked the hall slowly, all his attention strained backwards to listen as Angela led Toni's parents to the lunchroom.

"I hope you'll excuse the chaos in here today. It's production day, and unfortunately, it's our normal state." Angela didn't laugh, but the richness in her voice meant she smiled. Curt shook his head and grinned and said a silent prayer of thanks that Angela was his boss.

Toni hurtled through the door at the same moment Curt reached the end of the hall. She missed the latch for the gate and banged against it.

"Toni, there are some people here to see you. I have no idea who they are," Myrna said, "but it seems personal. You know, it's against company policy to conduct personal business on company time, don't you?"

"That's what Angela needs to talk to her about," Curt broke in, before Toni could do more than stop short and glare at the woman. He suddenly wanted to punch that superior little smirk off her face. "Oh, by the way, Myrna, Angela is investigating who handed out Sherwood's unlisted phone number last month. Whoever did it could be fired."

"But it was necessary for people to reach him," she protested.

"That's what those message pads are for." He pointed at the pink phone pads piled up on the desk, which Myrna used for shopping lists and practicing her origami when she wasn't putting customers through an inquisition about their personal lives.

"But—"

"Later." He hooked his arm through Toni's and led her to the back of the office at a jog.

"Thanks for saving me from breaking a couple knuckles," Toni muttered. "Am I dead meat?"

"Your folks still don't know about the White Rose."

Toni moaned and stopped short, just in front of the circulation office door. Curt shifted his grip so he could put his arm around her. She shuddered and leaned against him but stopped herself just as she started to clutch at his shirt with her gloved hand.

They met up with her parents as Angela was leading them back to her office. The five stopped short in front of the door. Andrew chose that moment to come out of the photography lab, where he was conferring with Loni over some prints for the front page. Curt couldn't decide if the introductions that delayed the final showdown were a blessing or an irritation.

"Well, it's good to see you again. Although, we conducted most of our business over the phone, didn't we, Ben?" Andrew chuckled heartily, wringing Mr. Napolitano's hand. "I have to tell you, your girl is a treasure. I can't tell you how encouraging it is to have her here on staff with us. It must be hard on her, working here with so many painful memories, and then having to cover the White Rose. Especially with those similarities between..." He trailed off, a frown forming two creases between his eyes. Curt could almost see the connections snapping to life behind his eyes. "Oh, dear."

He shook his head, and the look he gave Toni was a mixture of fatherly concern and disappointment. It was at times like these that Curt remembered what a sharp newspaperman Andrew had been in his own day. He wore his genial, sometimes bumbling personality like other men wore fishing hats, as a sign that he had retired.

"Something tells me you aren't here on a pleasure jaunt, are you, Ben? Your girl doesn't strike me as someone who takes silly risks. I'm sure that whatever her reasons, they're good ones." He shook Mr. Napolitano's hand once more, patted Toni on the shoulder, and continued down the hall to the lunchroom. After giving Angela a look that clearly said he wanted some answers as soon as possible.

"What's the White Rose?" Mrs. Napolitano asked once they were all in the office again. "I saw the name in the story you wrote but didn't read it. Didn't get a chance. That Myrna Calhoun is just as much a busybody as she was twenty years ago. You should have seen her in action, sticking her nose into other people's business, especially after—" She caught her breath and looked down at her intertwined fingers in her lap.

"Better to get it over with fast," Curt offered, as he unfolded the second folding chair for Toni. "Like yanking off a bandage."

She glared at him but nodded. She took a moment to settle herself on the chair, gripped the sides, took a deep breath, licked her lips.

"The White Rose is a serial killer. He gets his name from the white roses he leaves for the girls he stalks." She swallowed. Curt rested his hand on her shoulder, wishing he could give her more support than that. "He says he's in love with them and demands that they stay faithful to him. And when he thinks they've betrayed him..." She inhaled sharply, sounding like she fought a sob.

"The way he kills them reminded me of how Angel died," Curt said. He flinched when both Toni's parents turned their startled, hurting gazes on him. It was almost a physical blow.

"Of all the asinine—" Mr. Napolitano choked. He gripped the armrests of the chair hard enough Curt thought the chrome-plated bars would bend.

"That's what Curt and I both thought," Angela said.

"Then why didn't you tell her she was on a wild goose chase?"

"No, not that." She folded her hands on her desk, reminding Curt of the times she defused explosive confrontations between political rivals during pre-election interviews, right in this office. "We agreed with her theory. Curt had the same theory just before Toni showed up, looking for work. He was just looking for some more proof, some validation that he wasn't imagining it. What we thought was—as you put it, asinine—was her plan to do all the hunting by herself. Especially considering how much she resembles Angel, and the White Rose's targets all... resemble Angel. She was putting herself in a position to become the next target."

"Toni?" her mother whimpered.

"The White Rose doesn't go after girls who have relationships already," Curt hurried to say. "Toni agreed that if we let her come work here, she and I would pretend to be serious about each other. And considering how much time we spend together," he added with a grin that certainly felt wimpy on his face, "people would have gotten that idea eventually anyway, without any help from us."

"This isn't a crime-fighting TV show," Mr. Napolitano said.

Curt hoped the calmness he sensed filtering through the situation wasn't his imagination and didn't come from shock.

"So, you're supporting her in this?" his wife asked. She reached out and rested her hand on her husband's. He twisted his hand around to grip hers and they both stared at Angela, then at Curt, then back to Angela.

It was almost funny, Curt thought, that they ignored their daughter in their silent plea for answers and assurance.

"We agree with her theory. Maybe you don't remember, but Curt and I were both involved when Angel died. We want this resolved almost as much as you and Toni do," Angela said. "And this way, Toni is working *with* the police, instead of haring off on her own."

"We remember," Mrs. Napolitano said, nodding.

"Do you, Mom?" Toni scooted forward on her chair, hands gripping her knees, tears threatening in her eyes. "Because it seems like sometimes you don't want anybody to even know Angel existed."

"Antoinette!" her father barked.

"Look, this isn't the place for us to get into this." She blinked hard and jerked herself to her feet. "This is production day, and this is where I work, and Angela and Curt certainly don't need to get dragged into our family problems any more than they have already. And besides, do you really want Myrna Calhoun to blab about us all over town?"

"That woman wouldn't know the truth if it gave her two black eyes," her mother muttered. She managed a crooked smile for Angela. "I'm sorry. This is probably as uncomfortable for you as it is for us, but honestly, we had no idea how to find Toni! All we had was the address for the paper."

"Then maybe Toni should take you to her house and get you settled," Curt offered. He gripped her arm when she gave him a panicked look. "Then she has to get back to work and finish her stories for tomorrow and Thursday's papers. The three of you can cool off a little and think, and talk about it tonight when she gets off work, okay?"

"Pushy, like your father," Mr. Napolitano said with a grunt. He looked Curt over, head to foot before he stood up and nodded. "Think you know the best way to handle things, just like him. Ah, well, I always did like your father. Not often you can respect your business rival and be friends with him." He looked around the office. "Ms. Coffelt—"

"Angela, please," she said, and held out her hands to Toni's parents. "It just doesn't feel right to be so formal, when I can remember Trick-or-Treating at your house."

Curt sighed in relief when everyone managed a few chuckles.

~~~~~

Toni had no idea how she managed to get through the rest of the day. Curt proofed her stories and didn't send them back for corrections. Either he took pity on her and fixed all her gaffs and filled in the holes, or they weren't the totally incoherent drek she imagined. It was a blessing that she had to work so late into the evening, to prepare for two papers at the same time, but as far as she was concerned, she didn't work nearly late enough.

Stopping at Heinke's Grocery was another stalling tactic and she freely admitted it. On the other hand, she had very little to eat in the house. She didn't need a lecture from her mother on taking care of herself with good nutrition and having something nice to offer guests.

Especially male guests. Not that anyone ever came over her house except Curt, and he usually brought pizza or nacho chips or something.

Toni stopped in front of the ice cream display and put her head in her hands and silently groaned. She had seen that speculative look in her mother's eyes when Curt admitted they let people think they were interested in each other. If she knew her mother, Toni imagined plans for wedding invitations and bridal showers and party favors flitting through her mind, right that moment. Despite being told point-blank it was a protective measure, and not a real relationship.

"You okay?"

Curt's sudden appearance behind her startled a squeak out of her. Then she punched him in the arm when he just grinned at her.

"After everything that happened today, how can you even ask?"

"Feeding the folks, huh?" He gestured down at her half-full shopping cart. "Actually, it's pretty smart getting in here today to stock up. Everybody'll be doing their last-minute shopping tomorrow."

"New Year's Eve. I forgot." She fought another groan. "I know they'll be staying through New Year's. Why in the world did Mandy furnish the
~~~~~

place with a double bed and a sleeper sofa? If I had no place to put them, I could keep them in a hotel and..." Toni yanked open the freezer door and pulled out three cartons of ice cream. As long as it was chocolate, it would please all of them.

"Speaking of New Year's Eve." Curt caught the door when she let it go. He flashed her a grin as he leaned in and snagged a carton for himself.

"What about it?" She caught her breath. Was Curt about to ask her out for New Year's? No, that was ridiculous. He had to know she wouldn't leave her parents alone tomorrow night, much as she would love to.

"I talked to my folks." He rested a hand on her shoulder when she groaned in fearful anticipation of disaster. "Mom said she'd go over to your place and invite them over for New Year's. Lots of people coming over they'll remember. Could be fun."

"At least I won't be alone with them," she whispered. "You are saving my life."

"Hey, what are best pals for?" He slung his arm around her shoulders. "Now, how about inviting me over for dinner? I figure, double-teaming your folks is only fair, since they'll probably double-team you."

"You'd do that for me?" Toni forced a jaunty grin and a teasing tone. Otherwise, she might give in to the jangling sensations that filled her from the warmth of Curt's arm around her. When she had cried in his arms, she hadn't been coherent enough to notice and appreciate it. Now, she did.

"What are best pals for?" he repeated. He kept his arm around her all the way to the checkout, where they separated to side-by-side self-service stations. Toni felt cold once he let go of her, but at least she was able to stand on her own again.

If she stayed in Tabor very long, she was going to be in a lot of trouble.

But maybe the best tactic was to enjoy it while it lasted?

Chapter Sixteen

Tuesday, December 31

"So, how do you think it's going? Sorry." Curt laughed when Toni jumped. He had come up behind her in the archway between the living room and dining room of his parents' house. "Didn't mean to scare you."

"Just deep in thought."

He thought about telling her she looked fantastic in her calf-length, deep blue velvet dress, but the words caught in his throat. He knew how to ask questions to convince reluctant interviewees to spill their guts, but Curt had no idea how to give a compliment. The last time he tried, the girl involved had taken it as an insult and nearly punched him. That was four years ago.

That long since he'd tried dating?

"Your folks look like they're having a good time," he pointed out, to push the word "dating" out of his mind before it lodged there.

"Yeah, they are." Toni smiled up at him. "It was a great idea." She turned back to watching her parents in the living room, smiling and talking comfortably with people who had been their neighbors twenty years ago. "I owe you big time for this."

"Write my feature story next week?"

She laughed and shook her head and turned back to the buffet set up on the dining room table. Curt followed her. He winced only slightly when he saw his mother watching them with a very pleased smile.

"So, we didn't really get a chance to talk about it this morning." He lifted the lid on the Crock Pot full of broccoli cheese soup, sniffed, and decided to fill a mug for himself. "How did it go last night after I left?"

"Mom spent more time giving me suggestions for decorating my place. She wants to go shopping tomorrow, find me some furniture, curtains and rugs and that sort of thing."

"That's a good sign, right?" He offered her the first mug he filled and she thanked him with a smile that warmed him.

"Daddy doesn't like the idea of me hunting a murderer. They're still a little sore that I lied about where I was living and working. Other than that... I think they're almost relieved somebody forced the topic of Angel out in the open. Maybe some of the silence was my fault, too."

"Everybody's worried about upsetting everybody else, so nobody talks and everybody thinks nobody wants to talk."

"Does every family do that?" She forked a slice of ham onto her plate.

"Probably."

"Gee, it's nice to be normal, then."

They laughed together and finished filling their plates in silence. There were a few card tables set up in the family room, relatively quiet with the younger guests downstairs watching a movie and most of the parents in the living room. Toni chose a table and Curt debated holding out her chair for her, but he hesitated too long and she settled herself.

"What would you be doing tonight, if your parents hadn't shown up?" he had to ask.

"I was thinking about going to the Singles marathon at church. I've met a couple nice people." Toni sipped at a spoonful of soup, then put the mug aside. "That's another big change for me, actually. Having anything to do with church more than the worship service. If I went at all. For a long time, I always had an excuse... thanks for dragging me with you."

"What are best pals for?"

Curt choked when Toni leaned over and brushed a quick, light kiss against his cheek. He held very still until she settled back into her chair. A sideways glance showed her putting together her sandwich, acting as if nothing unusual had happened.

He knew he should be relieved, but somehow, he was disappointed.

Thursday, January 2

Donovan stopped at the *Picayune*'s office on his way home from work with news that made Curt alternately seethe and grin. The boy who had been blackmailed into setting fire to Xander and Hannah's new office was voluntarily working with the police, and today had led them to his contact. Curt watched Angela and Toni digest the news. They were just as torn as him between feelings of progress and the sensation the knot was getting more complicated. A homeless man paid the boy to set fire to the office and deliver roses to Hannah. He had a broken mind from some tragedy in his past and earned money running errands for people. There was no motivation for him to attack the law office, so everyone agreed he was the go-between for someone else.

Then Donovan told them about an encounter Hannah had with Toby Halm, a clerk at Montgomery & Associates law office. He had approached her in church at the New Year's Eve service and asked her out. He talked as if he had seen her and Xander quite often in the Singles class at church. The problem was, Hannah attended a different class on Sunday morning. From all indications, Halm had never stepped foot into their church until that evening. The question was where he got his inaccurate information about Hannah and why he had approached her at all.

"Hopefully we can link him with the arson and roses," Donovan said. "Let's hope we resolve the case before school starts next week."

Curt understood, like a punch in the chest. When the students returned to Butler-Williams University and the White Rose discovered his target hadn't returned, he would find a new love interest.

Please, God, he prayed silently as he watched understanding darken Toni's and Angela's faces. *Let this end soon, with no more deaths. Please. No more innocent girls hurt.*

Sunday, January 5

"Wonder where Hannah is," Curt muttered, as he and Toni walked past Xander on their way out of the sanctuary that morning.

Toni looked back, just long enough to catch the troubled look on Xander's face. She knew Hannah and Xander usually attended the service that had just ended, but she had looked for them both and hadn't seen either one. Until now. Curt and his family swept her along down the hall with them before she could suggest going back to ask Xander what was wrong. Maybe Hannah had decided to stay home today. If she had been going through the suspense Hannah had endured for nearly a month, she would have felt exhausted now that it was over.

Xander didn't look happy, even though Hannah's stalker had been caught. Toni wondered why not. Maybe Hannah and Xander were more tightly linked than they appeared, so it simply bothered him when she wasn't around. That had to be a sign of love.

She glanced at Curt, who laughed at something his father said, and wondered if it would be wrong to ask God for a boyfriend. Was that ridiculous? Curt was just as narrow-focused in his life as she had always been, no time for more than friendship. She honestly wondered if she had it in her to invest in a serious relationship. Curt probably felt the same.

They had so much in common, more than just their theory about the White Rose Killer and their shared pain over Angel. It would be nice, wouldn't it, if they could find something to keep them together once they had justice in their hands?

~~~~~

Where was she? His angel should have returned to school by now. Why wasn't she at school, where he could protect her?

He walked past her dormitory three times in the darkness, ignoring the cold, wet lash of the approaching storm. He circled the parking spot in the sheltered corner behind the dormitory building, close to the trash
~~~~~

collection bin, where no one else wanted to park. That was her parking spot. Why wasn't her car here? He returned to the front of the dormitory and watched her room.

A light came on, and his heart remembered to start beating. Tears warmed his frozen cheeks and he laughed into the storm. They lied, when they said his Angel wouldn't come back. She loved him. She had come back to him, just like she promised.

He waited, watching the movement between the light and the blinds covering the window. He wanted her to open the blinds and look out, to feed his starving heart with the sight of her pure, sweet, beautiful face.

A door opened, behind him across the street. He ducked into the shadows of the lightning-struck pine tree and watched the people coming out of the side door of the Mission. He relaxed, smiling, as he saw Claire Donnelly and her brother, Tommy, come out of the building. Tommy was a good boy, watching out for his sister. He admired Tommy, able to laugh and make others laugh, even though he was tied to a wheelchair for the rest of his life. Claire was good and kind and fierce when someone threatened the children under her care. He had seen her tackle and sit on a bully who climbed the fence of the Mission's playground to threaten the children. She was a good person, and she was nice to him. He was glad Claire and Tommy and the Mission were there to watch over his angel.

He waited until sister and brother worked the wheelchair lift and got Tommy into their van. He stayed in hiding until the taillights vanished into the snowy darkness. Then he stepped out to watch his angel's dormitory window. He smiled when the light finally went out. Good, she was asleep. She needed her sleep. School started this week, and she had to take care of herself, stay healthy, stay beautiful, and wait for him.

Would it be so bad if he went up to her room, just to look at her sleeping, just to wish her happy dreams? She wouldn't know he was there, but he would sleep better, knowing his angel was safe.

He had the keys for the back door of the dormitory out of his pocket before he finished thinking about it. He snorted disgust for the idiots who thought they could keep him away from her, just by changing the locks on the dormitory. He knew how to get all the keys. He was here to guard the whole town, so nothing could stay locked away from him for long.

Angel lived on the second floor. He crept up the back stairs, wincing every time his wet boots squeaked on the linoleum. Her door was second from the end, next to the empty lounge. He wished his angel would wake up and come into the lounge, so they could talk. She would be glad to see him. But the time wasn't right for them to be together. Not yet. She had to be tested a little longer.

He tried the doorknob of the dorm room and it turned easily. Unlocked. That pleased him, so a funny, happy, choking sensation filled his chest with warmth as he opened the door. Angel knew he was coming to visit, and she left her door open for him.

Cold tore the happy warmth away, making him hollow inside as he stared at the empty bed on the right side of the room, illuminated by the streak of light coming from the hallway. All his angel's books and posters, her computer and Teddy bears and her fluffy unicorn slippers -- gone.

"Where is she?" he growled and yanked the sleeping girl out of the other bed by her hair. She let out one squeak. He flung her across the room, so she slammed against the cinder block wall under the window. "Where is my angel?"

The girl wiped blood out of her eyes and stared up at him. She couldn't see his face, with the light coming from behind him. He would have to kill her if she had seen him. She wasn't pure. She wasn't allowed to see him. She wasn't his angel.

"Where is she?" He reached down to shake her until she talked.

"Tracy went home," she squeaked, and scrambled back away from his hands.

"Liar," he whispered, choking on something that wanted to come out as a scream.

For just a moment, he had Angel inside his hands, struggling and begging, crying, fighting to breathe. Pleading, swearing that the nasty stories were all lies, and he was the only boy she had ever kissed.

He swung, backhanding the roommate, so her head slammed against the cinderblock wall. She slumped, unconscious, without making a sound. Trembling, wanting to howl his pain and the old terror and guilt, he slipped out of the dorm room, pulled the door closed behind him, and skidded down the stairs. He almost forgot to lock up the back door behind himself again. He dropped the stolen keys and almost didn't go back for them. He almost ran right past his car, hidden on the other side of the trash bin.

She left him. She ran away. Why did she run away?

Monday, January 6

"What is that smell?" Toni demanded as she walked into the office. There was a definite wet, sewer smell hanging in the air. Partly chemical, partly rot. It made her glad she only had coffee and a slice of plain toast for breakfast, instead of the waffles with strawberries she had craved when she got out of bed.

Ty had switchboard duty this morning, thanks to his new school schedule. He grinned and finished his call. Toni waited, leaning against the counter.

"Toilets backed up."

"Oh, great." She frowned at him when he just grinned wider. "Ordinarily, that isn't something to smile about. What's the inside story?"

"Seems our sewage system is directly linked to the system of the building next door, which technically isn't next door, but just another part of this building. Owned by the same landlord."

"Okay," she prompted, when he paused for dramatic effect. Toni tried to remember if Ty was studying theater at BWU.

"The toilets next door backed up and broke a couple pipes and it's been raining on the bar downstairs all weekend."

"But they wouldn't know that until they got to work this morning, because they're closed for renovations." Her mouth stretched into a delighted grin. Toni had heard enough horror stories about the idiot customers of the previous bar downstairs, she could only imagine how much worse things would get when the bar's new incarnation opened again. Anything that delayed the opening suited her just fine.

"There is a God and He has a nasty sense of humor." Ty turned back to the ringing switchboard without losing a degree from his smile.

Angela met her in the hallway and gestured back to the front door. Toni immediately started putting her coat back on even before the editor started talking, her voice pitched low so no one else could overhear.

The White Rose had struck last night, invading the dormitory room of his latest target.

"But Tracy's gone," Toni protested.

"Her roommate was there. She's pretty shaken up. Chief Cooper thinks she'll be more open to talking to a woman. Taylor is on her way in, but we're closer. Can you get over to the Mission and help out?"

"The Mission?" Toni shook her head before Angela could explain. "I know where the Mission is. Why?"

"It's across the street from her dormitory, and it seems Tommy Donnelly is playing white knight." Angela shrugged. Her smile was bitter sweet. "Just go. Make sure the girl knows she's safe and people care, but get all the information from her that you can. Chief Cooper wants whatever you can find out."

Toni nodded and ran back out the door.

The Mission used to be the Eloise Elementary School, and Toni had gone to school there. She found it odd and a little amusing to park in the teachers' parking lot and ring the doorbell at the back entrance for admittance. Security issues being what they were anymore, Toni was glad to see that the doors weren't just hanging open for anyone who wanted to come into the building.

Claire Donnelly answered the door. Toni vaguely remembered seeing her at church once or twice, in the company of a broad-shouldered, dark-haired man in a wheelchair. Claire was tall and strawberry blonde and not prone to chatter. She offered no information as she walked Toni to the daycare center at the center of the building, right next to the office, where the school office used to be.

"Um, excuse me, maybe you got me mixed up with someone else," Toni said, when she looked through the tinted window in the door and saw the children playing Duck-Duck-Goose on mats on the floor in the center of the room.

"Samantha—that's the girl who got attacked," Claire said. "She's studying early childhood education and she's volunteered here. We thought being with the children would help her calm down a little."

That made a lot of sense. Especially the way the children giggled and wriggled and screamed encouragement to each other as they took turns getting their heads tapped and then chasing each other. When Claire opened the door and let her in the room, she saw a dark-haired girl with a bandage in stark white contrast to her hair, sitting on a pile of mats, chatting with the man in the wheelchair. He was Claire's brother, Tommy, and he held Samantha's hand.

Tommy turned out to be a comedian as well as a white knight. He made Samantha giggle, little snorts muffled through her nose, as he recounted how he rocketed across the street in his wheelchair and dragged her back to the Mission that morning.

"Man," he said, finishing up the story, "I don't know what's worse. Going without chains on my tires, or getting my hands torn up on the chains."

He sat there with a flat little grin, eyes sparkling with barely repressed mischief, waiting for someone to say something. The four of them were in what used to be the teacher's lounge, furnished now with three long couches, a refrigerator, microwave, and a tall, skinny cabinet full of paper plates, cups, and plastic utensils. Claire made hot chocolate for everyone and offered around a box of donuts while they got comfortable with each other.

Toni could well believe Tommy could go across the snowy street in his wheelchair without any help. His upper body was well developed, straining against his double-x sweatshirt with characters from VeggieTales across it. When she commented on his physique and asked if he lifted weights, he went into a long, involved, convoluted story about how he used to be on the wrestling team in high school and college and helped the team train on the weight machines.

"You know what was really fun, when I was in college? Besides doing the slalom going down the halls." Tommy glanced sideways under his thick, dark lashes at Samantha. She groaned and rolled her eyes, leading Toni to believe she had heard this story before. "You know, slalom?" He demonstrated, tipping his chair so it rested on the two back wheels, and waggled from side to side. "Swooshing down the hall, like they do with those gates in the Olympic skiing. The only problem is, in the hallways, the gates don't stand still, and they scream when you hit them," he added, with a straight face.

"You ought to do your routine on TV," Claire said from the open doorway. She leaned against the doorframe.

"Yeah, yeah." Tommy sighed dramatically. "My only sister just loves me so much. She wants me on television, so she—"

"Can turn you off," Claire cut in, with that precise timing that told Toni brother and sister teased each other in this way quite often.

Tears suddenly burned her eyes, anger and renewed grief. What would she and Angel have become together, if her sister had lived? Best friends? Friendly rivals? Watching out for each other or hating the sight of each other?

"Anyway," Tommy continued, "like I was saying, I loved going to the wrestling tournaments. Especially the road trips. There was always one guy on another team who'd be watching me for about an hour until he finally got up the guts to come over. And it was always, 'Hey, man, what happened to you?' And I'd look him over and say, 'You don't want to know.' And he'd say, 'Yeah, I do. What happened?' and I'd ask him what weight he wrestled at and he'd tell me and I'd say, 'Yeah, I thought so. I used to wrestle that weight.' Then I'd point at the guy on our team that he'd have to go against and say, 'Then I went up against him.' And the poor guy would get this terrified look on his face, like any minute now, he's going to scream 'I want my Mommy!' And then I'd say, 'It's a good thing he was in a good mood that day, because man, you do not want to go up against my brother when he's in a bad mood.' And the other guy would go, 'He's your brother and he did that to you?' and just about faint right there."

"Yeah, yeah, yeah," Claire muttered, and hid her grin in her cup of hot chocolate.

Samantha laughed, and Toni knew that was the point of the story.

Chapter Seventeen

After about an hour of chatting, Toni thought maybe she could bring up what had happened. The bandage on her forehead meant the girl had already had some official attention. The police knew what had happened. And besides, she had to get back to work eventually and work on her stories for the next edition.

"Samantha, have you been following the stories about the White Rose in the newspaper?" Toni asked, during a lull when Tommy had excused himself and wheeled out of the room, singing something about, "Gimme three steps," under his breath. This might be the best time to ask her about the attack, when there were no men in the room.

Samantha nodded, and her fingers clenched around her cup, so the Styrofoam squeaked.

"I'm going to tell you something, but I'm going to ask you not to tell anybody about this for now." She glanced up at Claire, including her in the request. Claire nodded, and when Toni looked back to her, Samantha nodded, too. "My sister, Angel, was strangled by her boyfriend because he thought she broke her promises to him." Toni waited for some sign that this was too hard for Samantha to take. The college girl just watched her, her eyes getting big and luminous with the threat of tears. "She kept her boyfriend secret from us, so nobody knew who he was. And after she was buried, he left white roses on her grave."

"This wasn't in the paper," Samantha said, her voice cracking a little.

"That's because it happened twenty years ago. Angel was twelve." Toni scooted over on the couch and wrapped her hands around Samantha's cold hands. "I believe the White Rose killed my sister. I want to stop him. Your roommate, Tracy, is safe from him now. And you're safe. And we need your help to try to figure out who he is, so nobody else will be in danger from him. Can you do that? Can you remember just one more time, so I can put the story in my file and add it to all the other clues?"

"He's going to go after someone else, isn't he?" she whispered. Samantha closed her eyes before Toni nodded. She tugged her hand free and knuckled her eyes dry and took a deep, loud breath. "Okay. What do you want to know?"

"You were asleep when he came into your room?" Toni waited for Samantha to open her eyes and nod. "What's the first thing you remember? Any smells, any sounds?"

Toni held Samantha's hand and scribbled one-handed on her notepad and slowly took her through those few terrifying moments in the dormitory when an angry stranger stepped out of the darkness, dragged her out of bed, and flung her against the wall. Tommy came back during the recitation and stayed out in the hallway, listening, slowly rocking back and forth on his wheels. Toni smiled at the tenderness he showed for Samantha. Everybody needed someone like Tommy. She wished she had been there to get a picture of him battling through the snowy street between the Mission and the dormitory to fetch Samantha to safety.

Claire came back from answering the phone. Samantha's parents were on their way and someone from university security wanted to talk to her again. Toni decided too many people present might not be a good thing, but she asked anyway if Samantha wanted her to stay.

"No, it's okay." Samantha looked more tired than anything. Toni wished the girl could be allowed to curl up and sleep. She had no doubt Tommy would keep guard over her. "Besides, you have to go back to the paper and write that story, to help the next girl stay safe."

"You bet." Impulsively, Toni reached out and hugged Samantha before she got up. The girl clung to her a few seconds, but she didn't shake or look teary when she let go.

Please, God, I don't ask for much. Maybe because I've been mad at You. But please, God, make Samantha okay now?

Toni didn't want to go back to the newspaper office. She didn't want to go back to the bickering and fraying nerves as deadlines drew near. To the sounds of hammering and drilling and cursing from the remodeling project downstairs. Or the smell of broken sewer pipes getting fixed. She needed to talk to someone who might understand what she was going through, what she felt.

Toni had a vague idea where Common Grounds Legal Clinic was, though she hadn't ventured down Pearl Road into that part of Padua yet. She kept track of the addresses as the numbers changed and barely noticed the snow was getting thicker as she drove further north toward Cleveland. Curt had mentioned it was on the left side of the street, in a former furniture store. Toni mentally slapped her own wrist for not venturing further out from Tabor Heights. She was as narrow-focused as Curt, obviously, centering her life around catching the White Rose Killer.

Her cell phone rang. She snarled at herself when she tapped the control on her steering wheel to accept the call, at the same moment she saw the sign for Common Grounds.

"Where are you?" Curt demanded when she distractedly answered the phone.

"I'm about to ask you that question." Toni glanced in her rearview mirror and saw she had a brief opening to get over into the next lane. She didn't hear what he said next. "What? Never mind. I'm in the middle of a snowstorm and trying to turn around because I missed my turn."

"Claire said you left the Mission twenty minutes ago. Why aren't you back here?"

"My stories are in fine shape. There's just this... errand I need to take care of, first."

"Toni, now that he knows Tracy is gone and not coming back, he's probably on a rampage. Look what he did to her roommate."

"He's not going to come after me in a snowstorm." Toni surprised herself by laughing.

"Where are you?"

"Somewhere on Pearl Road in Padua. Now get off the phone so I can figure out what I'm doing, okay?"

"Get back here right now."

"Yes, teacher." She stuck her tongue out as she pressed the button to cut the connection. The image of Curt having a snit because she ignored his order cheered her immensely.

She entertained herself wondering about the various ways he would express his anger, as she finally found a place to turn around. Five minutes after she made the turn, she saw the legal clinic coming up on her right, and the driveway between the buildings. Toni laughed in triumph as she pulled into the parking lot. The snow doubled in thickness as she trudged up from the back parking lot to the law office and tried to bluster in through the door with her.

The chime over the door startled her and she nearly stumbled across the threshold. It felt good just to stand there and let the heat of the office wrap around her while she stomped the snow off her boots. Hannah stood up from her desk on the far side of the reception area, smiling a little uncertainly. Toni wondered if she had heard about the attack. Maybe it wasn't such a good idea to tell her in this way?

She wondered if Curt was going to yell at her for this, too.

Hannah welcomed her into the reception area. It was empty of people, and looked like they had plenty to offer guests, with coffee, hot chocolate mix, tea, and cookies. Toni hadn't eaten all day, and it was long past lunch. How much time had she spent with Samantha, anyway? Maybe Curt had good reason to be concerned about her. Maybe it wasn't such a good idea coming here? Well, too late now. Hannah would think she was losing her mind if she turned around and just walked out without talking. Get it over with. Fast and simple. Then go back to the office and face Curt.

"Coffee?" Hannah continued. "Hot chocolate? It looks pretty vicious out there. I'm glad I got in before the heavy stuff hit us."

"The White Rose attacked Tracy Brickman's roommate." Toni

finished pulling her gloves off and raked her fingers through her snowy hair, shedding the last few flakes before she stepped off the rug.

"Is she—" Hannah went pale and sank down into her desk chair.

"Concussion, a dozen stitches, scared out of her skull and ready to quit school." Toni tried to smile. It was good news, actually, that Samantha was in the condition she was in. The poor girl could be dead, after all. "But very alive."

"He didn't believe Curt's story, that Tracy went home to stay," Hannah said, her eyes wide. "He thought he was going to find her in her room, and when he didn't—"

"He went ballistic. Well, at least we know it's a man now. No." Toni shook her head, guessing what Hannah was going to ask next. She dropped into the closest chair. "There wasn't enough light for her to get a description. She just got a general outline and the sound of his voice. Tall, baritone voice, really angry and raspy, big shoulders, dressed all in dark clothes. No mask, though. She was pretty sure there was no mask. Which doesn't make sense. Isn't he scared of anyone identifying him?"

"Maybe he was planning on snatching Tracy and didn't care if she recognized him later or not." Hannah paused. She looked like she might be feeling sick. "Because there wouldn't be a later." She rested her head in her slightly shaking hands. "When is this going to be over?" she asked in a voice that devolved to a whimper. Then she jerked her head up and looked guilt-stricken. "Oh, Toni, I'm so sorry. This has to be twenty times worse for you. Living it all over again."

"It'll be over when we catch the psychotic who killed my sister." A strange sense of calm filled her. Was this what they called an epiphany? This sudden sense that everything in her life had been one long, straight road, from the moment Curt found Angel's body in the park until now? It had never been over, had it? She had never been able to put it behind her. All these years had just been a long, silent wait, like a strange intermission, until the final act of the play unfolded. She nodded and stood up to go. "I thought you should know."

"Does—I don't even know her name. Does the roommate need any help? Someone to stay with her until she's feeling better? Has the university called her parents?"

"Taylor from the department is with her, and her name is Samantha. She's made friends with some of the folk across the street at the Mission, especially that guy in the wheelchair." A snort of something that came close to laughter escaped Toni. "He got across the street despite all that snow and barged his way into the RA's apartment and practically dragged her back across the street with him. Taylor says she's doing better, just surrounded by the kids. She wants to be a kindergarten teacher, so she loves kids. Claire—you know Claire, over at the Mission?" Toni waited for

Hannah to nod. "She says she'll take Samantha home with her tonight, and she's staying with them until her parents can get in from Vancouver."

"Good."

"I'll tell her you offered. All of us collateral damage folks have to stick together, y'know?" Toni reached for the door. She stopped, her heart in her throat, when a man appeared out of the heavy, blowing snow and yanked the door out of her grip.

For two seconds, she thought of Samantha's description of the White Rose Killer coming out of the darkness. He wouldn't have followed her here, would he? The snow wasn't nearly enough coverage.

Then she caught her breath, fighting not to laugh, as Curt's features, red with cold and hard with anger, emerged from the swirling white.

"Do you need someone to talk to? Somebody to stay with?" Hannah winced when an icy wind whipped through the office, disturbing papers, clothes, and hair.

"You are in so much trouble," Curt growled, grabbing hold of Toni's arm at the elbow.

"Thanks, but I don't think I need that." Toni smiled, her mouth twisting in an urge to laugh and burst into tears at the same time. How had Curt caught up with her so quickly? How had he even guessed she would be here? Why was she so glad he was here? She didn't even mind that he was going to chew her out until her ears rang. "My bodyguard just caught up with me."

"What did you think you were doing, just taking off like that? Hi, Hannah. Bye, Hannah. Say good-bye, Toni." Curt turned and pushed the door open.

"Curt thinks I'll be the next target, since I look so much like Angel. At least he cares that much!" She gasped a little as Curt dragged her out into the snow. "How did you get here so fast?"

"Already on my way," Curt admitted on a growl, after they walked twenty steps and reached the relative shelter of the alleyway between the two buildings.

"You thought Hannah should know?" Curt really was a considerate guy, even if he could be a big bully, like now.

"I was going to tell Xander, actually, and let him tell Hannah." He tightened his grip on her arm as they stepped out into the open again.

"How did you know I would be here? Curt, my car!" she protested, as he led her over to his car.

"We'll send somebody out to get it later. Right now, I want to be sure I know where you are every second of the day from now on." He unlocked the door and stopped just short of shoving her into the passenger seat. Then he stomped over to the driver's side and climbed in. "What are you grinning at?" he demanded, when she just looked at him. "Close the door before we freeze, will you?" And he punctuated his words by slamming his own door.

"You really do care, don't you? It's not just guilt over Angel, but you care about me." She pulled the door closed.

"I have no idea why..." He groaned and leaned his head back against the seat and closed his eyes. "Yeah. When I don't want to strangle you, I think I care. Okay? Satisfied?"

"Satisfied." She buckled the seatbelt and waited for him to start the car. "So, how did you know I'd be here?"

"Who else do you know in this part of town? Reporter's instincts."

"And my reporter's instincts tell me the White Rose won't come after me, now that he realizes Tracy isn't coming back. Everybody thinks I belong to you. I'm safe."

"Yeah, and Samantha thought she was safe. He broke his pattern, attacking someone who wasn't a threat to his ownership. From this point on, he could be completely unpredictable." He gunned the engine before shifting into gear.

Toni had to admit he was right, and right to be worried, but for some reason, she felt warm and safe. Almost invulnerable. Maybe that was what Lois Lane felt when she was with Clark Kent, before she knew he was Superman. Gut instinct, reporter's instinct, told her that despite his bumbling and seeming cluelessness, he would take care of her.

The problem with Curt was that he thought he was responsible for things that he couldn't have prevented. Could she make him see that? Should she even try? Maybe, like coming to see Hannah, it was something she had to do, and the sooner she got it over with, the better.

"You know, Curt..." Toni licked her lips, having second thoughts the moment the words slipped out. He glanced at her when they came to a stoplight.

"If you're going to apologize for scaring ten years off of my life, buy me dinner, okay?"

"Okay." She had to grin. Leave it to Curt to think of his stomach at a time like this. Come to think of it, she was getting a little hungry. Finally. "I was just thinking." She saw the spark of mischief in his eyes and hurried on. "And don't go saying that it's about time, either. I was just thinking that you've been blaming yourself for Angel, all these years. But there was nothing you could have done about it. You aren't to blame."

"Maybe if I hadn't kept trying to... I don't know. How do junior high boys think? Do they think at all?" He studied the street ahead of them, his face more tired than sad.

"If you hadn't come over to try to talk to Angel that day, we might not have found her body for another day. She was still warm. That meant a lot to my folks. She wasn't lying there, abandoned. And you weren't the one telling the nasty stories about her because you were jealous. So stop beating yourself up over it, okay?" She took a deep breath, swallowed hard, trying to take the taste of fear out of her mouth. "And stop riding me so hard because you feel guilty. You don't owe us anything. I'd much rather be your friend than your obligation. We're friends. Aren't we?"

Now he did look at her, just a glance because they were in the middle of moving traffic. Did she dare hope she saw a little bit of fear, some affection, something else to give her encouragement?

"Best pals, remember?" Curt reached over and gripped her hand, squeezing hard. "Even if I do want to pound you until you get some common sense."

"Yeah, you and whose army?" she shot back. Curt's grin and laughter made her want to melt into the seat.

Okay, God. He cares enough to be angry. Thanks. That's something, isn't it? But is it enough?

Thursday, January 9

Pure, sweet laughter rang out, bouncing off the ice coating the school playground. He stopped and leaned against the fence, dislodging snow from the chain links. He recognized that voice. It dragged him back to the happiest weeks of his life, the new boy in school meeting up with the shy, quiet girl, talking about books, meeting in the library, walking home from school together after choir practice or football games. His Angel had laughed like that.

She stood by the jungle-gym, laughing with two other girls. They slipped and slid, deliberately skidding their feet on the slick, black ice that had collected under the climbing tower, holding onto the bars to keep themselves upright. She wore fluffy white earmuffs and her long, straight, dark hair swung in the gentle breeze. Her cheeks were red. Her dark eyes sparkled with life and purity and joy. His angel, come back to him just as she had left him.

He knew exactly who she was, how to find her. No taking risks asking dangerous questions. No waiting outside her house or following her around town to learn her routine. He had been in her house before. How could he not have seen that she was his Angel, come back to him?

The other angels, the false angels, had distracted him. He was glad he had killed them. They deserved to die for keeping him from seeing her. But he had found her now. His Angel.

Friday, January 10

Three hours of searching got him into the school's computer system, to find his angel's locker number and her combination. He waited for her after school and watched her walk home, surrounded by giggling friends. He laughed when they stopped on the corner and had an impromptu snowball fight, and fought not to cheer when his Angel won.

When she was safely inside her home, he went back to the school, waved to the custodians as if he belonged there, and found her locker. He leaned against the locker door before he opened it, forehead pressed against the cold metal, remembering those happy days when he had walked down a hall just like this one to wait for her after school, after choir practice, after meetings.

It was a sign. It was a message. It was proof that this time, he had found his Angel and she would love him and stay faithful and they would finally be happy together.

His hands trembled as he spun the combination dial around and unlocked the door. He blinked back happy tears as he put the note inside her locker, on top of the books she hadn't taken with her for homework.

"I love you always and forever. Promise you'll be mine. I'll make you happy," he whispered in the darkness and quiet of the old school building, echoing the words of the note.

For fun, he had drawn hearts all over it in pink marker, just like his Angel used to do when she left notes for him at the old greenhouse and tucked them inside the ventilation slots of his locker during school.

His Angel would understand. She would be happy. She was his, now and forever.

Chapter Eighteen

Baxter Stemple stopped by the *Picayune* office and waited outside, catching Curt as he left for the day. He handed him an envelope with printouts and a CD each for him and Toni. He said nothing, just saluted and turned to saunter down the sidewalk to the end of the building and the sloped parking lot. Curt waited until he saw Baxter drive away and didn't even feel the cold wind wrap around him. Then he went to his car, got in, locked the doors, and called Toni.

"What are you doing tonight?" he asked, almost before she finished saying hello.

"You mean right now, or later on when I get my second wind?" She laughed.

"Want to help me check out some... research?" Curt grinned at himself in the mirror, amused at this sudden descent into cloak-and-dagger. He slid the key into the ignition and started the engine.

"Research, huh?" Toni's voice sounded tight. Did she understand what he hinted at? "Sounds like fun. You know I just can't get enough of research. Spaghetti sound good?" She laughed. "It's about all I have in the cupboard."

"Sounds fantastic. And maybe we'll head out for something fancy at Stay-A-While later, to celebrate." He barely glanced in the rearview mirror before backing out of his spot.

"Let's hope we really do have something to celebrate."

The spaghetti water barely started to boil before they had looked through the lists Baxter gave them. The list they handed Baxter had one hundred fifty-eight names of possible suspects, boys from the neighborhood, boys in school at the same time Angel had been there. Boys who had shown some interest in Angel or who merely had some contact with her from the day the Napolitanos moved to Tabor. Baxter's connections and superior searching methods narrowed that list down to thirty-five who were still alive and either living in Tabor, or close enough to the town to be convenient for them to stalk their chosen victims.

The printed sheets were the distilled versions of the reams of information Baxter put on the CDs for them. Curt looked through the spreadsheets and could only shake his head in admiration. All the hours he and Toni had invested to simply strike one suspect off the list, and Baxter had researched everyone and either eliminated them or kept them for further study in less than half the time.

"Did Donovan talk to you today?" Toni stepped over to the stove to take the pot off the burner and drain the spaghetti.

"No. About what?" Curt leaned back against the wall of the dining nook and watched her. He liked the comfortable, easy feeling of sitting here, working with Toni. He knew better than to examine it too closely. Like a captive butterfly, he could either sit and enjoy it, or try to find out more and end up killing whatever it was they had between them.

"He said someone finally got a brainstorm about that panel of plastic that replaced the window, where they found Annalee's body."

"Really? Any answers?" He sat up, alerted now and slightly peeved that Donovan had left the information with Toni and didn't bother making sure he heard it right away.

Then again, everyone understood Toni and Curt were partners, in the investigation and the increasing number of feature and government-related stories they were writing for the paper.

"It's a panel from a greenhouse. High quality, refracts light, intensifies radiation, just like glass. But doesn't break like glass would." She dumped the spaghetti from the colander back into the pot and ladled warmed sauce from a casserole through it. "I didn't see, but is there anybody on that list who has access to a greenhouse?"

"That'd be too easy, wouldn't it?" Curt murmured.

"Donovan said he'd get somebody started checking places that supply greenhouses, and places that would provide building materials. But wouldn't they report something like that being stolen?" She brought the pot over to the table, shoved aside a stack of papers, and put it on a trivet in the center of the table.

Curt inhaled deeply of the fragrant steam rising out of the pot and groaned. "That is not jar sauce. Please tell me you made it."

"Gotta have something to do when you're frustrated and you can't get to the gym." Toni blushed and grinned and stepped over to the refrigerator to pull out a big bowl of salad. "With a name like Napolitano, I better be able to make a decent pot of sauce."

"You are the perfect woman. Marry me."

Curt held his breath and went stone still, afraid to look at Toni. She, on the other hand, started dishing up the spaghetti as if she hadn't heard what he said. If she did hear, she didn't react. He slowly, cautiously released his breath, and congratulated himself that Toni knew him so well, she knew he was joking.

That was good, wasn't it?

"What if Donovan doesn't find any report of that greenhouse panel being stolen?" Toni continued, as she dished up her own spaghetti.

"How much surplus do you think anyone has sitting around?" He concentrated on twirling strands around his fork. He flinched when Toni reached over and slapped his hand.

"Bless the mess before you eat, okay?" She grinned at him when he looked up at her, startled and half-guilty.

Curt nearly took hold of her hands before he bowed his head to pray, just like he had seen dating couples do at Singles outings for church. That urge scared him, so he ended up clasping his hands together tightly in his lap. What was wrong with him lately?

For a few minutes after he said "amen," neither one said anything, busy with scooping up salad and putting dressing on it. He groaned at the first spicy, rich taste of the dark red spaghetti sauce. In college, he had lived on spaghetti and other inexpensive food, but instead of getting sick of it, Curt had turned himself into a connoisseur. Toni's creation ranked up there with the best he had ever tasted. She laughed when he said so.

"Flattery will get you a quart to take home, if you really like it that much."

"Forget about taking it home. I'll drink it instead of coffee."

"Low blood sugar. Definitely. You're getting loopy." She picked through her salad bowl for a moment. "Okay, the greenhouse panel. What if it was never reported stolen because the White Rose owns a greenhouse?"

"That'd make sense. They've been trying to use the roses as a lead, but no luck." Curt chewed for a minute or two while he thought it over. "He grows roses for himself, to give his victims."

"I didn't see anything about greenhouses or even belonging to a garden club, when I looked through the list. Did you?" Toni sighed and shrugged when Curt thought a moment and shook his head. "Got the feeling we'll spend the whole evening looking through those disks?"

"Just keep the spaghetti coming."

Toni laughed, and that suited Curt just fine.

Sunday, January 12

His angel played in the snow with her much younger cousins, helping them build a fort and then a row of snowmen-warriors to stand guard. He watched her, pausing only a few seconds at a time as he went past on his usual route. Even though he knew he had every right to be there, watching out for her, protecting the one who belonged to him, he also knew that others might not understand. So he went away and came back and went away again, always checking the neighborhood, ensuring it stayed safe for his angel.

He laughed, bubbling over with an excitement he hadn't felt in years.

Everything was right this time. Everything was perfect. His angel was safe, living under the eye of a police officer. He knew McGuire, his angel's guardian. He was a good man. The best man possible to keep her safe.

Best of all, McGuire was his friend.

Monday, January 13

He went into the school that evening, while the custodians and two women in the office were the only ones there. He kissed the note he wrote to his angel and put it in her locker. The first note was gone. He smiled as he imagined her excitement as she read his first note. Tomorrow, maybe, he would give her a rose. She would like that.

~~~~~

"Greenhouse supplies?" Officer Joe Watkins laughed when Toni sat up and clutched the notepad to her chest. "Thinking of going into business?"

She scolded herself for thinking of her stomach ahead of security. She shouldn't have gone to the Bluebird Café for dinner. She should have kept her work in the car or in her shoulderbag and not brought it out where anyone could see it as they walked by her table. Why did the Bluebird have to keep their lights so bright, anyway? Didn't they know what atmosphere and ambience were?

"My parents are coming back to Tabor." Toni shrugged and smiled. She really did like Joe, so helpful whenever she ran into him around town. He never laughed at her when she found out she was going in the wrong direction or had places and people mixed up yet again.

It was embarrassing admitting that she couldn't seem to keep things straight and kept trying to go to businesses that were closed or had moved to larger quarters. Just another sign that she needed to completely let go of the past.

"Mom has always wanted to have a little greenhouse. I thought if I could do the legwork, that might help them decide one way or another if they want to start up the business," she lied.

It wasn't like she was hiding a crime, so why did her heart thunder that way? Joe wasn't even in uniform, so technically she wasn't lying to a police officer, right?

"Wish I could help you, there." He shrugged and jammed his hands into the back pockets of his jeans. "My uncle used to own a greenhouse, but he sold it and the property it sat on to the greenhouse next door. Then about five years ago, they tore everything down and now it's just empty fields." He jerked his thumb over his shoulder, in the direction of Shorewood Township.
~~~~~

"So you know about the greenhouses that used to be around here, right?" Toni put the notepad down and picked up her pen.

Maybe it hadn't been such a big, stupid mistake to take her research work out in public after all. If Joe could give her a big lead in tracking down the greenhouses or even abandoned greenhouses in the area, she would have definite proof there was no such thing as coincidences.

"My uncle was into that stuff. Me, I have a registered brown thumb." Joe laughed, the sound warm and comforting, flowing over Toni like maple syrup. "You ought to see my house and what's left of the yard. Nothing but mile-high weeds." He seemed to take pity on her and the obvious disappointment on her face. "Tell you what, though. I'll dig through his old papers, see if there's some contact information anywhere. Might be a starting place, but I can't guarantee any of those places are still in business after all these years."

"Thanks, Joe. My mom would be so grateful. It's a dream she's had to put off for just years."

A dream of justice, Toni amended silently.

"Come to think of it, Evans might be able to help you. His uncle had a greenhouse, too. He went out of business about seven, eight years ago. Had a stroke, couldn't do the work. I'll ask him, too, if you want."

"That'd be great. Thanks." Toni waited until Joe walked away, then made notes. Both he and Duane Evans had been in school with Angel. She found it a little odd that both of them had relatives with greenhouses, but she honestly couldn't remember anything about those greenhouses in the information Baxter had found for them. Had she been lucky, running into Joe tonight, or should she be worried because it looked like there were still holes in her research?

Curt could hardly believe their good luck when she called him. She waited until she was in her car and on her way home, so no one would overhear her side of the conversation. They agreed that when Joe gave Toni the information, she would steer the conversation into reminiscing about the greenhouses that used to be in the area, and who ran them.

Tuesday, January 14

"You will always be safe," he whispered as he stood over Angel's bed. He smiled at the Teddy bear angel perched on her pillow. His smile faded as he looked around the room and saw posters for movies and singing groups. She couldn't love any of those men, could she? No, he decided a moment later. She was only looking for her true love. She would stop looking when he approached her and told her his name and reminded her that they had promised to always be together. She would remember him and be happy and love him.

For now, though, he left a note promising he would always watch over her and keep her safe, along with the first white rose.

Every day, from now on, he would leave a rose for her. At school. On the back step of the house when she took the garbage out for her aunt. In the tree house in the back yard. Anywhere she would go, she would find a rose, one every day. Until she was so much in love with him she would call him to come out of the shadows where he hid. She would beg him to come to her.

Then they would be together forever, just as they planned so long ago, and they would be happy. Because she would finally remember she loved him.

~~~~~

"Can't wait for Joe," Curt said, when Toni opened the cottage door that evening. He grinned at her and bustled in with a bucket of chicken dinner and a stack of old Chamber of Commerce directories. He gave her the bucket and spread the thin, grubby books across her table. "Had a brainstorm and stopped at the Chamber office on my way home, and they let me take these."

"To find the greenhouses that used to be in the area," she said, nodding. "But what if the White Rose has access to a private greenhouse? It's possible someone had one just for their own pleasure, not growing anything commercially."

"Maybe. But we can worry about that when Joe finally gets us that list. He has second shift patrol today and tomorrow, so I doubt he's going to get back to us until maybe this weekend."

"Okay." She stepped away to get dishes from the cupboard. "Thanks for saving me from cooking tonight, by the way."

"Oh. Sorry." Curt hated feeling his face heat up. Especially since he sensed Toni was amused at the way he just bustled in without asking. At least he had the sense to pick up some food instead of expecting her to feed him yet again. "You know, it just seems so natural. Us having dinner, working together. If you had plans —"

"No. I didn't. Just some TV and some downtime." She put the dishes on the table and patted his shoulder. "Thanks. It was a good idea. We make a great team."

Wish we could keep the team together, he thought, as he watched her step over to the refrigerator and pull out some bottles of fruit drink. His shoulder ached a little where she had patted him. He knew he was an idiot, but he wished she had hugged him instead.

His cell phone rang, startling him just as he picked up the first fragile, dirty old Chamber guide. He flinched, nearly ripping the book. Curt stifled a curse and dug out his phone.
~~~~~

"What's Xander doing, calling me?" he muttered, and flipped the phone open.

"Hey, Curt, just thought you should know. The chief will probably let you know tomorrow once we get the all clear." Xander sounded a little breathless. "The White Rose targeted Frank McGuire's niece, Sheila."

"Sheila?" Curt's voice cracked and rang off the old glass shade of the lamp hanging over the kitchen table. "She's what? Ten years old?"

"Thirteen. He left a couple notes in her locker—"

"He tracked her down at school? He got into the school? I can just see heads rolling when they find out about that." He sank into the closest chair. His heart raced and he found it hard to breathe.

"And she got home from school this afternoon to find a white rose on her bed. McGuire's furious. He got into his house, a cop's house."

"Is she okay? Please, Xander—" Curt nearly yelped when Toni rested her hands on his shoulders. He closed his eyes and took a couple deep breaths and listened as the lawyer filled him in on the rest of the details.

After he thanked him and broke the connection, Curt sat still and clenched his fists and tried to pray, but it was hard. He almost cried when Toni wrapped her arms around him from behind, rested her chin on his shoulder and pressed her cheek against his. She was warm and she smelled good, like fresh sugar cookies, and she had to understand exactly what he was feeling. After all these weeks working together, brainstorming together, sharing insights and frustrations, she had to understand.

They really were best pals, and that was crazy, because they both knew she wouldn't stay once they got what they wanted. How could he become best pals with someone who had been there such a short time?

"White Rose target number five is a thirteen-year-old who lives with her aunt and uncle." Curt spoke mostly to yank his thoughts in another direction.

"What are they doing about her?" Toni didn't sound as furious and frantic as Curt still felt, and he appreciated that. "You said Xander, right? Does that mean he and Hannah are involved? Did they get her away to a safe house, like they wanted for Annalee?"

"Exactly. Hannah's driving her to Indiana right now. With any luck, the White Rose won't even know she's gone until it's too late for him to do anything. He's only been leaving notes a couple days. Today was the first day for a rose." Curt took a deep breath. "Her name is Sheila and her uncle is Frank McGuire. A police officer," he said with extra emphasis. "I don't know why that should make her safer than anyone else, but the idea of the White Rose getting inside a cop's house to leave a rose on her bed—"

"It makes you sick and furious." She stepped around, still keeping contact with him by her hand on his shoulder, until she settled down into the chair facing him. "You know what we need to do? I rough drafted a story about Angel and the first time the White Rose killed. We should run it in Thursday's paper."

"No." Something turned to ice and shriveled up inside him at the thought of the White Rose reading that story. Curt's deepest gut instinct insisted that revealing the truth about his past would send the murderer on a rampage, and his first target would be Toni. "We tell Tabor about Sheila and how sick the White Rose is for picking on a little kid."

"You know, for him to have the gall to pick on a police officer's niece and go into his house..." Toni shuddered. "He has connections. He got into the dormitory at BWU. He got all sorts of information about the other girls. He knew they were trying to take Annalee away. He has sources. What if he realizes Hannah took her away? What if he figures out it's an Arc Foundation safe house, and he tracks her down there, despite all their security?"

"Then we warn Xander and Hannah and Arc and they double their security. The thing is, it'll take him time to figure that out, and more time to hack into their system." Curt took a deep breath. He felt better, having something to do, something to think through. "The first thing is, we tell Angela about the story we're going to write."

"You think she'll go for it?"

When they called Angela ten minutes later, Andrew said she was out riding. Curt and Toni ate their cooling chicken in the car as they drove out to the stables. When they got there, they saw Angela pacing in the open door of the long horse barn, arms wrapped tight around herself, as Curt had seen her do many times while working through a big, potentially dangerous story for the paper. Chief Cooper leaned against the door, watching her, his face a mask of stern determination.

"Did you two hear me thinking about you?" Angela called, when they got out of the car and walked over to the barn.

"We want to do a story about Sheila," Toni said. "It's time to remind people just what a monster the White Rose is."

"Do it."

Chapter Nineteen

Wednesday, January 15

He waited for his angel until the custodian came around to the front door of the school and chained it shut. He walked around to the side where the sports teams came out after practice and waited until dark, but she never emerged.

Where was she? Had she stayed home sick from school? He wanted to drive to McGuire's house and ask him, but he knew that wouldn't be a good tactic. McGuire was too good a cop not to get suspicious. He had watched McGuire give safety presentations in the elementary and middle schools, teaching the children how to avoid dangerous places and know when strangers were lying to them, trying to lure them into danger, to hurt them.

He wasn't going to hurt the girl. He loved her. But McGuire was too careful, too suspicious, to believe anyone. He admired McGuire for protecting the girl, his angel, so carefully. But that didn't help him now.

What was he going to do? He needed to see his angel every day.

Thursday, January 16

He had stopped reading the *Tabor Picayune*. He didn't like hearing the ugly things people said in letters to the editor or the small updates on the hunt for the White Rose copycat. Today, however, he bought a copy of the paper on his way home from work because he had overheard people discussing a story about the White Rose. Maybe there was news about his angel in there? No one was talking about her at the police station. He was afraid to ask questions. No one had any information at the school, and when he asked, he received odd looks that made him think something very bad had happened to his angel.

He needed to know. But he didn't want to know. Nobody knew the truth. They were all wrong, to be afraid of him. He never hurt anyone. Not the innocent ones. He only punished the evil ones, who lied to him and wouldn't obey. They deserved to be punished, didn't they?

So he bought the paper to find out what lies were being told about him. He made his supper and ate it in the silence and the shadows of his kitchen and listened for echoes of his aunt and uncle's voices and the sounds and smells of those happy, innocent days. Then he went out the back door, through the overgrown tangle of the backyard, to the small greenhouse that still functioned. The air was thick and sweet with the perfume of his roses. After his angel went away the first time, he had nothing in his life but the roses. He had learned from his aunt and uncle how to grow the roses and tend them, wrap them and feed them and trim them so he had roses blooming all year round. He stood in the middle of the darkened greenhouse and breathed the thick, humid, sweet, wine-potent air and let the perfume calm him.

Then he went to his desk and the plastic tub that stored and protected all his memories of his angel. He sat down at the desk and unfolded the paper and read.

The White Rose has now gone from a sick individual who terrorizes young women to a psychotic who threatens the safety of every child in our town, the story began.

"It's a lie," he whimpered, and nearly dropped the paper.

Dread fascination kept him reading.

The story took up the entire top half of the front page. In a few short paragraphs, the three writers who contributed to the story outlined the progression of events that started in October when Gretchen McKenzie received her first demanding love note. There were interviews with the two young men who asked her out on dates and received threatening notes from the White Rose, warning them they would be punished for trespassing and trying to steal the affections of the woman he had claimed as his own. The days of terror she experienced were dealt with in short sentences, listing each note and demand and rose like a list of crimes in an indictment.

"I loved her," he whispered, and couldn't stop reading.

The details of her death, how she had vanished and didn't reappear until five days later, and the forensic pathologist's report on how she had died, calling it cruel psychological, emotional, and physical torture, kept prisoner in some dirty, damp place until her tormenter strangled her.

"I gave her a chance to apologize and say she loved me." He stared through the greenhouse walls, heavy with condensation.

Echoes of her cries and screams and the fury in her weak voice came to him through the darkness. He had put her in the basement room under the greenhouse so she couldn't run away, so he could talk to her and convince her that she belonged to him. She had screamed every time he came near her. She had tried to run away, so he tied her to the moldy, rusty old pipes. It wasn't his fault that she bruised and tore the flesh of her wrists and ankles. She tried to escape when he told her not to. He gave her every chance to change her mind and realize she was wrong, but she refused. Her screams, her anger, made him angry. It was her fault he got so angry he hit her, so she slammed back against the wall, knocking her unconscious.

If he didn't love her, he wouldn't have strangled her while she was still unconscious.

If he didn't love her, he would have left her body in the dark, underground, but instead he took her outside and left her where people could find her and she could be buried decently. Even though she didn't deserve to be buried properly, because she was evil and cruel and she wouldn't let him love her.

Then the article talked about Katrina Harper and Sam Conrad, how he had tried to protect her by pretending he was her boyfriend, and how he was ambushed. It talked about how afraid Katrina was. Two psychology teachers from BWU added their analysis of the White Rose as someone who was immature and self-centered, who refused to earn love by meeting the object of his desire face-to-face, and who had such a low self-image he feared taking the risk or making the effort to earn that love.

The article spent three short paragraphs referring to modern literature, movies, and a passage of Scripture, all listing characteristics of love, and then showing how everything the White Rose did violated those standards of love.

He claims to love his victims, the article said, *but the only person the White Rose loves is himself, because he demands and takes instead of giving. He allows no choice or freedom. He punishes those who fear him when he has given them no reason to trust him. He demands love and admiration when he has done nothing to earn either.*

Then the article listed the measures taken by the police, the staff at the *Picayune* and Annalee's family, to protect her when the White Rose stalked her.

"I didn't stalk her," he insisted, and tore the page by gripping it too tightly. "I watched over her. I had to protect her, so no one would steal her from me. She tried to run away. I told her not to run away."

Fury brought tears to his eyes when he read how Hannah had worked as intermediary between the Arc Foundation and the Tabor police, to find a place where Annalee could go to be safe. How could Hannah do that to him? He thought she was his friend. How could she conspire to steal Annalee from him?

The article denounced him for breaking into the Gray house after dark, calling him a kidnapper because he took Annalee away from her home where she thought she was safe. It described her left alone in the darkness after he strangled her. Then it described how he left a love note for his next target the very next day, proving that he didn't love any of his victims, because he always found someone new to love before the bodies were even cold.

The article called him sadistic and cruel, terrorizing a college girl so she abandoned her education to protect her life. It described the stitches and bruises and terror the girl's roommate suffered when the White Rose broke into their college room, hunting her.

"I didn't attack her. She wouldn't help me. She lied to me. It's her fault I hit her," he choked out through an aching need to sob.

Then the article finished by describing the emotional distress Sheila McGuire felt when she got home from school and found the rose on her bed and realized a stranger had broken into the house while the family was away. It denounced the White Rose as a child molester and those same psychologists came back to speculate that the White Rose had been abused, emotionally, mentally, and sexually as a child, and calculated the chances that he was involved in child pornography.

"No!" he yelled, so his voice bounced off the panes of the semi-opaque roof. He ripped the paper into pieces and threw them on the floor and stomped on them.

The words he had read bounced through his mind, so he couldn't get rid of them. Sobbing, he dropped to his knees and hid his face in his crossed arms.

The moon hung high overhead, shining softly through a hazy threat of more snow, when he finally calmed and could get to his feet again. He stood a long time staring upward, as if he could climb the slope of the light and escape the aching that gnawed deeper into his spirit with every beat of his heart.

They were liars. Everyone was lying about him. Everyone had lied to him. No one kept their word. He was a friend to everyone, but no one was a friend to him.

He had to punish them.

He bent over, aching in every joint from spending so long curled up on the cold, damp cement floor, and picked up the fragments of the paper. One of the tears went through the byline of the lead story, so he could only read one name.

Angela Coffelt.

Yes, he would punish Angela. She was the editor of the paper. She made the decision to print all those lies about him and make people think that he was bad, that he was the criminal. The truth was that he was the victim. Nobody was his friend. Not even his angel.

He had to punish Angela. Then he would find someone else to punish, until everyone who kept him from finding his angel was gone.

Friday, January 17

Angela never came to work that morning, though he waited an hour in the parking lot of the shopping center across the street and watched the front door of the newspaper office. Fury and terror mixed in his chest. Had someone finally seen her evil nature and punished her?

The Coffelts lived in a quiet, tree-filled neighborhood in the old section of Tabor, where houses were two and three stories tall, driveways were gravel, the sidewalks were flagstone slabs instead of poured concrete, and basements were cellars that could be entered through rickety old doors set into the ground at the foundation. He knew where the Coffelts lived, because he had been there several times in junior and senior high through school activities.

It enraged him when he thought of Angela's cruelty and her betrayal in contributing to that article, so he gripped the steering wheel hard enough to bend it. Angela had been his friend. She had been Angel's friend when they were children. How could she say those things about him?

He pulled into a side street where he could see the Coffelt house, two stories, surrounded by old oak and maple trees, a wrap-around porch, all painted gray and white. The Christmas tree still sat in the front window and the sunlight sparkled on the colored lights and the icicle lights hanging from the eaves. He sat for a few minutes, studying the neighborhood.

All was silent. He got out of his car and walked around the back, aiming for the driveway of the house next door. He would cross the back yards and come into the house from the back door. He had his lock picks in his pocket and he could see Angela's car sitting in the driveway. He had to stop the lies now, today. How could he ever find his angel if people kept telling lies about him?

"Angel?" Andrew Coffelt stepped out onto the back porch and shaded his eyes against the bright sunshine sparkling on the snow.

He stopped, hiding in the shadows of the bushes in the side yard and watched. He shuddered, seeing movement in the garage, and realized Angela was working in the garage. What if she had seen him coming upon her? She didn't deserve any warning. She didn't deserve a chance to call for help. No warning, to try to run or fight to defend herself.

"Angel, are you okay?" the old man called again. He came down two steps and paused, still looking at the open garage door.

He shuddered as memories crashed down on him. His angel and Angela had laughed together about the similarities in their names. They had looked so much alike, and laughed when they chose clothes that were similar. Blue pleated skirts, white blouses, black loafers, red ribbons in their long, black hair.

Tears filled his eyes, turning everything into sparkling prisms as he watched Angela come out of the garage. His heart thudded in his ears, so he couldn't hear the old man and his daughter talk. A sob caught in his throat when the two embraced. He watched Angela take a grip on her father's arm and support him a little as he climbed the steps up to the porch.

Her father called her Angel.

Brilliant light seemed to burst into his mind and he sat back among the bushes, ignoring the snow that soaked through his pants and filled his boots.

Her father called her Angel.

Why hadn't he seen it before? She wasn't printing lies in the paper. She was trying to send him clues, trying to warn him. She was trying to get him to stop looking for his angel, because she was his angel. She always had been. She had been there, watching, waiting, when he thought he was in love with Angel. Could she even be jealous?

No, she couldn't be jealous. She was his angel, perfect and sweet and kind.

Saturday, January 18

Curt paused, halfway down the hall of the *Picayune*'s office. Something felt wrong. He couldn't define what it was, but it was there all the same.

"What's wrong?" Toni asked, nearly treading on his heels in the semi-darkness of the office.

They had beaten Chief Cooper and Angela to the office by about ten minutes. In the spirit of keeping this planning and analyzing session secret, Curt didn't turn on the lights when he unlocked the door. The overcast sky threatened a day of snow, and not much light came through the back windows, even bouncing off the coating of snow on the slanted roof directly below the windows.

"Something just doesn't feel right," he muttered, and started walking again. What he needed was a big mug of coffee, heavy on cream and sugar.

"What doesn't feel right is coming into the office at 8 a.m. on a Saturday morning." She poked him in the back with the corner of the box of donuts they had bought at Rick's Bakery after he picked her up at her house.

Curt decided she had to be right. He had made her laugh, recounting the times that something odd had happened, the strange smells and noises that had plagued the newspaper office in the days when DDT was still in business below them. She groaned when he recounted the times people walked into the newspaper at two in the afternoon, expecting to find an inside door to the bar, which wasn't open at that time of the day. Or the drunken customers who came upstairs to the newspaper on nights the reporters worked late, wanting to use the bathroom so they didn't have to wait for the people in line ahead of them. And on and on.

The sweet smell he thought he detected faded under the overpowering aroma of the fresh coffee Toni made. Curt forgot about it when Chief Cooper and Angela came in a few minutes later and they settled down at the table in the lunchroom to talk. Everyone seemed to be in a good mood. They were all still riding on the adrenaline of the full-exposure, heavy-hitting story about the White Rose that had run in Thursday's paper. The people of Tabor were warned. Angela had wisely stayed home from work on Friday to avoid the expected flood of calls in reaction to the story.

"So far, the general reaction is good," Chief Cooper said. "We hit the hundred mark on tips and suggestions and offers of help around one o'clock Thursday afternoon. Lots of strange things people noticed but didn't pay attention to at the time. Thanks to the stories of the targets, all together in one place, some people have noticed patterns they didn't see before."

"What percentage do we discount as mostly their imagination?" Angela said. Her smile went crooked as she met Chief Cooper's gaze. He sighed, smiling a little wider himself, and saluted her with a lift of his coffee mug.

I think Toni's right, Curt thought, watching their byplay. They reminded him of his parents, who seemed to read each other's minds, after all their years together. There was something more than friendship and a love of horses between Angela and the police chief.

They discussed what to put in next Thursday's paper for a follow-up. Angela wanted to keep running stories to warn the general public in Tabor, but not so often that they grew blasé about the whole subject.

"Do we want the White Rose to stay active, so we can finally get enough clues to catch him? Or do we want him to just go away, stop hunting, go into hibernation?" Toni remarked.

"What a choice." Angela drained her last mouthful of coffee. "I'm going to get a new notepad and a file for all our notes. Could somebody make another pot?" she asked as she headed for her office.

Curt was intrigued to note how quickly Chief Cooper leaped to do what she asked. Almost as if it was a comfortable old habit to make coffee and work together. He wondered what the setup at the stables was, if there was a kitchen or just a coffee machine, allowing them to sit and drink coffee and talk after riding together. How many Sunday afternoons did they spend together? He had assumed those few times he saw them, it was an occasional, chance thing. What if it was a regular habit?

Not that he was going to say anything about it.

"Ray?" Angela's voice didn't waver, but it sounded just slightly odd enough to make Curt leap to his feet and follow Chief Cooper to her office.

That odd, sweet smell Curt had noticed came from a vase full of white roses sitting in the middle of Angela's desk.

The three of them stood there in the doorway and just looked at the roses, until Toni joined them a moment later.

"We were the last ones out last night," she said, her voice tight and quiet. "Nobody brought those by before we left."

"And the custodian doesn't work on Friday nights," Curt had to add. He sidled around Angela, who seemed nailed to the spot in the doorway of her office.

"That's the vase we keep under the sink," Angela said. She put out an arm to stop Curt from going any further. "We all know who those are from."

"Angie..." Cooper grasped her shoulders and moved her aside just enough to slide past her. He approached the desk and bent over, bracing himself with his hands on his thighs so he didn't touch anything. "No note. Which is unusual. He usually starts with a note and leaves a rose on the second or third contact."

"Well, I think more than a dozen roses is a pretty big break from the pattern, too." Angela wrapped her arms around herself and gasped a little when Toni slid an arm around her shoulders. "That wasn't the reaction we were expecting when we decided to print the story."

Chapter Twenty

"I expected him to come after one of us or all of us," Toni said. She met Curt's eyes and he saw the misery, the guilt reflected in their dark depths. "Nothing like this."

"Oh, no..." he groaned.

"What?" Cooper came back to the doorway and gestured for them to move out. He led the way back to the lunchroom and pulled out his cell phone. "I don't care if it's Donovan's day off, he's the only one I trust to examine the scene." He scrolled through the phone book screen, searching for a number.

Curt gestured at Toni and Angela, who sat down together. Chief Cooper didn't see what he saw, and his questioning glance showed it.

"They could be close cousins, even sisters," Curt explained.

"Angel. Angela," Toni said, nodding.

"Okay. That's it." Cooper cancelled the number he had just punched in. "Anyone know Hannah's number off the top of their heads?"

"No." Angela stood up.

"Angie, it's the only smart thing to do."

"What?" Toni demanded.

"I agree with the chief," Curt said, understanding instantly. "Contact Hannah, get you out of town, to the safe house with Sheila."

"And when he sees I'm gone, he'll just pick someone else. Who do you want him to terrify next? Toni? Another schoolgirl?" Angela shook her head. "This has gone on far enough."

"That's one thing we agree on," Chief Cooper said.

"I am not running." She gestured toward the sign over her office door. "I vowed never to become part of the news, just report it. I swore that when Angel was murdered. I have to stay, Ray. I have to make sure it ends here. Now. I am certainly not going to run and let him choose someone else for his sick idea of paradise."

"Angie, just listen to—" He growled, throwing up his hands in frustration when Angela snatched up her coat and purse and stomped down the hall. He followed her, leaving his coat behind him.

"Wow," Curt muttered. "That's the first time Angela has ever run away from a fight."

"I don't think she was running." Toni shivered and wrapped her arms around herself. "She's right. It'd be wrong to run away and let the White

Rose pick someone else." She tried to laugh. "And not just because the next one might be me."

"He won't pick you." He gave in to his need and put his arm around her shoulders. "You and me, we're together, remember? Everybody who pays any attention thinks we're together, so the White Rose will leave you alone."

"He's ignored the fact that these girls don't want anything to do with him. What makes you think that a prior claim will stop him, once he decides someone is Angel, come back for him?" Toni shook her head and that hurting look in her eyes shifted to something hot, hard, and determined. "Too bad Angela and..."

"You know, I think you're right," he offered. Her puzzled little frown was almost amusing. "Angela and the chief. I think they're together, but they're so careful about it, nobody knows."

"Obviously, if the White Rose wants her now. You know, Curt... it's time for that last resort."

It took him a moment of thought, but he understood.

Time to tell the people of Tabor about Angel and how she had died and expose the White Rose's roots.

~~~~~

"Angie." Ray Cooper stood somewhere out in the aisle between the stalls. His shadow didn't fall into the stall.

Angela didn't turn around, and she was proud of herself that she didn't jump six feet in the air and fumble the saddle she had just lifted up off its bench. She finished settling the saddle on her horse's back and turned to him.

In the twenty minutes between leaving the newspaper office and him following her here to the stables, he had aged ten years, maybe more. She wanted to go to him, wrap her arms around him, try to drive away that chilled, aching look from his eyes. But how could she, when she felt so cold inside that not even the hottest afternoon Ohio produced could ever warm her again? They would both freeze together, stuck there. Wouldn't that be a lovely way for the rest of the world to learn how they felt about each other? She could just see the picture in some other newspaper, the two of them locked in an embrace, with icicles hanging off their elbows and noses.

She refused to break her cardinal rule, even in death, though she definitely had no intentions of dying just yet. No, the Coffelts reported the news. They never became the news.

"I think it's time," Ray said. He stayed out in the aisle, though he did take a step closer and braced both hands on the posts of the stall door.

"Time?"

"We've been edging around the issue for a while now. I love you, and
~~~~~

you love me. And everything that's going on, it kind of woke me up to what I want in life, and what I need. And I'm hoping you need me just as much."

"Ray—"

"I want to marry you, Angie."

She wanted to laugh. She wanted to scream. She seriously considered scooping up the brush she had pulled out, to remind her to buy a new one next time she went to the tack store and lobbing it at him.

"How about we make it official?" he hurried on, taking one step into the stall. "Shock the whole town, put our engagement announcement in Tuesday's paper?"

"I suppose you want it on the front page." Angela opted for laughing.

"No, that'd be slapping him in the face a little too much. But he has to know."

"This isn't about us, is it? This is about the White Rose."

"It's definitely about us. And you wouldn't be in danger from him right now if we had both had the guts to take our feelings for each other out into broad daylight." Some of the chill left his eyes, and she realized that mixed in with his fear for her was shame.

"Ray, don't blame yourself—"

"You bet I blame myself. I love you, Angie. What kind of an idiot lets some stupid small-town politics push him into hiding his feelings for the most incredible woman—" He choked and finally let go of the door posts to take another step closer to her,.

"You want to use our engagement to scare the White Rose away. But what if it just pushes him to strike?" she hurried on, when he opened his mouth to respond. "Ray, I've thought about what you said before, wondering just how healthy our relationship is, if we hide it. But even more, I've been thinking about Sam Conrad."

"What does he have to do with this?" He rested his hands on her shoulders. Just like always, his touch sent a jolt of warmth through her, and gave her a feeling of steadiness, of solidity that she had been missing since she saw those roses on her desk.

"What if the White Rose attacks you? I can't risk it."

"What about the risk to you?"

"Ray..." She fought down the thick sense of pressure in her throat and was stunned when the feeling turned into choked laughter. The sound grew stronger when his eyes widened, just as stunned as her. "This is so idiotic..." Angela sighed and rested her hands on his upper arms. "I know I've said I don't care about romance, but honestly, this is the worst reason to get married that I've ever heard of."

"I can't think of a better reason to get married, than to protect the woman who means more to me than anyone or anything." He let out a groan, just a second after he turned into a teary blur in her eyes and wrapped his arms tight around her.

Angela admitted in that moment, as the ice fled her bones and the warm, clean, cotton-and-leather scent of him filled her lungs, he couldn't have done anything more persuasive. Even before the White Rose Killer emerged from the shadows of the past, being held in Ray Cooper's arms for the rest of her life had become a temptation that was harder to resist with every day that passed.

She wasn't sure if it would be wise to admit that to him. Even after they were married. And just considering the possibility of that shocked and amused her, and sent a throb of longing through her, as well.

"Well it's about time," Diane Cooper drawled, just about the same time Angela registered the sound of footsteps in the straw of the aisle.

"Di—" Ray began. He held onto Angela when she tried to step back out of his arms.

"For heaven's sake, Daddy, do you two honestly think I don't know? Okay, you're a cop, the king of secrecy and all that garbage, but..." She jammed her fists into her hips, and the glare she aimed at them was ruined by the laughter in her eyes. "I approve, okay? Stop using me as an excuse to be a coward."

"An excuse—"

"But I think maybe we'd all be more comfortable if I didn't call Angela 'Mom,' okay?" She winked at them.

"Okay," Angela managed to say. She wanted to laugh, but Ray was still staring at his daughter as if he couldn't translate what she had just said. "So I'm guessing we have your blessing?"

"Just don't make me wear a dorky bridesmaid dress. That's all I ask." Diane raised her arms in the universal gesture of "whatever," and backed away. "I'm gonna get out of here and give you some privacy, but I want some hard facts by the end of the month. A date, the honeymoon spot, and if I should call Mr. Coffelt 'Grandpa' or something else." She giggled as she vanished down the aisle.

Angela and Ray stood there a few seconds, listening to the sound of Diane's boots racing down the aisle and out of the stables. They looked at each other, their smiles growing a little wider with every heartbeat. Then they laughed, and he drew her against his chest again, squeezing her almost to the point of threatening her breath.

"Well, that's one less excuse," he muttered.

"I don't want excuses anymore," she admitted.

"Then—"

"All I want is to wait until this is all cleared up." Her voice caught. "It has to be over soon."

"I promise," he growled, pressing his face into her hair.

"Promise me you'll wait until this is all over, and life is boring again. Then you can ask me." She took a deep breath. "And I won't be hurt if you don't ask."

"I'll ask. I'll be there with witnesses when they haul the White Rose off to jail."

~~~~~

Toni and Curt both had obligations Saturday afternoon, so they met again at his apartment Saturday evening to work on the story. She was flattered that he liked the rough draft she had done. If it weren't for the grimness of the subject matter and their objective, she would have enjoyed the quiet evening at the table in his kitchen, munching on popcorn and making revisions and then revisions of revisions.

The story took far fewer words than she had expected when she first conceived of the idea. Toni was almost surprised to do a word count and see how short it was. It felt so huge. It took so much time and effort to revise and refine.

She imagined Angel's spirit, watching over her shoulder. Would her sister approve of this last-ditch effort to get through to the boy who had loved her and murdered her in pitiful, adolescent jealous rage?

"You know what the hard part of this is going to be?" Curt said, when he came back to the table. He had decided to order Chinese takeout to celebrate the final draft and completion of their story.

"Convincing Angela to let us run it," Toni said, not needing to guess. "Maybe you should just slot it into the paper without asking her."

"I should. She'll refuse to run it for the same reason she refused to go to the safe house."

"To protect anyone else who looks like Angel." She nodded, managing a smile. Suddenly, she was so tired her bones ached. "What made him choose her, after all this time? She's been there at the front lines, so to speak, writing about him. And those few times the TV reporters caught up with the chief and she was with him, she didn't hang back. Why didn't he pick on her until now?"

"We can figure that out after we catch him." Curt cupped her cheek and the gentle, warm touch took her breath away. "You gotta understand something, Toni. I'm only doing this because I know it has to be done. I still think running the story will get him stirred up enough to put you, specifically, in danger."

"You'll protect me, won't you?" She tried to smile. Her only choices were to either make a joke or cry. She refused to cry. That would give another victory to the White Rose, and she had cried too many tears because of him already.

"You better believe it." He pulled her up out of her chair and wrapped his arms around her. They stood there in silence, holding each other, until
~~~~~

the delivery girl from the Chinese restaurant rang the doorbell.

Later, as she curled up in her chilly bed and stared at the light reflecting from the streetlights, Toni decided the only thing that could have made that moment perfect was if Curt had kissed her. And not that comforting brush of a kiss across her forehead. She wanted a real kiss, lips meeting and warmth and tingles up and down her spine.

Would Curt run away or laugh if she told him?

Monday, January 20

All hopes of hiding the White Rose's attentions shattered when the staff showed up for work and a bouquet of roses lay on the floor in front of Angela's locked office door. Curt snarled at Loni when she bent to pick up the paper-wrapped bundle, saying she would put them in a vase of water for Angela. He silently cursed himself for not coming to work even ten minutes sooner.

"Nobody can touch those," he said, after muttering an apology to the photographer.

"But they're so pretty. Even if they are white, which is pretty bad taste, considering everything that's been going on with white roses lately. Whoever sent them... wait a minute. I unlocked the door. I was the first one in." Loni's face paled and she took a step back. "They're from him, aren't they?"

Fortunately, Loni wasn't someone who fell apart in bad situations. She stood guard over the roses while Curt called Donovan.

Unfortunately, the police officer hadn't come into the office yet. Curt went through three different officers, all offering to help. Each time he explained it had to do with the White Rose, the men he spoke to wanted to know if any progress had been made. Curt appreciated the fact that Chief Cooper had trimmed the number of people who were handling the information, to avoid security leaks, but it made things difficult. Everyone wanted to know what was going on. Curt hated irritating someone who might be a source in the future. He especially hated saying no to someone who had been helpful in the past.

He finally got someone who said Donovan had just walked into the station. After that, it was a matter of moments to explain and for the officer to promise he was on his way over. Donovan had come in on his day off to take the vase of roses from Angela's office and examine the entire room for evidence of the White Rose's presence. Her office was locked now because it was a mess with fingerprint powder, and to avoid losing any clues that hadn't been discovered yet. Curt had no idea how Angela was going to do her job today, without access to her office. He could only hope that would make it easier to sneak his and Toni's expose into the paper tonight.

Chief Cooper followed Angela into the office and they had an argument that couldn't be hidden behind the closed door of the supply room. His urging her to leave town for the safe house turned into an order.

No one gave Angela Coffelt orders.

Once he was gone, Angela called a staff meeting, including the people at the front of the office. Curt breathed a sigh of relief that Myrna wasn't working today. If the old woman stayed true to form, she would dominate the meeting and turn everything around to how Angela's situation affected *her*. Then, she would ignore her phone duties and the front desk and spend the rest of the day on the phone, spreading an exaggerated and warped version of the facts to everyone she knew in the county.

"Some of you may have noticed a little tension between Chief Cooper and me," Angela said.

She flinched when Andrew came into the newsroom and put his arm around her shoulders. From the look on the old man's face, Curt guessed the police chief had intercepted him on the way in and told him about this latest development.

"You may have noticed my door is closed, which isn't usual for Mondays." Angela looked around the room, at the somber faces. Curt noticed she avoided looking at him and Toni. "We have discovered new information about the White Rose, only some of which was included in last week's story. He's looking for a specific girl, and it seems that now I fit the criteria."

The gasps, curses, muttered comments, and generally horrified and angry expressions that filled the room were gratifying to Curt. Despite their occasional differences, they were a family at the *Tabor Picayune*. He knew Angela would be able to count on them for discretion and emotional support through the days that followed.

If he and Toni had anything to do with it, those days would be very short and the White Rose Killer wouldn't leave any more roses for Angela.

He and Toni both stayed quiet as Angela outlined the precautions that she had agreed to with Chief Cooper. She would never be alone anywhere. The telephone system and her home phone were due to have wiretaps and tracers installed, in case the White Rose continued to break his pattern and called her. No deliveries for Angela would be accepted until a police officer looked through them first.

"And I'm asking all of you to keep this entirely secret. We are not going to tell anyone what is going on here. The White Rose is probably watching and knows about the police activity here at the office, but we're going to tone everything down and go on with life as usual. As much as we're able," she added with a short-lived, crooked smile.

"That's the spirit," Andrew muttered.

"Angela?" Loni took a step away from the wall where she had been leaning. "Wouldn't it be safer to just go to a safe house, get out of town for a while, like Tracy Brickman and Sheila McGuire?"

"I don't have that option." Angela raised a hand, silencing the comments before they burst out. "I have a newspaper to run. I'm not a schoolgirl without obligations. And as we've seen amply demonstrated, as soon as the White Rose realizes his true love has deserted him, he finds someone else."

"Try the classifieds for a change," Ted muttered, just loudly enough it was obviously intended for everyone to hear. "You get better results."

Angela's shoulders shook, as if she started to laugh and choked on it. Curt didn't really like Ted, but at that moment, he could have hugged the abrasive salesman in pure gratitude. The atmosphere lightened measurably.

"We don't want him targeting someone else," Angela said, looking around the room and meeting everyone's eyes, including Curt and Toni this time. "We're going to take what we learned with the other targets and we're going to use it to lead the White Rose into a trap. This ends here and it ends... I wish I could say *when* it will end, but God help us, it *will* end soon." Her eyes glistened with the first hint of tears, and she turned to go into her office. She paused for a long, painful moment in front of the closed door. Then she grasped the handle, turned it, and went inside. Andrew never released contact with her, keeping a hand on her shoulder.

"It ends tomorrow," Toni murmured, standing so close behind him, Curt felt the warmth of her breath against his ear. "As soon as the first paper hits the street."

Chapter Twenty-One

Their plan required creating a duplicate set of layout pages for the newspaper and deciding which pieces to bump to make room for Toni's story to run. They put it on the front page, but on the bottom half. It took some juggling and refiguring to take the two stories that were originally slated for the front page and put them further into the paper. They ended up trimming the community focus column and entirely deleting two of the events calendars. Curt wondered how many oblivious people would call to complain that their club meeting didn't appear and totally ignore the significance and seriousness of Angel's story.

Angela sent the master layout sheets via courier to the printing company that handled the *Picayune* at 7:30, just before Chief Cooper came to escort her and Andrew home. Curt called the printer at 7:35, when everyone else had left the office, and said something had changed at the last minute, so ignore the first set of sheets. Then he transmitted the new story, the trimmed column, and the kill order for the two pieces over the Internet connection. He and Toni drove the new sheets out to the printer, an hour away, and waited until the front page came off the presses.

"That's pretty rough," the shift foreman commented after looking over the page proof with them. "It's all true?"

"All true," Curt said. Toni could only nod, her eyes bright with angry tears.

"Hope they catch that creep and string him up," the man growled.

"That's the plan." He put his arm around Toni, thanked the foreman, and led her out to his car.

"We are so dead, once Angela finds out," she muttered as she slid into the passenger seat.

"Just as long as it's us, and our jobs, and not Angela."

Tuesday, January 21

ANGEL IS DEAD
The truth about the White Rose Murders

By Antoinette Napolitano

With Curt Mehdlang

My parents, my sister, Angelique and I moved to Tabor twenty-two years ago this spring. Angel was ten. We went to Eloise Elementary, where the Mission is now.

Our parents loved Tabor because it was so quiet and safe, and they didn't worry when Angel and I walked down to the corner store for candy by ourselves. We liked our new home. Angel was very popular because she was smart and pretty and kind to everyone, but nobody understood how painfully shy she was. Some girls thought she was a snob because she didn't run around with them. The fact was, Angel was afraid. She didn't like big, noisy groups. She didn't feel comfortable with more than three or four people, because she had a little bit of a hearing problem and she couldn't keep up with conversations in large groups.

I said all this to make it easier to understand what happened the fall Angel turned twelve. The whole boy-girl thing got going in earnest from the first day of seventh grade and every boy in town seemed to want Angel to be his girlfriend. They followed her home from school and left notes and little presents in her locker and they came by on the weekends. Some girls hated her because she could have had any boy she wanted, but other girls realized how hard all this was on her, and they tried to be her friends and offer advice.

All that pressure just made Angel retreat even more. And the faster someone runs, the harder people try to catch her. It's human nature. Boys kept trying to make her their girlfriend and Angel kept saying no. I think seventh grade was the most miserable time of her life. Our parents didn't understand. They thought it was adolescence. I didn't understand, because I wasn't in the same building, let alone the same classes.

Then something changed. Angel smiled more, and every time I looked in her room, she was writing in her diary. The boys who came by our house didn't bother her anymore, because she was hardly ever there when they came to see her. She went to the library and the park by herself as often as she could and stayed away from home for hours at a time.

Angel had a boyfriend. A secret boyfriend.

He made her very happy.

I found her diary later, and all the notes her boyfriend sent to her. She had a shoebox full of little trinkets that he gave her, gumball machine rings and dried flowers and candy bar wrappers and all sorts of little things that a junior high boy could afford.

Angel was in love and she was happy. And I hate to say it, but I was jealous. Normally, I would have tattled on her to my parents. Especially when she made me walk home from school alone, or when she left the house without telling anyone. But I was so angry, I kept it to myself. Maybe I was hoping that she would get caught and get in trouble. And despite being jealous, I didn't want her to blame me when my parents caught her and ended it.

I should have tattled. I should have followed her and spied to see who her boyfriend was.

The jealous girls told lies about Angel. And the boys who couldn't get anywhere with her called her a tramp and made up their own lies.

Angel's boyfriend got jealous. He didn't believe her when she said the rumors were all lies. He thought he owned Angel. He thought she lied to him when she promised that he was the only boy she would ever love.

On Saturday, May 15, Angel went to the park to meet her boyfriend. Her diary entry that morning said she was frustrated with him because he still wouldn't believe her. She didn't know what to do to convince him that he was the only boy she had ever kissed. There were tearstains on the page when I read it only a few weeks later.

Angel didn't come home. Her boyfriend strangled her and left her lying in the mud in the park. Dead.

No one knew who Angel's boyfriend was. No one knew she had a boyfriend, except me, and she never told me his name. She never wrote his name down in her diary. He never signed his name on any of the notes. Why did he need to sign his name to love letters and Valentines and cards on presents, if he was the only one she loved?

He never identified himself to my family. If he came to the funeral home and the cemetery, he never told us. He left white roses on her grave, and he nearly killed one boy who told lies about her. He attacked that boy from behind, in the dark, so his victim never saw his face.

Just like his victims today have never seen his face.

I know who Angel's boyfriend is. I know who killed Angel, my big sister.

He is the White Rose Killer.

He is the man who terrorized and stalked and threatened Gretchen McKenzie, Katrina Harper, Annalee Gray, Tracy Brickman and Sheila McGuire. He is the man who killed Gretchen, Katrina and Annalee after he claimed he loved them.

The White Rose is a murderer. He is a criminal. He is evil. He does not know how to love. He has done nothing to earn the love of anyone.

The only one who ever loved him was Angel, my sister, and he killed her, first.

~~~~~

"Explain to me why I shouldn't fire both of you?" Angela said.

Toni's heart ached for her. Angela leaned against her desk, both hands braced on either side of the front page. She looked tired, more than furious. The printer wouldn't have called Angela about the switch in layout because Curt had the authority to make those changes. The only thing that could have awakened her in the middle of the night and stolen her sleep was thinking about the White Rose calling her his true love.

Maybe later, when the shock had worn off, Angela would get angry. Toni felt a strange, calm sense of fascination, wondering how she would act when she was angry. The woman was such a class act, it was hard to imagine her furious with anyone.

"Maybe you should." Curt stood three steps back from Angela's desk, instead of sitting in his usual chair facing her, with his arms crossed over
~~~~~

his chest. "Insubordination and all that rot. I agree. I'd probably urge you to fire someone else, under the circumstances. But it's those circumstances that make me think this was the right thing to do."

"And you can't really fire me," Toni added. "I'm only here temporarily. Until the White Rose is caught. And like you said, this has to end. This story will help bring it to an end. We all but called him a coward and a liar and dared him to reveal his face and his name."

"And brought you forward to become his next target. Think about Sam Conrad, who got in his way and Bobby Hollander. I remember Bobby now." Angela's eyes went distant. "Nobody knew why he was beat up and left hanging in a tree in the park, until your parents found Angel's diary, and she named him as someone who told lies about her. Bobby was in the hospital for a week with stitches and a concussion and broken fingers. That was what a teenage boy did to him. Imagine what that grown man can do to you today, to punish you for telling the world about him." Angela took a deep breath, visibly fighting for calm. "Such a story shouldn't have been used except as a last resort."

"And it's time for that last resort," Curt said.

"No, it isn't." She paused as the sound of the phone ringing echoed down the hall. "The storm is just starting to hit. I don't know if it's a blessing to have Myrna on the phones today to fight with people, or if she'll just make things worse. Don't talk to anyone about this story, do you hear me? No TV reporters, no one in this office, no one in town. If you have to go home and hide in your basement—"

"Apartment," Curt said with a shrug. "No basement."

Angela picked up her desk calendar and flung it at him. A tiny, gasping laugh escaped her and she sank down in her chair. "Get out of here. Both of you. Call it a personal day. Mental health day."

"Only if you take one for yourself," Toni said. "You need it even more than we do."

To her surprise and relief, Angela nodded and laughed, with tears in her eyes.

~~~~~

When he got to work that morning, to prepare for the afternoon shift, the police station seemed to ring with excitement. The buzz of energy in the air vibrated unpleasantly against the contentment that had filled him ever since he realized his true angel, Angela, had been waiting for him all these years. His first love letter to her waited in the trunk of his car, ready to be delivered to her house this evening after he got off work.

"Did you read the *Picayune*?" Joe asked when he approached the front desk.

"What about it?" Not that he cared what the *Picayune* said. It was all lies. He shrugged and kept walking toward the squad room, to read the
~~~~~

duty roster and find out if anything had changed. He had to get hold of Donovan before the man went off duty and try to learn if anything new was being done in the hunt for the White Rose. He had to protect himself, after all, so he could protect his angel.

"News about the White Rose." Joe rapped the folded paper against the counter. "Sheds a whole new light on things. Man, I thought the guy was sick before. Now I know he's a psycho. Hard to believe he's been living here all these years, just waiting to bust out and—"

Joe snapped to attention and the gleeful expression shifted to serious. Turning, he saw Chief Cooper cross from his office and approach the front desk.

"Watkins, call everybody into the squad room," Chief Cooper said. His gaze barely skimmed over the other men standing around the desk. "I have an important announcement to make."

Ten minutes later, every available officer had crammed into the squad room. The usual chatter and joking were missing, driven away by the sight of Chief Cooper standing by the podium, hands clasped behind his back, head bowed.

"By now," Chief Cooper began, "most of you have probably read the story in today's paper. I want you all to know it is true. I've been working with the reporters who wrote the story. We've suspected for quite some time now that the White Rose Killer was responsible for the death of Angelique Napolitano twenty years ago, and his current murder streak is related to her death."

Sitting in the back of the room, he felt as if a wall of ice had slammed down on him and encased him from head to toe. He couldn't breathe, couldn't move, couldn't even blink. He wanted to turn his head so he wouldn't see Chief Cooper's lying face, so serious, so calm, as if he spoke the truth instead of the cruel, vicious lies coming out of his mouth. He wanted to put his fingers in his ears to keep from hearing. He wanted to shout and drown out the sound. But he couldn't do anything.

"I'm sure all of you are deeply angered that Officer Frank McGuire's niece, Sheila, was targeted by the White Rose. I'm sure Frank will appreciate your support and encouragement at this time. Be assured that Sheila is safe. We acted quickly and got her out of town before anything happened more drastic than a couple notes. But we have a serious problem here, people. The White Rose has access to our schools. He got into the dormitories at the university, to stalk his victim. All indications are he had keys. There was no breaking and entering. He got into the middle school and left notes in Sheila's locker." Chief Cooper stepped back from the podium, holding it at arm's length for a moment. He closed his eyes and swallowed hard. Even from the back of the room, his struggle for composure was visible.

The White Rose thought he could hear every officer breathing, hear their heartbeats, the silence was so deep and pervasive in the room.

"I know all of you have taken these attacks on the women of our community personally, and you have helped in every way possible. Because of evident security leaks, Officer Donovan and I have cut most of you out of the loop. Well, now we're opening that loop wide. Because the White Rose is hitting home more personally than I can express. His new target is Angela Coffelt, editor of the *Picayune*. Angela is more than a friend to me. I'm asking you as your commander, and I'm asking you as your friend, help me find the White Rose and stop him, because now he's threatening the woman I love."

He didn't hear anything more, though he was vaguely aware that Chief Cooper continued to speak. Then Donovan stepped forward to speak, and some of the officers in the room asked questions that both men answered.

No. It wasn't true. It was all lies. Chief Cooper wasn't in love with Angela. Angela didn't love Chief Cooper. Angela loved *him*, had loved him ever since middle school, had wanted him and waited for him even when he was an idiot and chased Angel Napolitano.

"Hey, you okay?" Mike Nichols slapped his arm with the folded paper he had carried into the squad room.

"Hmm? Oh, yeah. Thanks." He stood up and looked around. The room was empty. "Just stunned, I guess."

"Man, that's the truth. Who would have thought the chief was getting it on with anybody?" Hobbs said, catching up with them as they went down the hall to the outer office of the station. "Of course, being the chief and Ms. Coffelt being the classy lady she is and working at the paper, it's no wonder they kept it hush-hush." He nodded. Eagerness gleamed in his eyes. "When the news hits the street..." He whistled. "You can bet those slimebag politicians are going to have a field day with this. Anything they can use against the chief or the paper, they will." He nodded and trotted back to his post at the front desk.

He watched Hobbs go and didn't even try to repress his sneer. If anybody was going to spread the gossip, it would be Hobbs. The man couldn't keep his mouth shut for ten minutes. The chief had probably instituted security lockup because of Hobbs.

The chief. What was he going to do about the chief? How could the chief have betrayed him like this, stealing his true love?

She had betrayed him. She had to be punished. She didn't deserve to live, after what she had done. She had lied to him and betrayed him, just like all the others.

Just like before.

From the very beginning.

"Some story, huh?" Steve Peters stepped up next to him. "I went to school with Angel. I remember Bob Hollander, shooting off his filthy mouth, claiming he could get Angel to do the nasty with him when she wouldn't look at anyone else. Everybody knew he was a liar. Remember that trouble he got in, when we were in tenth grade? Glad to see that jerk leave town." He unfolded the paper and scowled down at the story spread out on it. "I guess the White Rose was the only idiot who believed him. Man, what kind of sicko kills a girl who loves him?"

"Can I see that?" It took all his self-control to hold out a steady hand for the paper and not snatch it. He thanked Steve with a nod and concentrated on strolling, no hurry in the world, to the locker room.

He read the story through three times before it sank in. Most of the words turned into a jumble in front of his eyes, a foreign language that he had to read over and over to force a translation. He thought about the story as he changed into his uniform. He thought about Toni, how she had been so nice to him when they were children, and how she had been so nice to him now.

She was a liar. She lied about Angel. She had told lies to all his angels and made them afraid and made them hate him. She had to be punished.

Chapter Twenty-Two

"You're serious?" Toni laughed, and that felt strange after the tension of the morning.

The phones had been ringing off the hook when they left the office on Angela's orders. Myrna was in her usual form, playing "authority on everything worth knowing" while Max and Ty and the entire circulation staff scrambled to handle the phones that she let ring and ring and ring. Curt's phone had been ringing when they retreated to his apartment, reasoning that the security door would keep most intruders away. There were already ten messages on his answering machine. Even when he turned off the ringer, the constant stream of messages being left on his machine couldn't be ignored.

Two types of people called. There were the ones who wanted to get more information from Curt for their own investigations: TV and newspaper reporters, true crime novelists, and private investigators. Toni couldn't understand why private eyes would involve themselves in the White Rose case. Maybe make a name for themselves by solving it? And there were those who wanted to offer their theories about the White Rose and their memories of the Napolitano family and Angel's death.

When the fifth message began, from someone who wouldn't identify herself, her voice shrill with self-importance, Curt grabbed Toni's arm and fled.

At her house, amazingly, there were no messages. They had a blessed half hour of quiet to sit and make coffee and try to settle down to watch a movie. Then the curious and stubborn managed to find her phone number. Her answering machine was in the kitchen. They turned off the ringer and closed the sliding door leading to the living room, but that only offered so much insulation. They still heard the loud voices, even if they couldn't make out the words.

They watched a movie, then took a chance on the news and were relieved that the story on the White Rose hadn't made the news. Maybe the stations were waiting for the noon broadcast, and to get a little more information together.

The prospect of watching another movie, afraid to go into her own kitchen and hear those messages coming in on her answering machine, almost felt like torture. Then Curt made his totally ridiculous suggestion.

"I'm serious," Curt said, grinning like a bad boy bent on mischief.

"Run away." Toni flinched as the answering machine clicked on and a man with an old-sounding, creaky voice started explaining how he knew her family. She wanted to hit the delete button, to stop the message before it recorded. Doing that would hang up the phone and let the caller know someone was home.

"Eventually, they're going to get tired of leaving messages and they're going to come here. I say we make our escape while we can." Curt hooked his thumb over his shoulder at the kitchen door and outside.

"And go where?" she challenged.

Strange, how light-hearted she felt in the middle of all this chaos. Maybe it was the weird sense of knowing how celebrities felt. Would they be surrounded by paparazzi soon?

"How about the zoo?"

"In January?"

"Why not? Nobody else will be there. We can take lunch and have a picnic."

"Again I say: in January?"

"There's the Rainforest. They have a café. We can bring food with us, take our time seeing all the exhibits without a thousand kids getting in the way, make faces at the monkeys, whatever we want. And we can eat indoors."

"You're serious about the picnic?" When Curt nodded, she pointed at the door leading down into the cellar. "The last tenants left a picnic basket down there. Get it for me, will you? I'll ransack this place to see what I've got worth eating."

"We could just stop at KFC and get a bucket," he grumbled, but he grinned and opened the door and started down the stairs.

"That wouldn't be half as much fun," she called after him.

"Yeah, but how much fun will you have if the monster in the basement eats me?" He stomped extra hard on the steps.

Toni laughed, the sound catching in her throat when it hit her how much she would miss Curt when she had to leave Tabor Heights. She didn't want to leave, but after the stunt they had pulled with the story, would Angela give her a chance? Sure, she got along great with Curt. They were best pals. They worked well together. He worried about her. But was it enough to prompt him to ask her to stay? She had already made a fool out of herself once, pursuing a man who wasn't interested in her enough to make things work. Toni refused to ruin this friendship with Curt by hounding him. Better to lose him because she moved away, and still have some hope, some sense of "might have been," rather than drive him away.

At least, she had herself *mostly* convinced that was true.

The knock on the door startled her so she dropped the jar of peanut butter. It bounced on the counter and hit the rag rug in front of the counter.

Fortunately, the jar was plastic. She picked it up and slid it back onto the counter before going to the front door. She paused just before she stepped into the living room, remembering what Curt had said about people coming to her home. What if Myrna had gotten irritated with all the people looking for her and Curt, and started handing out her address?

Toni peeked between the living room curtains. The sight of a police cruiser made her heart skip a few beats. She couldn't see who was standing on the front step. Probably Donovan, with news.

She pulled the door open, then wondered: wouldn't Donovan have called Curt's cell phone? For a moment, she stood and blinked at the officer standing there. She knew him, but since she didn't expect him, it threw her off balance.

"Got a minute?" He wore that crooked grin from the first time they met. "Wanted to talk to you about the story you wrote about Angel."

"Oh, please..." Toni groaned. It turned into a chuckle and she stepped back. "Come on in. You caught me just in time. I'm getting — "

"Liar," he growled, and backhanded her. Pain exploded black through her face as she stumbled backward and hit the photo collage on the wall with the back of her head. It fell and shattered. The front door slammed before she could even take a breath through the jagged sensation that blinded her, and she slid to her knees. "Liar," he shouted, and kicked her in the ribs.

The White Rose. Through the hot, paralyzing agony and the taste of blood in her mouth, Toni finally knew. It made all the sense in the world.

The new kid in town.

He stomped on her hand. She screamed.

~~~~~

The thud from upstairs made Curt jerk while he was on his knees, reaching under the dust-crusted shelving. He banged his head on the shelf above him. Wincing, he pressed his hand against the back of his head. Right above where he had those stitches. Life certainly was exciting with Toni around.

He listened and heard her footsteps moving through the kitchen over his head. He saw light through some spots in the floorboards above his head. If Toni was going to stay here, he would have to see about improving the insulation and other things. Sure, it was a rental, but Mandy was a good landlord who only needed to be told once that her property needed fixing. And what if Toni decided to make it a rent-to-own? He liked the idea of Toni buying this cottage. Spending lots of evenings together, talking about stories, watching movies, making plans for goofing off.

All right, he made himself face it. He wanted Toni to stick around after the White Rose was caught. Nothing wrong with that.
~~~~~

A man spoke, the words muffled. Curt was on his feet, responding to the sudden shiver down his back before he realized Toni had moved far to the right overhead, to the front door. She hadn't let anyone in the house, had she?

"Liar!" a man shouted.

Footsteps banged overhead. He heard a thud, then a crash of glass breaking, just as his feet hit the stairs.

Curt hit the top step and skidded on the kitchen floor. Toni screamed. He banged against the kitchen counter before he could turn. A tall, broad-shouldered, dark-haired shape in a blue uniform kicked Toni in the ribs.

"Toni!" Curt roared and slipped on the throw rug on the floor.

The man picked up Toni by her hair and dragged her halfway to her feet, then bent to put her over his shoulder. Curt flew across the living room and tackled them. They went down in a tangle. He tried to yank Toni out of the man's arms. She writhed, fighting him, pulling them both off balance. The man swore, a low, animal sound. Curt got a fist in his face, a boot in his gut. Toni screamed again. Something cracked and snapped and thudded against a wall. The door suddenly slammed him in the face. Heat gushed across his face, with a blossoming ache in his nose. Curt fought off the spinning sensation and clawed at the wall to try to get upright. Somehow, he was upside down, with his blood flowing from his nose into his eyes. He heard an engine roar and tires spinning. Blinking blood out of his eyes, he rolled over and scrambled on hands and knees to the open door. He saw the tail end of a black-and-white roar down the street and turn into the police station parking lot.

"He's a cop." He spat blood. Curt sat back, struggling to catch his breath. Sharp aches blossomed through his body.

Toni. She was hurt. She had screamed. He had felt the hot stickiness of her blood on his hands when he tackled her and the White Rose.

"No," he growled, when he turned and saw her lying in a crumpled heap, like a rag doll left out in the rain and mud. Curt curled himself around her, needing to hold her, afraid to move her. There was blood all over her face, her clothes. Was her neck twisted wrong?

It took painful effort to clear his thoughts enough to think and pull out his cell phone and dial 911. Ridiculous, to use the phone when the police were just across the street.

But a police officer had tried to kill Toni. His brain caught on that fact and wouldn't let him match up the pieces and put a name to the face.

He couldn't leave Toni. He wouldn't let go of her. He had kept the White Rose from taking her away. Curt made himself concentrate on that.

When he finally got the dispatcher off the phone, he called Donovan. His friend swore for the first time Curt could ever remember, and they had grown up together.

Donovan ran across the street. Curt thought maybe he would laugh about it later. He sat in Toni's doorway, wrapped around her as much as he could be without moving her, and watched Donovan break all speed records to race up the street.

"EMTs are on their way," Donovan blurted before he dropped to his knees next to Toni. He ran his hands over her face, down her neck, checking her ribs. "I think something's broken here. Ribs," he hurried to say, when Curt muffled a moan, imagining the worst.

Toni whimpered, and both men grinned at each other at that sign of life.

"Toni, can you hear me?" Donovan leaned over her, gently brushing bloody hair out of her face. She whimpered something and her eyes started to flutter. "Just hold still. You're okay."

"Not," she groaned. "Head's ready to bust."

"Yeah, well, it looks a lot worse," Curt offered. He felt giddy, and that was ridiculous.

"He — gone?"

"Yeah, he's gone."

"My hero." She got her eyes open and tried to lift her head. She moaned, her eyes rolled back and she subsided into a limp pile.

"Told her to hold still," Donovan said. "Want to tell me what happened?" He looked up as a siren sounded down the street.

"The White Rose is a cop." Any other time, Curt would have laughed at the open-mouthed shock on Donovan's face.

"No."

"I saw a blue uniform. I saw the Tabor badge on his shoulder. Toni wouldn't have opened her door to anyone but a cop."

"Did you see —"

"Yeah, I got bits of his face, but I can't put a name on him." Curt growled and slammed his fist into his thigh. "I saw his car drive away and turn into the lot, with a dozen other cruisers. Lost in seconds. Hidden." He reached for the porch post and levered himself to his feet.

"Where do you think you're going?" Donovan grabbed his arm to stop him.

"Maybe he's still there, laying low —" He groaned when his sudden movement made his head ache and spin.

"You're not going anywhere, except to the hospital with Toni." He stood up when the sound of the siren got closer. "The only thing you're allowed to do is watch out for her, hear me? Two less people we have to worry about." Donovan's face went icy calm and pale, and gut instinct told Curt there was something his friend hadn't told him yet.

"What is it?"

"The chief held a meeting, not half an hour ago, everyone on duty and coming on duty. He asked them to help us end this because the White Rose was threatening Angela. He told us all that he loved her."

"Oh, I bet the White Rose loved hearing that." He sat down again, feeling like his stomach would empty. Visions of how the White Rose Killer had captured and killed his previous victims raced through his mind. "Angela won't suspect anything, just like Toni didn't. He can grab her in broad daylight."

"I'm on it. You stick with Toni." Donovan pulled his cell phone out of his pocket and hurried back across the street as the EMT truck slid around the corner.

~~~~~

The newspaper office was in chaos and it took all his self-control not to reach for his nightstick when the animals filling the reception area turned to him, demanding answers. He hated them for expecting him to fix everything, just because he wore a police uniform. He wasn't there for them. He only existed to make the town safe enough for Angel to return.

Angela had lied. Just like all the others.

She had to be punished.

"I have a message for Miss Coffelt from Chief Cooper," he said, pushing through the crowd to the counter. "Where is she?"

Myrna Calhoun stood up, her scowling mouth bright in the same disgusting orange lipstick she had worn when she was his teacher in high school. He wished he had hit her with more baseballs. She would look better with a broken nose. He had heard that if the nose was hit hard enough, at just the right angle, splinters of bone would penetrate the brain and bring instant death. He should have tried it years ago. He would be a hero in Tabor Heights, rescuing generations of innocent children from Myrna Calhoun's arrogance.

Everyone was calling him a murderer, and it was Angela Coffelt's fault.

Why did she lie about him? Why did she lie to him?

"The chief ought to know where she is. They spend far too much time together." Myrna sniffed. "If you ask me, there's something unethical about the chief of police and the newspaper editor spending so much social time together." She narrowed her eyes. "I know you, don't I?"

"No."

"Well you tell the chief that he's doing a lousy job of protecting this town if he can't keep track of a woman who practically lives at his stables. It's undignified, how she comes in here smelling of horses."

"You wouldn't know dignified if it gave you a black eye," he growled, and backed away when he wanted to reach across the counter and throttle her. "Somebody should have given you one a long time ago."

"How dare you!" Myrna screeched, the sound nearly drowned out by
~~~~~

laughter from half the people crowded into the reception area.

The looks of admiration, the sense of being a hero, didn't soothe the aching fury that shot through him in rhythm with his laboring heart. He fled the office, fighting to breathe, hating the certainty that he would burst into tears like the pitiful, badgered boy he had been so many years ago.

Everything would be all right soon. He knew where to find Angela. Once he punished her, everything would be all right again. And maybe when she was gone, his Angel would finally come for him.

~~~~~

Toni was asleep when the nurse finally let Curt into her hospital room to sit with her. The woman reported her prognosis looked good. He couldn't get comfortable in the chair by the side of her bed, so he lowered the bed rail and sat on the side of the mattress, legs folded up against his chest and his arms wrapped around his legs, so he could rest his chin on his knees. The pain lines had softened and in the shadows of the room, her bruises and the swelling didn't look quite so bad.

Curt relived her scream, the feeling of her blood on his hands. He was positive most of the blood staining his clothes was hers, not his.

The White Rose Killer was a police officer. Hiding in plain sight. Hiding where he could get the information on all the efforts to protect his victims. He could walk all over Tabor and spy on his victims and nobody would think anything of it. He could get into any public building, get keys from maintenance and security people without anyone questioning why he needed them. People would tell him anything he wanted to know. He probably talked to all his victims a dozen times a day and they never suspected a thing. Because innocent people trusted the police.

Toni had opened the door to him because he wore a uniform. She trusted him, just like Angel had trusted him when he was a kid in junior high and said he loved her.

Curt wracked his brains for the details of the boys who had grown up in Tabor, trying to remember which ones had become police officers. Thinking made his head hurt. Would it make any difference if he could or couldn't come up with the names? Donovan knew, and he would protect Angela. That would have to be enough for now.

The silence was comforting. It let him hear the soft, whispering sound of Toni breathing. Curt ignored the ache in his back from the position he sat in, and the wet spots in his clothes where he had tried to rinse out the blood. None of that mattered. As long as he could touch Toni and keep watch over her, and sit between her and the door, she was safe.

~~~~~

"It's Evans," Donovan reported over the phone, as Ray Cooper hurried up the sidewalk to the front door of the *Tabor Picayune*.

"You're sure?" He clutched his cell phone hard enough the plastic case groaned.

"He's the only one who hasn't responded to Taylor's call to check in."

"All right. I'm at the paper. I'll bring Angela over if I have to hog-tie her." He eyed the door and the big picture window of the newspaper office. "Bring in some off-duty men if you have to. No uniforms. We don't want him to know we know."

Ray barely heard Donovan confirm his orders before closing his phone and yanking the office door open.

Inside the reception area, people lined up three deep at the counter. Every phone in the office seemed to be ringing off the hook. Myrna Calhoun was in an argument with three different people and barely looked at him as he slid around people and opened the gate to step into the office. Several people called his name or, "Excuse me, officer." He ignored them. As he strode down the long hallway to Angela's office, he decided he didn't recognize more than three of those faces. A good guess was that all those strangers were here to get inside information on the story that had appeared in today's paper, most likely for TV stations and bigger newspapers. There was some irony here, he supposed, in the local newspaper being harassed by other representatives of the media.

The smell of pizza surrounded him as he reached the intersection of editorial room, lunchroom/kitchen, and Angela's dark office. Most of the reporters and the salespeople were gathered around Sherwood Gaines' desk. Everyone looked grim. A college-age girl he vaguely recognized from church stepped out of the lunchroom and looked around.

"Lunch?" she said, taking a step toward the cluster of reporters.

"Where's Angela?" he barked, only vaguely pleased when nearly everyone in the office jumped. Without waiting for an answer, he slammed the door of Angela's office open and slapped his hand against the wall, turning the lights on. A ridiculous move, because obviously she wasn't there. Then he stalked back out into editorial and fought not to snarl for someone to confess. Why wasn't Angela safe in her office, where there were people to keep an eye on her?

Chapter Twenty-Three

"Riding," Max Randolph said.

He only half-heard her as he stalked into the lunchroom, hoping to find Andrew lounging at the table with a cup of coffee and examining that day's paper.

"Chief," she said, following him into the room, "do you know anything about—"

"Toni is still unconscious and Curt is with her. That's all I know." He turned to head back down the hall. His heart doubled its pace.

"What's going on?" she demanded, grabbing his arm to stop him.

"The White Rose is after Angela. I told my men we had to catch him now, because she's his target and I love her." A sharp ache shot through him, making his heart miss a beat. He would never forgive himself. How could he have let anything come between him and making a life with Angela, when he knew he loved her? "And the White Rose was there. Do you know what that means?" He tore his arm free of Max's grip and hurried down the hallway.

He had to get to the stables. Angela was going to the Arc Foundation's women's shelter if he had to tie her up and throw her in his trunk and drive her across the state line himself.

"Chief Cooper." Myrna slithered away from her desk, waving for one of the strangers who had been talking to her to be quiet. The frustration on his face was almost comical. "I want to register a complaint about the rudeness of your officers. One of your men was just in here, and he threatened to hit me."

He swallowed down a retort that he was on the verge of hitting her himself. Then that seething heat in his gut turned to ice.

"What did he want?"

"He claimed he was bringing a message here from you."

"What did he want?"

"To speak to Angela, of course." She sniffed. "I told him that there was something wrong with the police department if you couldn't keep track of Angela, with all the time you two spend together."

"Did you tell him she was riding?"

"She didn't even tell me where she was going!" Her eyes widened with indignation. She sniffed and stomped back to her desk. "I told him and I'll tell you, it's beneath her dignity to spend so much time at your stables, coming in here smelling of horses like she does."

"If Angela doesn't fire you and your idiot mouth—" He was too aware of all the silent, staring people watching and listening. "Do your job for a change, Myrna." He yanked the gate open and stalked out, slamming it shut, while the aggravating old woman gasped and stammered.

He snapped his phone open and nearly stabbed his finger through the keypad as he dialed Donovan.

"He's going after Angela at my stables. Get someone out there now. No radio."

~~~~~

Angela thought about calling Ray, just to let him know where she was. Then she pushed the thought aside for probably the fifth time since she had changed into jeans, sweatshirt, and riding boots, and headed out here. There was something almost sinfully decadent about spending the day at the stables instead of fielding the usual complaints and inanity of the newspaper office on delivery day.

Her father and the editorial staff knew where she was. If anyone needed to get hold of her, they would call. She wondered how long her stern warning to Myrna, not to call her unless the town was on fire, would last. She really did need to fire the frustrating old woman, but Angela was willing to admit that Myrna did prove useful at times. Some of the most irritating people in town refused to call the newspaper on the days Myrna had phone duty. Whenever something in the newspaper got their dander up, they had to wait a full day to call and complain, which meant they had time to calm down and actually think.

Not that Angela would ever tell Myrna she was a valuable employee. Then the woman would be completely impossible, instead of just mostly impossible.

After three hours, she finished all the fussy little chores she never had time for during her weekend rides. She had tended to the hooves of her horse, as well as the Coopers' horses, mucked out all their stalls, and gave all her tack a good cleaning. There was something comforting about the smell of saddle soap. She had her horse tethered to the fence as she curried him, enjoying the bright sunshine and almost balmy breeze. Soon, she would be able to saddle up and head out. Maybe she would call Ray and invite him to play hooky and ride with her.

Grinning, feeling like a rebellious child, she pulled her cell phone out of her saddlebag and turned it on. Her heart skipped a beat when she saw seven messages waiting on the display.

"So help me, Myrna, if you gave out my new cell number again, I don't care how much I need you as pest-repellent—"

Her phone rang and she jumped, almost fumbling it. The display held newspaper's main number. One of the bands of tension she had
~~~~~

managed to loosen with all her labors slipped back into place. Then she sighed and closed her eyes and flipped her phone open.

"This had better be good." She knew it wouldn't be.

"Angela," Myrna said, with her put-upon-longsuffering-school-teacher voice, "I have a Mr. Phillips here who wants to talk to you. I'll put him on the phone—"

"No. I'm not talking to anyone right now."

"But Angela, your duties—"

"Don't tell me what my duties are. I said I was taking the day off. The only reason I have this phone turned on is to get important calls from people I actually want to talk to. Do you understand me?"

"You don't have to be nasty." For emphasis, she sniffed.

"If you break the office rules one more time, you'll find out just how nasty I can be. Don't call me again!"

There was only so much force she could use in closing her cell phone. Angela glared at it and contemplated the satisfaction of flinging it across the stable yard, into the half-frozen mud and under the hooves of those slowly plodding horses out enjoying the sunshine. A few moments of glee versus the annoyance of having to replace the phone and re-enter all those contact numbers and other information. She jammed the phone into her pocket, rather than putting it back into the saddlebag. It rang again, just as she lifted her saddle off the fence.

She let it ring twice before she put the saddle back on the fence and checked the number. The newspaper again. Most of the editorial staff had her cell number, but she trusted them not to call her unless it was an emergency. She put it on the top of the fence post and let it ring. When it stopped, she would check her messages and then turn it off. Chances were good they all were from Myrna, passing on messages from people she didn't want to talk to and could leave until tomorrow. Or maybe next week.

~~~~~

He pulled into the driveway slowly, creating as little noise as possible, and parked in a clump of shaggy evergreens, just before the asphalt paving turned into gravel. He watched Angela through the trees as she saddled her horse. No other cars in sight but hers. He thought about checking out the house and attached garage, several hundred yards away from the stables. It wouldn't do to have witnesses when he brought Angela her just punishment.

After a few moments, moving from the cover of one bush and evergreen to another, he decided there was nothing to fear. Even if someone was in the house, the stable blocked all view of Angela and the horse she was saddling. No one would see him. He would finish his unpleasant chore and leave, with no one the wiser. He could have wished
~~~~~

for falling snow to cover his tracks, and darkness to match the vile soul he had to destroy, but he refused to wait any longer. Angela wasn't his angel, and for that she deserved to die.

A tune chimed softly through the air, over and over again. He used the sound of it to cover up his footsteps as he reached the stable yard and crossed the muddy, icy gravel. The song stopped briefly, then started up again. Now he saw her cell phone sitting on the fence post. Angela talked in a soft, soothing voice to her horse as she adjusted her saddle, and he choked on a threat of tears. How could she sound so sweet, so caring and warm, when she was such a filthy, lying whore?

He reached the stable before she finished her chore, and slipped inside before she turned around. The phone fell silent, and he watched from the safety of the shadows as Angela snatched it off the fence post. She looked irritated, and he was glad. The phone rang again just as she flipped it open, and she snarled something unintelligible.

"Whoever you are, you have no business calling this number," she snapped. She paused to listen. "Mr. Phillips. Didn't my *former* receptionist tell you I was taking the day off?" Angela tapped her foot as she listened again. "I'm sure you feel it is a matter of life and death to get exclusive rights to the White Rose story, but I disagree. I need this phone line open for important calls, and quite frankly, yours doesn't qualify." She held the phone out at arm's length and flipped it closed. "Remind me to hang up on you, next time you call me." She pressed a button until a *whoosh* indicated the phone was powering down, then put it back on the fence post and reached for her saddlebag.

As she flung it over the saddle and fussed with the cords to attach it, he crept quickly from the stable to snatch up the phone. He refused to let anything interrupt what he had to do. And what if she resisted him and got hold of her phone and managed to call for help before he could punish her? She didn't deserve even that much mercy.

She turned around and let out a little gasp as their gazes met. He offered his warmest smile, the shy boy mask he had learned to wear in school, to fool people into thinking he was harmless and weak. He slipped her phone into his pocket.

"Sorry about that," he offered with a chuckle.

"What happened?"

For a moment, he had no idea what she meant. Then he looked down at himself and realized that she thought he was there on city business, since he was wearing his uniform. He could use that. After all, liars deserved nothing but lies. "Nothing. I'm here to look after you. Make sure you're taken care of."

She sighed, glanced up at the house, then around the stable yard. He froze for a moment when her gaze slid over the empty fence post. She didn't react, didn't seem to notice her phone was gone.

"Ray, so help me..." A smile softened her face, brightened her eyes, and sent a jolt of pain through him. Why couldn't she look like that at him? "You mother hen," Angela muttered, then nodded. "Can you ride?"

"Oh, yeah. Love it." He hated horses.

"Good. Because I need to ride, and if you plan on playing bodyguard, you'd better be able to keep up with me. Come on." She beckoned and led him inside the stable.

~~~~~

Ray snapped his phone shut when the car Donovan was driving pulled into his driveway. He saw the black-and-white partially hidden among the evergreens, halfway between the house and the stables. Angela wasn't answering her phone, and he prayed for the dozenth time since meeting up with Donovan at the station that she had turned it off because of too many frivolous phone calls. Another patrol car pulled in behind them.

He was going to think of something nasty to do to Myrna Calhoun, and then convince Angela to fire the aggravating woman. If it wasn't for her, Angela wouldn't have to ignore her phone.

"It's Evans' car," Mike Nichols said only a few seconds later, as he and his partner, Todd James, joined him and Donovan in the cover of the evergreens.

"We've got three more teams coming up through the park road," James reported, holding his phone to his ear.

They had elected to keep all communications to phones, rather than use the police dispatch system, to keep Evans from knowing what they were doing.

"Please, Lord, keep her safe," Ray whispered, as the four checked their weapons.

"Amen," Mike said, just as softly.

"Okay, here's what we have." He squatted in front of an untouched patch of snow and drew a rough map of his yard and the stables with his bare finger. In moments, they divided up and moved in.

~~~~~

He watched Angela sort through the saddles waiting to be used in the tack room. It irritated him that she seemed amused and not worried at all. She should be worried. Didn't her sins weigh on her conscience? She had to know that he would come to punish her for deceiving him, tricking him into loving her. Did she think she was so valuable that Chief Cooper would actually send her a bodyguard?

At the very least, someone should have called her to tell her that he had attacked Toni and Curt. He might have managed to kill Toni, but he knew Curt was still conscious when he fled. He should have called for help by now.

His hand slid into his pocket to look at her cell phone. She had been ignoring her phone. There was probably a message in there, warning her. Maybe Curt had even recognized him and there was an APB out for him right now.

Why hadn't he killed them both?

He had been startled when Curt appeared. He thought Toni was alone.

Why was everyone so cruel to him?

He reached into his other pocket and pulled out the zipper bag with the chloroform cloth. Everything worked fine when he followed his plan, rather than letting his wounded heart rule.

"I think I'll put you on Buster," Angela said, turning around with a saddle in her hands. "He's Di's horse. She won't mind. Come on." She gestured with a tip of her head and led the way down the aisle to the box stall closest to the door.

He stepped up behind her as she bent to put the saddle down on the bench in front of the stall, and he brought the chloroform cloth from the bag. Just a few more seconds now, and he could throw her in his car and be on his way. No one the wiser.

Angela turned, reaching for a bridle hanging on a peg above her head. She hesitated a moment, her face hidden by her arm, and he shivered, suddenly afraid. He shifted to the left and their gazes met and locked.

He lunged, reaching for her head with his free hand, the cloth ready to slap over her face.

Angela snatched at the bridle and turned, slapping at him with the leather straps. He went down, momentarily blinded, and let out a howl. Lunging to his feet again, reaching for her, he saw the flash of silver and ducked. The bit caught his cheek, stunning him for two seconds in a black flash of heat and pain. Angela ran, her boots making muffled thuds in the straw-strewn aisle.

"Angel!" he roared, wiping away the blood with one hand and reaching for his gun with the other. "Come back!"

~~~~~~

"You've got to be kidding," Angela gasped, and stumbled out of the stable, into the bright sunlight.

She saw the dark body and swung the bridle before she recognized Donovan. He ducked, eyes wide, and caught the bridle straps. She opened her mouth to shout warning, and a hand clamped over her mouth, an arm wrapped around her, and she was yanked back against a hard chest. She raised one foot to kick backwards.

"Angie," Ray whispered, freezing her, and stepped back, pulling her
~~~~~~

out of the doorway.

A gunshot rang out and horses neighed.

"Angel!" the White Rose screamed again, and his footsteps hammered down the aisle.

"I know him, but I don't," Angela said as they scrambled around the side of the stable. She stared as six more uniforms appeared from around the fence, through the trees, from behind the tarpaulin-covered bales of straw. One was Lindsay Tinnerman. Curt had done a feature story on her only a few months ago when she won a marksmanship medal. Angela shivered. If she had to, Lindsay would kill the White Rose.

"Duane Evans," Donovan whispered, crouching down next to her. "He came to town to live with his aunt and uncle about three months before Angel died."

"His files say he was abused before they got custody of him," Ray said, as he tightened his arm around her, making her lean against him. She didn't mind in the least. She needed his warmth, his solidity.

"Angel!" Evans shouted as he burst from the doorway. He skidded to a stop, kicking up gravel and mud. He looked at the horses, trotting and snorting beyond the fence. Then he turned in their direction.

Donovan jumped up, turning with his whole body, swinging the bridle so all the straps slapped Evans' face. He screamed and staggered backwards, clutching at his face. Mike raced across the gravel yard as Donovan lunged at the man, bringing him down. Between them, they pinned the writhing, screaming Evans, while Todd raced up and pried the gun from his hand.

"Give it up, Evans." Donovan slammed the man's shoulders into the gravel for the third time. "It's over."

"Angel," Evans sobbed, opening his eyes and turning to look directly at Angela. "Please, my angel..."

"I'm okay," Angela whispered. Ray helped her to her feet, and kept his arm tight around her. He didn't resist, but stayed with her when she walked toward Evans — the White Rose Killer — and stared down at him.

"My angel... why?"

"I'm not yours," she said, breathless with the effort not to snarl or burst into tears. She wasn't ashamed of the urge to kick him in the teeth. "I'm not Angel. You killed Angel. She loved you, and you killed her."

"No. No, I didn't." He let out a muffled wail as Todd slapped his hand down over his mouth.

"Ray..." Angela turned her head. She leaned into him. "Get me out of here."

"Anything you say." Ray's mouth was grim.

He kept his arm tight around her as they hurried across the yard to his house, not to her car or his. That suited her just fine. Behind them,

Evans let out a few more yelps and wails, and from the thumps and other sounds of struggle, Angela imagined he was giving his captors a hard time, and they were giving him an even harder time in return.

"About that promise I made you," Ray said, as they reached the porch.

"Not yet." She tried to laugh as he turned her to face him, gripping her shoulders. "Life isn't boring yet."

He nodded, trying to smile, but one corner of his mouth trembled too much. He groaned and wrapped his arms hard around her. She hid her face in his shoulder. If they stood there like that for the rest of the day, she wouldn't mind at all.

~~~~~

A nurse came in to check on Toni. She shook her head and smiled when she saw Curt perched on the end of the bed, but she didn't order him to get off. She checked Toni's pulse and peeled back the bandages to check the stitches on her cheekbone and forehead, and lifted the blankets to check the bandages on her ribs.

"Toni?" She gripped her shoulder and gently shook. "Time to wake up, sweetheart." She turned on the brighter light over the bed.

Toni murmured and turned her head away. Curt grinned, thinking this was probably how she woke up in the morning. He thought maybe he wouldn't mind struggling to wake her up every morning.

"We have to wake her up regularly, because of her concussion," the nurse explained.

"Toni? Time to go to work." Curt caught hold of her hand and squeezed it.

"Curt?" Toni whimpered.

"Yeah, it's me."

"What're you doing here?" Her eyelids fluttered, but he could see she was still half-asleep.

"Where do you think you are?" He shared a grin with the nurse.

"Home?"

"You're in the hospital."

"Hospi—" Toni's eyes opened and she started struggling to sit up. The nurse stopped her, a hand on her shoulder. Curt saw the moment when memories caught up with her. He squeezed her hand harder and she twined her fingers with his in turn. Neither one said anything until the nurse finished her examination, patted Toni's shoulder, and left, closing the door behind her.

"You're going to be okay," Curt said.

"He's a cop," she whispered, and her voice broke.

"I know. Donovan knows, and he's told the chief by now, and they're going to catch him."
~~~~~

She took another shaky breath. "He called me a liar and just hit me. No warning. Nothing."

"Hey, it's okay." Curt wrapped his arms around her, pulling her up to a sitting position. Toni clung to him. "You're safe now. I won't let him hurt you."

"You were right. He came after me, just like you thought."

"Yeah, well, sometimes I get lucky." Curt grinned, blinking back stupid tears when she managed a shaky giggle at his words.

"Wonder what would have happened if we wrote that story a month ago. Two months ago, before he killed Annalee," she whispered against his shoulder.

"Can't change the past." He tightened his arms around her. She felt good in his arms. "What matters is that it's over."

"Yeah. Over." She took a deep breath and tried to push free of his arms.

"Where are you going?" he teased, and reluctantly let go.

"That's just it. I made a promise. I'll be heading out soon." Toni knuckled her eyes and blinked rapidly, fighting the bright gleam in them.

You're a sick man, Curt scolded himself, when he realized that light feeling was glee that she was upset when she talked about leaving.

"Not so fast. We make a pretty good team, don't we?"

"But I promised that once this was over and we knew who the White Rose was and he was caught... I promised I'd get out of your hair."

"Yeah, well, tough. You're not leaving." He caught hold of her hand again and they just grinned at each other for a few seconds. Curt thought maybe he could like this silly, slightly unbalanced feeling. He liked worrying about Toni. Besides, didn't Lois Lane and Clark Kent end up together, eventually? "I'm not letting you leave. Okay?"

"Okay," she whispered.

Toni blushed bright red when he raised the hand he was holding to his lips and kissed her knuckles. Funny, but he had never seen that side of her before. He decided he liked it.

Curt leaned closer and she blushed even deeper. A soft, breathy giggle escaped her lips just before he kissed her. It tickled against his mouth. He liked that.

"Duane," she whispered.

"Huh?"

"Duane Evans. I remember him. He was new to town."

"Yeah." Curt sat back, hating that dropping sensation, when all the pieces came together in his mind. "I remember him."

"Call Donovan. It probably won't make any difference, but tell him. Okay?"

"You're back to normal. Pushy." He grinned, and swooped in for a quick kiss before he sat back and pulled his cell phone out of his pocket. Her stunned grin made him want to laugh, made him feel like he floated about three feet off the ground.

<center>~~~~~</center>

Toni scooted around in the bed, trying to get comfortable as she listened to Curt's side of the conversation. From the relaxing of the lines around his mouth and eyes, the news was all good. He nodded and mumbled responses, but most of the talking seemed to be on Donovan's end of the conversation.

Now she had time to think about what had just happened. She wondered if the concussion affected her, that in the face of Angel's murderer finally having a name, all that mattered was that Curt wanted her to stay. Curt had kissed her. He was a good kisser. Definitely, she had brain damage, that such a small detail mattered so much.

Curt wanted her to stay. Maybe to make a life together.

How could she be so bruised and achy and slightly sick to her stomach, and yet feel so good?

Well, maybe this was what love felt like. It was nice.

Curt hung up the phone and got out of the chair and reached for her hands. She liked the warmth and strength in his hands. She pretty much liked everything about Curt. Even when he was bossy and nearly smothering her with protectiveness.

"Angela's safe." He took a deep, loud breath. "It's finally over."

THE END

THANK YOU!

Thank you for reading this book from Mt. Zion Ridge Press.

If you enjoyed the experience, learned something, gained a new perspective, or made new friends through story, could you do us a favor and write a review on Goodreads or wherever you bought the book?

Thanks! We and our authors appreciate it.

We invite you to visit our website, MtZionRidgePress.com, and explore other titles in fiction and non-fiction. We always have something coming up that's new and off the beaten path.

And please check out our podcast, **Books on the Ridge,** where we chat with our authors and give them a chance to share what was in their hearts while they wrote their book, as well as fun anecdotes and glimpses into their lives and experiences and the writing process. And we always discuss a very important topic: *Tea!*

You can listen to the podcast on our website or find it at most of the usual places where podcasts are available online. Please subscribe so you don't miss a single episode!

Thanks for reading. We hope to see you again soon!

About the Author

On the road to publication, Michelle fell into fandom in college and has 40+ stories in various SF and fantasy universes. She has a bunch of useless degrees in theater, English, film/communication, and writing. Even worse, she has over 100 books and novellas with multiple small presses, in science fiction and fantasy, YA, suspense, women's fiction, and sub-genres of romance.

Her official launch into publishing came with winning first place in the Writers of the Future contest in 1990. She was a finalist in the EPIC Awards competition multiple times, winning with *Lorien* in 2006 and *The Meruk Episodes, I-V,* in 2010, and was a finalist in the Realm Awards competition, in conjunction with the Realm Makers convention.

Her training includes the Institute for Children's Literature; proofreading at an advertising agency; and working at a community newspaper. She is a tea snob and freelance edits for a living (MichelleLevigne@gmail.com for info/rates), but only enough to give her time to write. Her newest crime against the literary world is to be co-managing editor at Mt. Zion Ridge Press and launching the publishing co-op, Ye Olde Dragon Books. Be afraid … be very afraid.

And please check out her newest venture: Ye Olde Dragon's Library, the storytelling podcast. Each week, listeners are invited to join Michelle on her blog to ask questions and give feedback and suggestions. Interspersed between the chapters will be interviews with authors of fantastical fiction. Listen to the podcast on your favorite podcast app or listen on the website: www.YeOldeDragonBooks.com, and click on the Ye Olde Dragon's Library link. Then go to her blog to interact: www.MichelleLevigne.blogspot.com

www.Mlevigne.com
www.MichelleLevigne.blogspot.com
www.YeOldeDragonBooks.com
www.MtZionRidgePress.com

Look for Michelle's Goodreads groups:

Guardians of Neighborlee
Voyages of the AFV Defender

NEWSLETTER:
Want to learn about upcoming books, book launch parties, inside information, and cover reveals?
Go to Michelle's website or blog to sign up.

Thanks for reading!
If you enjoyed this book, would you help Michelle by posting a review on Goodreads?

Are you a member of Book Bub? If so, please follow Michelle on Book Bub, and you'll get alerts when new books are coming out.

As a way of saying thanks, Michelle invites you to the Goodies page on her website. It will change regularly, offering you a free short story, a sample audiobook chapter, sneak peeks at new cover art, inside information on discounts and new release dates, etc.

Please go to: Mlevigne.com/good-stuff.html

Also by Michelle L. Levigne

Guardians of the Time Stream: 4-book Steampunk series
The Match Girls: Humorous inspirational romance series starting with **A Match (Not) Made in Heaven**
Sarai's Journey: A 2-book biblical fiction series
Tabor Heights: 18-book inspirational small town romance series.
Quarry Hall: 11-book women's fiction/suspense series
For Sale: Wedding Dress. Never Used: inspirational romance
Crooked Creek: Fun Fables About Critters and Kids: Children's short stories.
Do Yourself a Favor: Tips and Quips on the Writing Life. A book of writing advice.
To Eternity (and beyond): *Writing Spec Fic Good for Your Soul.* A book defending speculative fiction.
Killing His Alter-Ego: contemporary romance/suspense, taking place in fandom.
The Commonwealth Universe: SF series, 25 books and growing
The Hunt: 5-book YA fantasy series
Faxinor: Fantasy series, 4 books and growing

Wildvine: Fantasy series, 14 books when all released
Neighborlee: Humorous fantasy series
Zygradon: 5-book Arthurian fantasy series
AFV Defender: SF adventure series
Young Defenders: Middle Grade SF series, spin-off of *AFV Defender*
Magic to Spare: Fantasy series
Book & Mug Mysteries: cozy mystery series
Quest for the Crescent Moon: fantasy series
Steward's World: fantasy series reboot and expansion
The Enchanted Castle Archives: fantasy series